S. S. Copeman

Thoughts on Life

from modern writers

S. S. Copeman

Thoughts on Life
from modern writers

ISBN/EAN: 9783337385736

Printed in Europe, USA, Canada, Australia, Japan

Cover: Foto ©Andreas Hilbeck / pixelio.de

More available books at **www.hansebooks.com**

THOUGHTS ON LIFE

FROM

MODERN WRITERS.

EDITED BY

S. S. COPEMAN.

"Great thoughts are the precious life-blood of master spirits embalmed for a life
beyond life."—MILTON.

"Our thoughts are ours, their ends none of our own."—SHAKESPEARE.

LONDON:

SWAN SONNENSCHEIN, Le BAS & LOWREY,

PATERNOSTER SQUARE.

1886.

Printed by Hazell, Watson, & Viney, Ld. London and Aylesbury

PREFACE.

In placing this volume in the hands of the public, the compiler would take the opportunity of thanking the Authors and Publishers for the kind and courteous way in which they have given her permission to make extracts from books, the copyrights of which are their property. She trusts that in the choice of selections she has made they will not have cause to regret the confidence thus placed in her.

THE following Authors desire that it should be stated from which of their works the "Thoughts" have been selected:—

Those by Dean Church, pp. 205, 244, from "Sermons at Oxford." By the Rev. J. Pulsford, pp. 8, 23, 32, 35, 44, 51, 55, 57, 59, 106, 154, 156, 159, 174, 191, 193, 202, 206, 219, 220, 229, 231, 233, 234, 241, 243, from "Quiet Hours." By the Rev. A. Maclaren, pp. 81, 103, 128, 151, from "Sermons in Union Church," Manchester. Pp. 114, 212, from "Week Day Evening Addresses." Special permission has been granted by Messrs. Cassell & Co. for the "Thoughts" from Archdeacon Farrar's "Life of St. Paul," pp. 14, 22; also from the Rev. P. B. Powers' "Heart Chords." By Messrs. Macmillan & Co., from Archdeacon Farrar's "Life of Christ," p. 77; "The Temple of God," p. 211; "In the Days of thy Youth," pp. 216, 222, 224. By Messrs. Hodder & Stoughton, for those from Professor Drummond's "Natural Law in the Spiritual World." By Messrs. Strahan & Co. for those from Dr. George Macdonald's "Annals of a Quiet Neighbourhood," pp. 11, 97, 174, 194, 240. By Messrs. Smith, Elder, & Co., that from "Sir Gibbie," p. 75.

THOUGHTS ON LIFE.

"How all Nature and Life are but one Garment, a 'Living Garment,' woven and ever a-weaving in the 'Loom of Time.'"

"Our life is compassed round with Necessity; yet is the meaning of Life itself no other than Freedom, than Voluntary Force: thus have we a warfare; in the beginning, especially, a hard-fought battle. For the God-given mandate, Work thou in Well-doing, lies mysteriously written, in Promethean Prophetic Characters, in our hearts; and leaves us no rest, night or day, till it be deciphered and obeyed; till it burn forth, in our conduct, a visible, acted Gospel of Freedom. And as the clay-given mandate, Eat thou, and be filled, at the same time persuasively proclaims itself through every nerve,—must not there be a confusion, a contest, before the better Influence can become the upper?"

"By benignant fever-paroxysms is Life rooting out the deep-seated chronic Disease, and triumphs over Death. On the roaring billows of Time, thou art not engulfed, but borne aloft into the azure of Eternity. Love not pleasure; love God. This is the Everlasting Yea, wherein all contradiction is solved: wherein whoso walks and works, it is well with him."

"What is Man himself, and his whole terrestrial Life, but an Emblem; a clothing or visible Garment for that divine Me of his, cast hither, like a light-particle, down from Heaven?"

Thomas Carlyle.

I

"Of the Divine Spirit holiness is the rule, and of all spirit love is the power, without which there can be no movement forth upon objects and beings around, nothing to stir the self-centred repose, or in any way to turn pure being into the definite and successive action of a true life."

James Martineau, D.D.

"Life is a battle, a struggle, the cultivation of a stubborn soil, a service in an enemy's country in time of war, where carelessness is danger, and sleep is death."

Archdeacon F. W. Farrar, D.D.

"Whether it may seem paradoxical or not, it is a fact in our nature that, without endurance, life ceases to be enjoyable ; without pains accepted, pleasure will not be permanent."

"Man's life, his true and proper life, his health, is of such grandeur, of such intensity and scope, that it would absorb, and turn into the servitors of its joy, all that we now find intolerable pain, all agony and loss."

"Man's perfect life is a life in which love can be perfect, and find no limitation ; it is a life so truly lived in others, so participant with them, that utter and unbounded sacrifice is possible ; the limitations of this mortal state bounding us no more."

"A beautiful external life is the fruit of life within, especially of that life which dwells in joy."   *James Hinton.*

"Every man has a plan in life marked for him by God, and it is his duty to discover it, and his safety to fulfil it ; and if you talk to me about the tyranny of circumstances, and ask how you can escape them, I answer : ' If circumstances crush feeble men, strong men use circumstances, and fortune is at the feet of the strong.' "   *Bishop Thorold.*

"Let us do our work as well,
    Both the unseen and the seen ;
Make the house, where Gods may dwell,
    Beautiful, entire, and clean.

Else our lives are incomplete,
    Standing in these walls of Time,
Broken stairways, where the feet
    Stumble as they seek to climb.

Build to-day, then, strong and sure,
With a firm and ample base;
And ascending and secure
Shall to-morrow find its place."

Henry W. Longfellow.

'To live in the Spirit is the·right condition of man, his normal condition, out of which he is out of order; and to live in the Spirit is to live with God—hearing Him, and knowing Him, and loving Him, and delighting to do His will."

Thomas Erskine.

" Life is only bright when it proceedeth
Towards a truer, deeper life above;
Human love is sweetest when it leadeth
To a more Divine and perfect Love."

Adelaide Procter.

" Life consists in first being stirred to do, and then learning how to do." *Charlotte M. Yonge.*

" What is our life? It is a mission to go into every corner we can reach, and reconquer for God's beatitude His unhappy world back to Him. It is a devotion of ourselves to the bliss of the Divine Life, by the beautiful apostolate of kindness."

F. W. Faber, D.D.

" All life is a mere progression, a pressing on and on; and death itself, we Christians believe, but a higher development into more perfect life." *Dinah M. Muloch.*

" Life itself passes by many births
To happier heights and purging off of sins."

" Life, which all can take but none can give,
Life, which all creatures love and strive to keep,
Wonderful, dear, and pleasant unto each,
Even to the meanest; yea, a boon to all
Where pity is, for pity makes the world
Soft to the weak and noble for the strong."

Edwin Arnold.

" Life is a succession of lessons which must be lived to be understood."

" Life brings to each his task, and, whatever art you select,—algebra, planting, architecture, poems, commerce, politics,—all are attainable, even to the miraculous triumphs, on the same terms, of selecting that for which you are apt;—begin at the beginning, proceed in order, step by step. 'Tis as easy to hoist iron anchors, and braid cannons, as to braid straw, to boil granite as to boil water, if you take all the steps in order. Wherever there is failure, there is some giddiness, some superstition about luck, some step omitted, which Nature never pardons. The happy conditions of life may be had on the same terms. Their attraction for you is the pledge that they are within your reach. Our prayers are prophets. There must be fidelity, and there must be adherence."

" Life would be twice or ten times life, if spent with wise and fruitful companions."

"Life is hardly respectable—is it?—if it has no generous, guaranteeing task, no duties, or affections, that constitute a necessity of existing. Every man's task is his life-preserver. The conviction that his work is dear to God, and cannot be spared, defends him."

Ralph Waldo Emerson.

> " Is life a groping and a guess,
>   A vain cry in a wilderness,
>   No light of home at distance seen ?
> And do our hearts, like fallen trees,
>   Drift down the rivers to the seas,
>   Though hope hath once exalted been?
>
> We are not driftwood on the wave ;
> But like the ships, that tempests brave,
>   Our hearts upon their voyage stand :
> We utter no unheeded cry,
>   ' Where is my God ? '   Lo, He is nigh,
>   And says, ' Take, child, thy Father's hand.' "

Rev. T. T. Lynch.

" Life must be regarded in the light of all that is to grow out of it. Seeds of things are planted here, foundations are laid, perhaps only ground is cleared. There is eternity to work out the results." *Rev. J. Baldwin Brown.*

" The life of Christ looks indeed a broken life, when we think how brief it was, cut off like the foam upon the waters while He was yet in the bloom and vigour of His manhood. It looks a broken life, yet it was the only whole life ever lived on earth; the only one whose task was perfectly finished ere its days were ended." *Walter C. Smith, D.D.*

" Christian education should strive that the soul, from the beginning, should grow up a plant of grace, budding and shooting higher, each year, till, in mature life, it comes to a strong and natural flowering." *J. Cunningham Geikie, D.D.*

" Every life should begin in Eden, should have its blest traditions to return to, its holy places on which an eternal consecration rests. The dew of the birth of each most hallowed, most human thought and impulse within us is of the womb of the morning, and there is surely a literal meaning in our Saviour's words, ' Unless ye become like little children, ye cannot *enter* the kingdom of heaven.' " *Dora Greenwell.*

" Nothing can live in a state in which God did not intend it to live." *Canon Kingsley.*

" There is no worship comparable with a right life ; a life lived as in the sight of God, and in constant dependence on His aid. No higher aim can man place before him—no grander ambition can stir his zeal than to be A Man ; a man as God made him— for he was made in the image of his Creator."

" The most sacred thing in life is work, of whatever kind it be, done as to the Lord, in which we serve not men, nor self, but the Lord Jesus ; and for which we shall receive the reward of the inheritance ; the inheritance of a true moral manhood, of greater self-respect, of a deepening Christliness, and, at the last, of a Paradise regained." *James McCann, D.D.*

" We need the beautiful varieties of the seasons in our lives, if
we are to become worthy servants of the eternal Master."

Hubert Bower.

" In all other kind of energies except that of man's mind, there
is no question as to what is life, and what is not. Vital sensibility,
whether vegetable or animal, may, indeed, be reduced to so great
feebleness, as to render its existence a matter of question, but
when it is evident at all, it is evident as such : there is no
mistaking any imitation or pretence of it for the life itself; no
mechanism nor galvanism can take its place ; nor is any resemblance of it so striking as to involve even hesitation in the
judgment ; although many occur which the human imagination
takes pleasure in exalting, without for an instant losing sight
of the real nature of the dead things it animates ; but rejoicing
rather in its own excessive life, which puts gesture into clouds,
and joy into waves, and voices into rocks. But when we begin
to be concerned with the energies of man, we find ourselves
instantly dealing with a double creature. Most part of his being
seems to have a fictitious counterpart, which it is at his peril if
he do not cast off and deny. Thus he has a true and false
(otherwise called a living and dead, or a feigned or unfeigned)
faith. He has a true and a false hope, a true and a false charity,
and, finally, a true and a false life. His true life is like that of
lower organic beings, the independent force by which he moulds
and governs external things ; it is a force of assimilation which
converts everything around him into food, or into instruments ;
and which, however humbly or obediently it may listen to or
follow the guidance of superior intelligence, never forfeits its own
authority as a judging principle, as a will capable either of obeying
or rebelling. His false life is, indeed, but one of the conditions
of death or stupor, but it acts, even when it cannot be said to
animate, and is not always easily known from the true. It is that
life of custom and accident in which many of us pass much of
our time in the world ; that life in which we do what we have not
purposed, and speak what we do not mean, and assent to what
we do not understand ; that life which is overlaid by the weight
of things external to it, and is moulded by them, instead of

assimilating them ; that, which instead of growing and blossoming under any wholesome dew, is crystallised over with it, as with hoarfrost, and becomes to the true life what an arborescence is to a tree, a candied agglomeration of thoughts and habits foreign to it, brittle, obstinate, and icy, which can neither bend nor grow, but must be crushed and broken to bits, if it stand in our way. All men are liable to be in some degree frost-bitten in this sort ; all are partly encumbered and crusted over with idle matter ; only, if they have real life in them, they are always breaking this bark away in noble rents, until it becomes, like the black strips upon the birch-tree, only a witness of their own inward strength."

John Ruskin.

" Long fed on boundless hopes, O race of man,
    How angrily thou spurn'st all simpler fare !
' Christ,' some one says, ' was human as we are ;
    No judge eyes us from Heaven, our sin to scan ;

' We live no more, when we have done our Span.'
    ' Well, then, for Christ,' thou answerest, ' who can care ?
From sin, which Heaven records not, why forbear ?
    Live we like brutes our life without a plan !'

So answerest thou ; but why not rather say :
' Hath man no second life ?—Pitch this one high !
Sits there no judge in Heaven, our sin to see ?

More strictly, then, the inward judge obey !
Was Christ a man like us ? Ah ! let us try
If we then, too, can be such men as He !' "

Matthew Arnold.

" The self-life feeds on ashes, for it is the law of every life, that it shall taste its own quality. The self-life is self-love, but within the inmost soul of self-love lurks the fear of evil. For if a man is the subject of his own individual will, instead of being the subject of the universal law, then all highest powers and operations are against him ; and though his senses move in a ' fool's paradise,' his spirit moves in a ' horror of great darkness,' foreboding miserable things. Because the self-life is cold, straitened, and incapable of blessedness, God seeks to vanquish

it, in order that His Love may take its place, and that man, being
delivered from his selfishness, may sit down to the feast of
Eternity."   *Rev. John Pulsford.*

"It is one of the features of religious life that as men grow in
holiness they grow in humility."

Bishop W. Boyd Carpenter.

"No life is a failure which is lived for God, and all lives are
failures which are lived for any other end."

F. W. Faber, D.D.

"Is it not true that everything has to help something else to
live, whether it knows it or not?   That not a plant or an animal can
turn again to its dust without giving food and existence to other
plants, other animals?   That the very tiger, seemingly the most
useless tyrant of all tyrants, is still of use, when, after sending out
of the world suddenly, and all but painlessly, many an animal
which would without him have starved in misery through a diseased
old age, he himself dies, and in dying gives, by his own carcase,
the means of life and of enjoyment to a thousandfold more living
creatures than ever his paws destroyed?"

> "Ah! could you kill that ever-craving lust
> For bliss, which kills all bliss, and lose your life,
> Your barren, unit life, to find again
> A thousand lives in those for whom you die—
> So were you men and women, and should hold
> Your rightful rank in God's great universe,
> Wherein, in heaven and earth, by will or nature,
> Nought lives for self.   All, all from crown to base—
> The Lamb, before the world's foundation slain—
> The angels, ministers to God's elect—
> The sun, who only shines to light the worlds—
> The clouds, whose glory is to die in showers—
> The fleeting streams, who in their ocean-graves
> Flee the decay of stagnant self-content—
> The oak, ennobled by the shipwright's axe—
> The soil, which yields its marrow to the flower—
> The flower, which feeds a thousand velvet worms,

Born, only to be prey to every bird—
All spend themselves for others.   And shall man,
Earth's rosy blossom—image of his God—
Whose two-fold being is the mystic knot
Which couples earth and heaven—doubly bound
As being both worm and angel, to that service
By which both worms and angels hold their life,—
Shall he, whose every breath is debt on debt,
Refuse, without some hope of further wage,
Which he calls Heaven, to be what God has made him ?
No ! let him show himself the creatures' lord
By free-will gift of that self-sacrifice
Which they, perforce, by Nature's laws endure."

Canon Kingsley.

" Longing moulds in clay what Life
    Carves in the marble Real ;
To let the new life in, we know,
    Desire must ope the portal ;
Perhaps the longing to be so
    Helps make the soul immortal.
Longing is God's fresh heavenward will
    With our poor earthward striving ;
We quench it that we may be still
    Content with merely living ;
But, would we learn that heart's full scope
    Which we are hourly wronging,
Our lives must climb from hope to hope
    And realize our longing."

J. Russell Lowell.

"The spiritual life of man is something like his natural life reversed.   He has to live himself back into a little child, to be educated down into an infant.   Instead of being sophisticated into all the arts and schemes of man-life, he has to be simplified into the artlessness and purity of child-life.   Instead of being conformed to the world and fitted for its plans, the world has to be disenchanted of its charm for him, and he has to be untwined from it.   And this process of teaching the heart is just the reverse order of the teaching of the head, through which we pass in worldly life. Our earth-schooling consists in training the child into a man ; the spiritual schooling of the Divine life trains the man into a child. Hence, then, the order is reversed. The three tabernacles are taken backwards. In the education of the natural man for natural life we have home, school, business ; love, discipline, duty ; Christ, Elias, Moses. But in the education of the spiritual man for spiritual life, we begin where we left off before, and leave off where we began. Now, it is business, school, home ; law, discipline, love ; Moses, Elias, Christ."

Rev. Arthur Mursell.

"The greatest results in life are usually attained by simple means, and the exercise of ordinary qualities. The common life of every day, with its cares, necessities, and duties, affords ample opportunity for acquiring experience of the best kind ; and its most beaten paths provide the true worker with abundant scope for effort, and room for self-improvement. The road of human welfare lies along the old highway of steadfast well-doing ; and they who are the most persistent, and work in the truest spirit, will usually be the most successful. Fortune has often been blamed for her blindness ; but fortune is not so blind as men are. Those who look into practical life will find that fortune is usually on the side of the industrious, as the winds and waves are on the side of the best navigators. In the pursuit of even the highest branches of human inquiry, the commoner qualities are found the most useful—such as common sense, attention, application, and perseverance. Genius may not be necessary, though even genius of the highest sort does not disdain the use of these ordinary qualities."

Samuel Smiles.

"Our life is no poor cisterned store
The lavish years are draining low ;
But living streams that, welling o'er,
Fresh from the living Fountain flow
For ever."

Elizabeth Charles.

" It is just as true for us, as for the crystal, that the nobleness of life depends on its consistency,—clearness of purpose,—quiet and ceaseless energy. All doubt, and repenting, and botching, and retouching, and wondering what it will be best to do next, are vice, as well as misery.

" If, on looking back, your whole life should seem rugged as a palm-tree stem ; still, never mind, so long as it has been growing ; and has its grand green shade of leaves, and weight of honeyed fruit at top. . . . Nothing is ever done beautifully which is done in rivalship ; nor nobly, which is done in pride."

John Ruskin.

" It is a most earnest thing to be alive in this world ; to die is not sport for a man. Man's life never was a sport to him ; it was stern reality, altogether a serious matter to be alive ! "

Thomas Carlyle.

" Life is a constant sunrise, which death cannot interrupt, any more than the night can swallow up the sun."

" To live carelessly-divine, duty-doing, fearless, loving, self-forgetting lives—is not that more than to know both good and evil—lives in which the good, like Aaron's rod, has swallowed up the evil, and turned it into good ? "

George MacDonald, LL.D.

" The presence of the spirit which culminates in your own life, shows itself in dawning, wherever the dust of the earth begins to assume any orderly and lovely state. You will find it impossible to separate this idea of gradated manifestation from that of the vital power. Things are not either wholly alive, or wholly dead. They are less or more alive. Take the nearest, most easily examined instance—the life of a flower. Notice what a different degree and kind of life there is in the calyx and the corolla. The calyx is nothing but the swaddling clothes of the flower ; the child-blossom is bound up in it, hand and foot ; guarded in it, restrained by it, till the time of birth. The shell is hardly more subordinate to the germ in the egg, than the calyx to the blossom. It bursts at last ; but it never lives as the corolla does. It may fall at the moment its task is fulfilled, as in the poppy ; or wither gradually, as in the buttercup ; or persist in a ligneous apathy, after the flower is dead, as in the rose; or harmonise itself so as to share in the aspect of the real flower, as in the lily; but it never shares in the corolla's bright passion of life. And the gradations which thus exist between the different members of organic creatures, exist no less between the different ranges of organism. We know no higher or more energetic life than our own; but there seems to me this great good in the idea of gradation of life—it admits the idea of a life above us, in other creatures, as much nobler than ours, as ours is nobler than that of the dust."   *John Ruskin.*

"Our life is consentaneous and far-related. This knot of nature is so well tied, that nobody was ever cunning enough to find the two ends."   *Ralph Waldo Emerson.*

"Life became inexpressibly precious to men who believed, and who knew that they had a right to believe, that out of the pain and travail of the present, a future of glorious liberty, power, and joy was being born."   *Rev. J. Baldwin Brown.*

"One of the most painful experiences of life is to meet with a true man of the world, who sees no evil, save in what shocks the foundation of society, and who measures sin not by moral pollution, but by political results. This lowered sense is the result of a view narrowed to this earth by the amputation of the spiritual world. A wider view would lead to a sterner repugnance to sin, as a thing charged with destructive force. The higher the ascent we can climb, the more clearly shall we see which is the right way to choose. From the vantage-ground of the loftier eminence many a path which promised fair is perceived to lead to dangerous declivities and profitless wastes. The waters which appeared to glimmer refreshingly, in front are found to be illusions, the corn-fields are discovered to be mere prodigality of gorse, and the beaten track to lose itself in dreary marshland. The circumscribed view is ever deceptive."

                        Bishop W. Boyd Carpenter.

"In the very spirit of Promethean ambition, man has practised something on the lifeless corpse, and has imitated the fitful workings of apparent existence—the distorted writhings of galvanic life ; but the spirit that has fled would not listen to his invitations to return, and the blood would not resume its pulse at his bidding. Life, the unattainable object of his far-reaching ambition, has returned to heights beyond him ; and whether he chisel, or paint, or galvanise, the result of all experience only proclaims more forcibly the impressive truth—that life is the gift of God." *W. Morley Punshon, D.D.*

"The abiding spirit of a man's life, more than his special actions and peculiar theories, is that by which other men are moved and admonished." *Frances A. Kemble.*

"To be devout means to live always with the consciousness of God's presence ; to walk with Him, as the old Scriptures put it, so that all thoughts and acts are thought and done before Him, and ordered so as to be in tune with His character. It means to live in worship of Him, so that honour is paid in everything to that which is God, to truth and mercy, justice and purity. And this, smitten into reality in a life, is a life of prayer." *Rev. Stopford A. Brooke.*

> "The sexton, tolling his bell at noon,
> Deems not that great Napoleon
> Stops his horse, and lists with delight,
> Whilst his files sweep round yon Alpine height ;
> Nor knowest thou what argument
> Thy life to thy neighbour's creed has lent.
> All are needed by each one ;
> Nothing is fair or good alone."
> *Ralph Waldo Emerson.*

"Human life is like the wheel which Ezekiel saw in vision. Its aspects and relations, external and internal, are continually changing ; one spoke of the wheel is always ascending while another is descending ; one part is grating on the ground while another is aloft in the air.

"Action and reaction is the law of man's life." *Rev. Hugh Macmillan.*

"Dying, we do but pass to the very source and home of life." *James Martineau, D.D.*

"Whether we will or no, the greater part of life is passed alone; and if we know any truth about ourselves at all, we know how much depends on the upward guidance of solitary thought."
Canon H. P. Liddon, D.D.

"Would it be 'far better' either to leave this actual tangible life, throbbing with hopes and passions, to leave its busy, Christ-like working, its quiet joys, its very sorrows which are near and human, for a nap of several ages, or even for a vague, lazy, half-alive, disembodied existence?"   *Elizabeth S. Phelps.*

"Man's lifetime is a mere moment; nay, the past history of our race, with all its great and varied events, is but a handbreadth compared with the orbit of our solar system.

"Step by step the ideal exemplar, the divine archetype, first embodied in the fishes of the earliest seas, was modified into higher and yet higher forms of life, until at last it was arrayed in that costly vesture of humanity that has been found worthy to clothe the incarnate Redeemer."   *Rev. Hugh Macmillan.*

"Without real trial, how soon we find rust upon our arms, and sloth upon our souls, and the paltry difficulties of common life weigh like chains upon us, instead of being brushed away like cobwebs."   *Rev. F. W. Robertson.*

"Why is it that people do perpetually live below their own pitch?"   *Frances A. Kemble.*

"Is there a climbing element in life
　Which is at war with rest, alternates strife with strife,
　Whereby we reach eternal seas upon whose shores unstirr'd
　Ev'n Joy can sleep,—because no moan like this
　　　Within those waves is heard?"
Robert Buchanan.

"The life of a Christian is a life in Christ, and rises transcendently above the minutiæ of ritual, or the self-torments of asceticism. 'The kingdom of God'—such is the axiom which He lays down for the decision of all such questions—'is not meat and drink; but righteousness, and peace, and joy in the Holy Ghost.'"   *Archdeacon F. W. Farrar, D.D.*

" Every man's life has its apocrypha."

Philip James Bailey.

" Him

In whom Life's tangled, broken threads complete
Are gathered up, its wasted things made meet
For holier use, its roughness smoothed, its bitter
turned to sweet ! " *Dora Greenwell.*

" Knowledge of God, likeness to God, appropriation of God
through spiritual communion with God—and He is presented to
the heart in Christ—this is the essence of life eternal. It may be
experienced in a prison here, or in a Paradise yonder. It matters
little, it is a state, not a place in the Divine presence ; a loving
trust suffuses the whole being, silences doubt, and casts out fear,
and the heart is at rest." *Rev. H. R. Haweis.*

" What is this spiritual life, or its great development, as Christ
has taught it to us ? It is . . . in the living recognition of the
Fatherhood of God, of the Leadership of Christ, of the Brotherhood of Men. He in whom these are living root apprehensions
is spiritually alive, is born again, has entered upon the fulness of
his manhood, and must, sooner or later, bear the fruits thereof."

E. Campbell Tainsh.

" There is a subtle law of assimilation whereby man, in his
deepest life, receives an impress from the object on which his
gaze is habitually fixed. Those who gaze heavenward are, as the
Apostle tells us, changed by the Image of Perfect Beauty from
one to another degree of glory. Those who look downwards
and earthwards receive as certainly the stamp and likeness of
the things beneath them ; they lose their hold by a progressive
declension on all that sublimates and ennobles human life."

Canon H. P. Liddon, D.D.

" That which is to teach us to live, is itself life—not precepts,
not rules. alone, but these clothing themselves in the flesh and
blood of action and of suffering. . . . .Life stretches out on every
side, and on every side loses itself in the infinite."

Archbishop R. C. Trench.

" Better to share the Spirit's bitterest aches—
Better to be the weakest wave that breaks
On a wild Ocean of tempestuous Life."

Robert Buchanan.

" It is not ignoble to feel that the fuller life which a sad experience has brought us is worth our own personal share of pain ; surely it is not possible to feel otherwise, any more than it would be possible for a man with cataract to regret the painful process by which his dim, blurred sight of men as trees walking had been exchanged for clear outline and effulgent day. The growth of higher feeling within us is like the growth of faculty, bringing with it a sense of added strength ; we can no more wish to return to a narrower sympathy, than a painter or a musician can wish to return to his cruder manner, or a philosopher to his less complete formula."   *George Eliot.*

" To live in any amusement is to be the slave of it.   And the Christian should spurn any such dependence."

Dean Goulburn, D.D.

" It is the peculiarity of the Christ-life that it may be lived in its utmost grandeur in the humblest worldly circumstances."

James Culross, D.D.

" Life is a train of moods like a string of beads, and, as we pass through them, they prove to be many-coloured lenses which paint the world their own hue, and each shows only what lies in its focus."   *Ralph Waldo Emerson.*

" Amid the tragedies of life, in the haste of sudden grief or the crises of appalling suspense, the quick and vehement waves of passion that sweep within us break angrily against the steadfast sternness of nature ; we resent its silence, we deprecate its periodicity, we are in despair at its calmness, and say, ' It is the face of the blind ' : we forget the long years quickened by the felt life and love of God, and the high moments kindled by his freshest inspiration ; for it is strange and sad how small and brief a darkness may quench for us an everlasting Sun.   The healthy mind has no deeper assurance, none closer to the very springs of its energy, than that it is entrusted with itself, able to rise with wing that strengthens in the flight, or to drop in un-fathomable fall. But when the moral nerve relaxes, and life is looked at more than lived, sickly subtleties invade us, and, fitting us into the universal mechanism, oppress us with the ancient nightmare of fate."   *James Martineau, D.D.*

> "We are hasty builders incomplete ;
>   Our Master follows after, far more slow
>   And far more sure than we, for frost and heat,
>   And winds that breathe, and waters in their flow
>   Work with Him silently ; we stand too near
>   The part as yet to look upon the whole ;
>   That thing which shall be doth not yet appear ;
>   It is not with the eye but with the soul
>   That we must view God's work."
>
>   *Dora Greenwell.*

"Now, in this life, is the time of growth in the capacity for receiving that boundless love of God. God makes every common thing serve, if thou wilt, to enlarge that capacity of bliss in His love. Not a prayer, not an act of faithfulness in your calling, not a self-denying or kind word or deed, done out of love for Him-self; not an act of study done purely for His love; not a weariness or painfulness endured patiently ; not a duty performed ; not a temptation resisted,—but it enlarges the whole soul for the endless capacity of the love of God, and of God."

                          Edward B. Pusey, D.D.

"The faint outlines of ideas that have at any time visited my brain about this tremendous mystery of human life have all been sad and dreary, and most bitterly and oppressively unsatisfactory ; and, therefore, I rejoice that no mental fascination rivets my thoughts to the brink of this dark and unfathomable abyss, but that it is, on the contrary, the tendency of my nature to rest in hope, or rather in faith in God's mercy and power ; and moreover to think that the perception we have (or as you would say, imagine we·have) of DUTY, of right to be done and wrong to be avoided, gives significance enough to our existence to make it worth both love and humour, though it should consist of but one conscious

2

day in which that noble perception might be sincerely followed, and though absolute annihilation were its termination. The whole value and meaning of life, to me, lies in the single sense of conscience—duty ; and that is here, present, now, enough for the best of us—God knows how much too much for me."

Frances A. Kemble.

" All men are endued with an immortal, conscious, self-determining principle of life. Or rather, that principle is each man's true self, around which all else that belongs to him is clustered, and to which it stands in the relation of a property, or it may be of an accident." *Canon H. P. Liddon, D.D.*

> " It matters not
> To him who holds the mastery o'er his spirit,
> And can suppress its workings, till endurance
> Becomes as nature. We can tame ourselves
> To all extremes, and there is that in life
> To which we cling with most tenacious grasp,
> Even when its lofty climes are all reduced
> To the poor common privilege of breathing."

Felicia Hemans.

" A true life in this world is indeed the best preparation for the world to come, but it must not be forgotten that the chief duties in this world are spiritual, and that spiritual heavens over-arch this world as well as the next."

Rev. Theodore T. Munger.

" Life is movement, but motion upward or downward is the alternative. If, as we go on in years, we go forward towards maturity, then we are saving treasure as well as training faculty ; winning reward as well as waiting till our school-term has expired."

Rev. T. T. Lynch.

" That man is very strong and powerful who has no more hopes for himself, who looks not to be loved any more, to be admired any more, to have any more honour or dignity, and who cares not for gratitude ; but whose sole thought is for others, and who only lives on for them." *Sir Arthur Helps.*

"I do not believe that any human creature, called by God into this life, is without some notion of a Divinity, no matter how mean, how unworthy, how seldom thought of, how habitually forgotten. Superstition, terror, hope, misery, joy—every one of these sentiments brings paroxysms in every man's life when *some* idea of God is seized upon, no matter of what value, no matter how soon relinquished, how evanescent. Eternity is long enough for the progress of those that we see lowest in our moral scale."

Frances A. Kemble.

"We set out in life upon our pilgrimage with ideals we are not destined apparently to realise; we throw all our energy into some work which shall be accomplished, and which shall place upon our career at length its crown. The fields seem to us ripe for the harvest, and we have only to go into them and reap; we have all had our ideals, but by-and-bye we find that the highest joy and bliss of life is in setting our disappointments themselves to music, and that this is what all the greatest singers have done. It is not the success of life, often, so much as its unsuccess, which is grandest and most hopeful, and proves its greatness. Each of us has his own heaven, tent, endowment, and force. See that one 'grinding in the mill of industry'; see that one climbing the giddy Alpine heights of science; see that one toiling in the dark and crooked ways of trade; see that one dashed frequently, it seems almost to pieces, in strife and war with his fellows, but starting up and pursuing his work again. The glory of life is in the purpose that rules it, and finds at last, by faith, that a Divine purpose rules all life." *Rev. E. Paxton Hood.*

> "All through life I see a Cross,
>   Where sons of God yield up their breath:
> There is no gain except by loss,
>   There is no life except by death,
>   There is no vision but by Faith,
> Nor glory but by bearing shame,
> Nor justice but by taking blame;
>   And that Eternal Passion saith,
> 'Be emptied of glory, and right, and name.'"

Walter C. Smith, D.D.

" In the depths of our mortal nature lies a dark unsunned well, too deep sunk for the events of common life to stir and touch it, the waters of which, *when troubled*, reflect the Cross, and prepare man's heart for the cardinal doctrine of Christianity—*i.e., deliverance through a work not his own.* Life's deepest moments rouse man from lethargy which its ordinary course weaves round him, and bid him listen for the footstep of Reuben coming to release him, where he lies tied and bound, and incapable of effort, at the bottom of the pit, 'wherein is no water.' "

Dora Greenwell.

" By thought alone can no man find God : he may find the solitude in which God dwells, and feel how awful and immeasurable it is ; but he must 'live' to know the living God ; and we do not fully live unless we act. . . . We must take in 'stuff' from the crude dark world, and work with it ; then meditation is manufacture ; else we may have the 'steam up' and the wheels whirling, but there being no cotton, there will be no clothes ; and though busy in speculations, we go about naked and ashamed, and among the naked whom we might have clothed, and therefore the more ashamed. We are only 'godly' as we are 'partakers of the Divine nature,' and that, in its pure, simple, and sweet, though intense, essence, is revealed and given in Christ, whose life was as busy as it was holy."

Rev. T. T. Lynch.

" There is only one plain rule of life eternally binding, and independent of all variations in creeds, and in the interpretations of creeds, embracing equally the greatest moralities and the smallest ; it is this—try thyself unweariedly till thou findest the highest thing thou art capable of doing, faculties and outward circumstances being both duly considered, and then DO IT."

John Stuart Mill.

" Our daily familiar life is but a hiding of ourselves from each other behind a screen of trivial words and deeds, and those who sit with us at the same hearth are often the farthest off from the deep human soul within us, full of unspoken evil and unacted good."

George Eliot.

" A dark and boundless deep,
 And a blind height above,
 Untrodden fields of sleep,
 Wherein no force may move,
 Where every sound is still,
 Nor breathes a living breath ;—
These are the heights, these are the depths, these
   are the voids of Death.
 But slowly on the lifeless plain
 There wakes a far-sent ray, a little star,
 A tiny spark of Being from afar,
 A throb of precious pain.
It is done, it has been, it has risen, the glimmer
   of Life,
 The dark void withdrawing around,
 It breaks with a whisper of sound,
 Through the wastes of silence and sleep,
 There is no more stillness nor death,
The great Universe wakes with a deep-drawn
   singultient breath.
The great orbs cohere and spin on their measureless
   ways—
The great suns awaken and shine, ringed with
   girdles of fire every one—
All the worlds are on fire and ablaze—
The flaming globes circle and whirl each one round
   its sun,
The hot seas seethe and bellow, the fixed hills glow,
And the fire of Creation burns fierce while the
   centuries grow ;
 And Life and Time have begun ! "

      Lewis Morris.

 " This earthly life, when seen hereafter from heaven, will seem
like an hour passed long ago, and dimly remembered ;—that long,
laborious, full of joys and sorrows as it is, it will then have
dwindled down to a mere point, hardly visible to the far-reaching
ken of the disembodied spirit."   *Henry W. Longfellow.*

"There is much heroism in life, however humble, in every well-conducted struggle, though it be but a struggle for bread; and in the effort to obtain knowledge, however limited our powers and gloomy our prospects, there is always something noble; and those higher conflicts of the moral and spiritual life —conflicts in which every man may be successful—are dignified and great by whomsoever enterprised."

Rev. H. Stowell Brown.

"Beware, that thou dost not hasten thy seedling life-tree into bloom. Hasty development is fatal to mature fruit."

Rev. John Pulsford.

"This little islet of our life—with deep calling to deep round it, for ever, and the tide covering it, moment by moment—is too small for any neglect. Eternity comes up like the night, hiding all things, and blotting out the sun. There is no time for trifling. The true Pactolus, with every sand golden, is life."

J. Cunningham Geikie, D.D.

"We, here in England, like the old Greeks and Romans, dwellers in the busy mart of civilized life, have got to regard mere bustle as so integral an element of human life, that we consider a love of solitude a mark of eccentricity, and, if we meet any one who loves to be alone, are afraid that he must needs be going mad. That with too great solitude comes the danger of too great self-consciousness, and even at last of insanity, none can doubt; but still we must remember, on the other hand, that without solitude, without contemplation, without habitual collection and recollection of our own selves from time to time, no great purpose is carried out, and no great work can be done, and that it is the bustle and hurry of our modern life which causes shallow thought, unstable purpose, and wasted energy, in too many who would be better and wiser, stronger and happier, if they would devote more time to silence and meditation; if they would commune with their own heart in their chamber, and be still." *Canon Kingsley.*

"Practise in life whatever thou prayest for, and God will give it thee more abundantly." *Edward B. Pusey, D.D.*

"Whatever you win in life you must conquer by your own efforts, and then it is yours—a part of yourself."

James A. Garfield.

"All storing up of force is a nutrition; all liberation of it is the effecting of a function. To see the world as it is, we must carry this picture in our eye; to feel it rightly, our hearts must cast all things into this mould. For it is not in the material alone that this law has its place. It extends as widely, and soars as high as life; it is the key above all to our own. All strife and failure, all subjection, baffling, wrong;—these are nutrition, they are the instruments of life, the prophecies of its perfect ends. They store up the power, they make the organization; and where these are, the function shall not fail. Life is in that which we call failure, which we feel as loss, which throws us back upon ourselves in anguish, which crushes us with despair: it is in aspirations baffled, hopes destroyed, efforts that win no goal. It is in the cross taken up. The silent flowers, the lilies of the field, teach us this lesson too. Nature takes up her cross; loses her life to gain it."

James Hinton.

"From idealised presentments of the lives of our fellow-servants, there would be but little for us to learn; but we do learn the greatest and most important of all lessons when we mark in a struggling soul the triumph of the grace of God—when we see a man, weak like ourselves, tempted like ourselves, erring like ourselves, enabled by the force of a sacred purpose to conquer temptation, to trample on selfishness, to rear even upon sins and failures the superstructure of a great and holy life,—to build, as it were, 'the cities of Judah out of the ruined fortresses of Samaria.'"

Archdeacon F. W. Farrar, D.D.

"The sun, as he dips beneath the ocean in a cloudless sky, displays a splendour with which nothing else in nature can compare: and yet in our eyes his glory is fairer and more persuasive when he sinks amid clouds which he bathes through and through with rays of fire,—clouds, which linger over his resting-place, like the tragic memories of a human life, in pathetic and fading beauty, to tell us what he was and is, whom we no longer see."

Canon H. P. Liddon, D.D.

"Having life in its abundance, there is no break in its current at death; there is no waste of even endless ages. If joined to the Divine Life, every change must be to more life."

Rev. Theodore T. Munger.

"Life in its finest effluences comes to those whose susceptibility is keen to affection." *Rev. T. T. Lynch.*

"We, like the leaf, the summit, or the wave,
   Reflect the light our common nature gave;
   But every sunbeam, falling from her throne,
   Wears on our hearts some colouring of our own;
   Chilled in the slave, and burning in the free,
   Like the sealed cavern by the sparkling sea;
   Lost, like the lightning, in the sullen clod,
   Or shedding radiance, like the smiles of God,
   Pure, pale in virtue, as the star above,
   Or quivering roseate on the leaves of Love;
   Glaring like noontide, where it glows upon
   Ambition's sands,—the desert in the sun;
   Or soft suffusing o'er the varied scene
   Life's common colouring,—intellectual green."

Oliver Wendell Holmes.

"Life is ceaselessly repeating itself, yet anything but monotony is the result." *Caroline Fox.*

"Life does not wait for our higher moments."

J. Tulloch, D.D.

"Life is for action, not for questioning.

Edward B. Pusey, D.D.

"We live in deeds, not years, in thoughts, not breaths;
   In feelings, not in figures on a dial.
   He should count time by heart-throbs. He lives most
   Who thinks most, feels the noblest, acts the best."

Philip J. Bailey.

"It is the instinctive acquaintance with God which constitutes the very essence of eternal life." *Rev. Henry Simon.*

" All life, it has been truly said, is thatched with illusions ; but few illusions are more common and delusive than the idea that the glory and the happiness of the deed in life depends rather upon the conspicuousness of the sphere in which the work is wrought than the moral elevation of the spirit in which it is achieved. The grandeur and power of life is in ' being a whole man, to be one thing at one time '; we cannot guess or gauge the value of what we say or do. ' Set me,' the young man says, ' some great task, ye gods, and I will show my spirit.' Not so ; we must plod and plough, vamp up old shoes, and mend old coats, weave our small threads, and trust that great affairs will come by-and-by. ' Everything,' it is said, ' comes to him who waits '; and if we weave the slightest work in all humility, perhaps, in the long hereafter, we may find that the thing had within it the seminal glory of diadem and stars." *Rev. E. Paxton Hood.*

" There are some days in our higher life when the winds of the Spirit seem to blow and waft us leagues towards the heavenly country: these are the strong moments of our existence."
W. C. Smith, D.D.

" Men's proper business in this world falls mainly into three divisions : First, to know themselves, and the existing state of the things they have to do with.

" Secondly, to be happy in themselves, and in the existing state of things.

" Thirdly, to mend themselves, and the existing state of things, as far as either are marred and mendable." *John Ruskin.*

" As in each man the man's breath or spirit is the life of the body, so in each man there is a certain holy breath or spirit which is the life of his soul ; whence also cometh every good thought and deed into the man." *E. A. Abbott, D.D.*

" In our lives we are always weaving novels, and we manage to keep the different tales distinct. A man does, in truth, remember that which it interests him to remember ; and when we hear that memory has gone as age has come on, we should understand that the capacity for interest in the matter concerned has perished."
Anthony Trollope.

"Life is cumulative in all ways. A steady purpose is like a river, that gathers volume and momentum by flowing on. The successful man is not one who can do many things indifferently, but one thing in a superior manner. Versatility is overpraised. There is a certain value in having many strings to one's bow, but there is more value in having a bow and a string, a hand and an eye, that will every time send the arrow into the bull's eye of the target."   *Rev. Theodore T. Munger.*

"There is a period in our lives, of several years, in which we are, or should be, slowly exchanging the qualities of one state for those of the other. During this intermediate state, then, we should expect to find persons become less teachable, less ignorant, less selfish, less thoughtless."   *Thomas Arnold, D.D.*

"Life seems to me so strange, that the chain of events which forms even the most commonplace existence has, in its unexpectedness, something of the marvellous."   *Frances A. Kemble.*

"The gleam of noble actions, generosity, and heroism, may for a moment gild the current of a life while its native hues are dark, cold, and polluted. It is the direction of the great heart-tide within which must be regarded. Splendid deeds are the ornaments of a life, but they cannot be taken as substitutes for its general tone and tenor. They may illuminate the surface for an instant, but the tide moves on unchanged."
          Bishop W. Boyd Carpenter.

"How solemn is the life that now is! There is greatness even in its trifles; for they are agencies, all of them, for good or evil. The cairn is heaped high by each one flinging a pebble; and the living well is worn by the diligent flow of the brook; and the shoal that has wrecked a navy is only the work of a colony of worms. And in the moral world surely there can be no trifles at all. Nourish the unrecorded thought of ill, and it shall ripen into the full deed by-and-bye. Hug the sin to the bosom, and cry, 'Is it not a little one?' and the one demon will go out only to bring a brotherhood of seven home. Trifles! They have fixed a destiny, and have sealed a doom many a time."
          W. Morley Punshon, D.D.

"What is a Christian life but a lingering death, of which physical death is but the last consummating act ; and if it be not all for Christ, how is it a Christian life ? "

F. W. Faber, D.D.

" What mortal, when he saw,
  Life's voyage done, his heavenly Friend,
  Could ever yet dare.tell Him fearlessly :
' I have kept unfringed my nature's law ;
  The inly-written chart Thou gavest me
  To guide me, I have steer'd by to the end '?

Ah ! let us make no claim,
  On life's incognisable sea,
  To too exact a steering of our way ;
  Let us not fret and fear to miss our aim,
  If some fair coast has lured us to make stay,
  Or some friend hail'd us to keep company.

Ay ! we would each fain drive
  At random, and not steer by rule.
  Weakness ! and worse, weakness bestow'd in vain !
  Winds from our side the unsuiting consort rive,
  We rush by coasts where we had lief remain ;
  Man cannot, though he would, live chance's fool.

No ! as the foaming swath
  Of torn-up water, on the main,
  Falls heavily away with long-drawn roar
  On either side the black deep-furrow'd path,
  Cut by an onward-labouring vessel's prore,
  And never touches the ship-side again ;

Even so we leave behind,
  As, charter'd by some unknown Powers,
  We stem across the sea of life by night,
  The joys which were not for our use design'd,—
  The friends to whom we had no natural right,
  The homes that were not destined to be ours."

Matthew Arnold.

> " Is the life, that bears its fruitage best,
>   One neither of supremacy nor rest ? "
>
> *John Ruskin.*

" To the Christian life, as Christ taught it, a certain thorough-
ness, which can alone spring from enthusiasm, is absolutely
indispensable." *Rev. H. R. Haweis.*

"It's plain enough you get into the wrong road i' this life if you
run after this and that only for the sake o' making things easy
and pleasant to yourself." *George Eliot.*

" There is, in the lives of thousands, a period when a change
takes place more or less outwardly visible and sudden, but attaining in either case the same result—a change wonderful as that
which our modern geologists, of the school of Darwin, would have
us think may have taken place when the unprogressive animals
gave birth to the unknown 'primates' of our race, endowed with
the first faint twilight of reason and possibility of progress. There
is a change from a lower to a higher stage of progress; from
stable equilibrium to an unstable equilibrium. To suppose (as
pedants have done) that this change consists in a passage to a
condition of perfection, is to mistake its nature altogether. Rather
does the introduction of the new element into life involve apparent
fresh imperfection and disorder. The infinite aspirations awakened
in the heart throw out of proportion all the former conditions of
existence, and time must intervene before harmony can be re-
established between the inner life and the outer; while even at the
end of all and at his highest achievement of virtue, the regenerated
man must feel his own imperfection, feel (as while unregenerate
he could never do) that there is infinity between him and the
perfection of God." *Frances P. Cobbe.*

" The poor copies of Christ's life which are presented to us even
in the lives of the most sincere Christians, resemble the copies
of good pictures made by little children. The proportions are
all faulty, and the colours do not blend together. There is a
likeness, but so imperfect a one, that we must not take pattern
by the copy, but ascend up to the original, and study its every
feature there, where alone it is perfect." *Maria Hare.*

" The strength of this spiritual life within us may be increased or lessened by our own conduct ; it varies from time to time, as physical strength varies ; it is summoned on different occasions by our will, and dejected by our distress, or our sin ; but it is always equally human, and equally Divine. We are men, and not mere animals, because a special form of it is with us always ; we are nobler and baser men, as it is with us more or less ; but it is never given to us in any degree which can make us more than men."   *John Ruskin.*

" The lost days of my life until to-day,
    What were they, could I see them on the street
    Lie as they fell ?   Would they be ears of wheat
    Sown once for food but trodden into clay ?
    Or golden coins squandered and still to pay ?
    Or drops of blood dabbling the guilty feet ?
    Or such spilt water as in dreams must cheat
    The undying throats of Hell, athirst alway ?

    I do not see them here ; but after death
    God knows I know the faces I shall see,
    Each one a murdered self, with low last breath.
    ' I am thyself,—what hast thou done to me ? '
    ' And I—and I—thyself' (lo ! each one saith),
    ' And thou thyself to all eternity ! ' "
                        Dante G. Rossetti.

" God looks more at the ' why ' of life, than at the ' what ' of life."   *James McCann, D.D.*

" What is life worth without a heart to feel
    The great and lovely, and the poetry
    And sacredness of things ?   For all things are
    Sacred,—the eye of God is on them all,
    And hallows all unto it.   It is fine
    To stand upon some lofty mountain-thought
    And feel the spirit stretch into a view ;
    To joy in what might be if will and power
    For good would work together but one hour."
                        Philip James Bailey.

" Love excites the profoundest life of man; and each lower degree of love prepares the way for one which is higher. The love of God is the end of all, and I suppose that all must drop off, leaf by leaf, till that fruit is matured. The *withering*, no doubt, is often exquisitely painful; still we find that the heart cannot grow here of itself, and that it retains to the last its strong necessity of loving. In the ordinary appointment this goes on gradually through the successive stages of filial tenderness, fraternal affection, intense love, wedded purity and confidence, friendship, patriotism. In other cases it is done by wrenches, as there are some flowers that blossom with a loud crack, when the old covering, once green and tender, falls off; and the great thing, then, seems to be to go on to the next stage humbly, if one has been missed, instead of sinking to the same level again."

Rev. F. W. Robertson.

" The pleasure of life is according to the man that lives it, and not according to the work or the place."

Ralph Waldo Emerson.

" It is most true that when the spirit is completely right, all life is a harmony of pleasurable activity; but it is also most true that, till the spirit is right, its action will generate sorrows. . . . In spiritual life, distresses are a sign of evil that exists, but of good that has come into a new and high activity to put it away."

Rev. T. T. Lynch.

" Still hope ! still act ! Be sure that life,
　　The source and strength of every good,
Wastes down in feeling's empty strife,
　　And dies in dreaming's sickly mood.

To toil in tasks, however mean,
　　For all we know of right and true—
In this alone our worth is seen ;
　　'Tis this we were ordained to do.

So shalt thou find in work and thought
　　The peace that sorrow cannot give ;
Though grief's worst pangs to thee be taught,
　　By thee let others nobler live." 　*John Sterling.*

" Life is indeed probation, but the judgment that decides is in perpetual session ; not for one moment is it adjourned ; every hour it renders the awards that angels fulfil ; daily and for ever does the Christ of humanity judge according to the deeds done in this present life of humanity, and send to right or left hand destinies. There is no day of eternity auguster than that which now is. There is nothing in the way of consequence to be awaited that is not now enacting, no sweetness that may not now be tasted, no bitterness that is not now felt. What comes after will be but the increment of what now is, for even now we are in the eternal world. The kingdom of heaven has come, and is ever coming ; its powers and processes, its rewards and punishments are to-day in full activity, mounting into ever higher expression, but never more real in one moment of time than in another. Thus seen, life begins to get meaning and dignity, and this world becomes a full theatre of God's action ; for here and now is His throne of judgment set in the heart of every man and in every nation. And so *life* is the single theme of the Christ—life and its fulness. God gives His children one perfect, all-comprehending gift—*life*. It is His own image, His very substance shared with His creatures. Life carries everything with it ; if true, it may be trusted to the uttermost ; all things belong to it. By its own law it is endless ; why should life ever cease to be life? It has but one enemy,—sin. So long as life is true to its own laws and relations, it knows no diminution of its forces."   *Rev. Theodore T. Munger.*

" He only is advancing in life whose heart is getting softer, whose blood warmer, whose brain quicker, whose spirit is entering into living peace."   *John Ruskin.*

"Amid all life's quests
There seems but worthy one—to do men good.
It matters not how long we live, but how."
                         Philip J. Bailey.

"Your life is part of the great human life whose movement onwards in God you retard when you cease to move."
                         Rev. Stopford A. Brooke.

"When the Burning Bush of Holy Scripture, and the burning bush of a man's life meet together, thenceforward he is a seer of the invisible, and his life transcends the world. He becomes a Mount Horeb man, he makes excursions into eternity, he talks with God. The fiery Bush is for man, yet he stands in awe before it. It is his own high, august life, that he stands in awe of. It may open upon him suddenly, but he cannot suddenly get used to it. The day will come, when even in heaven, which is God's Bush—full of glory in the highest, he will feel like a child at home. For the Lord of Glory will change him from glory to glory, until complete congeniality is brought about between him and the Eternal Glory." *Rev. John Pulsford.*

"We do but guess
At one another darkly, 'mid the stir
That thickens round us; in this life of ours
We are like players, knowing not the powers
Nor compass of the instruments we vex,
And by our rash, unskilful touch perplex
To straining discord, needing still the key
To seek, and all our being heedfully
To tune to one another's." *Dora Greenwell.*

"This wonderfully woven life of ours shall not be broken by death in a single strand of it; it shall run on and on, an unbroken life, upheld by the will of the Eternal. Death cannot break it, but it shall change it. It shall draw from it all perishable dross, While the life remains the same, some elements of which its strands are woven shall be changed; instead of the silver cord shall be the thread of gold; for the corruptible shall be the incorruptible; and there shall be no more entanglement and imperfection, no more strain upon any strand of it; the flesh shall not chafe against the spirit, nor the spirit against the flesh, but there shall be at last the one perfectly accorded, incorruptible, and beautiful life." *Rev. Newman Smyth.*

"The spontaneous life of emotion and imagination ends in powerlessness and emptiness, and mere slavery to outward impressions, unless its free movements be not indeed suppressed, but regulated towards distinct ends. *John Sterling.*

" We shape ourselves the joy or fear
  Of which the coming life is made,
And fill our Future's atmosphere
  With sunshine or with shade.

The tissue of the life to be
  We weave with colours all our own,
And in the field of Destiny
  We reap as we have sown."   *J. G. Whittier.*

"Life has its point of view as well as Art; God, the great
Painter, contemplates His pictures from His own standing-point,
not from ours; but He does not require from us more than that
we should work on and ' wait,' and ' Rest ' in Him."
                                   Rev. George Dawson.

" The main feature of life is not its sorrow or its joy, nor even
its right or wrong doing. 'Its main feature is that, starting at the
bare point of existence, it grows with such stride and rapidity that
it yields first a person, and then reaches up to God, into whose
affinities and likeness it enters as a partaker."
                                   Rev. Theodore T. Munger.

" We are placed, as it were, in the presence of an Isis—a veiled
glory. The heavenly tabernacle is about us, but we know it not.
We live, and move, and have our being in the midst of its eternal
realities, but they are covered with the badger's skin of familiar
uses and commonplace enjoyments, veiled with the blue wrappings
of sky and sea, and the purple and scarlet veils of mountain and
flower. Our whole life is spent in the effort to see more of heaven
in nature and in revelation. Now and then, while we work and
pray, the covering is partially lifted, and we obtain a glimpse of
the hidden effulgence."   *Rev. Hugh Macmillan.*

" The universal life bears man's destiny within it ; and not the
meanest labour, the most trivial accident, fails in contributing its
part. If, . . . to understand our life, we must look beyond the
seeming, we see here the guide by which we may interpret it.
The carrying out of a change in man, this is the meaning of it ;
this the unseen fact."   *James Hinton.*

"Future life does not depend upon the *preservation* of the physical body, but rather upon its loss.

The butterfly emerges from the chrysalis—a perfect creature —not by working up the substance of the worm into itself, but by a growth within it. At a certain stage, the chrysalis may be opened, and the members of the winged insect may be seen, two bodies in one ; one fed through the agency of the other, but not identical with it. The butterfly gains its perfect form, not by assimilating the worm, but by getting rid of it. It is the most beautiful analogy in nature, its very gospel upon the resurrection, —at first a creeping thing, dull and earth-bound, a slight period of dormancy, and then a winged creature floating upon the air and feeding upon flowers ; one life, yet possessing from the first the potency of two forms."   *Rev. Theodore T. Munger.*

" This life's a mystery.
The value of a thought cannot be told ;
But it is clearly worth a thousand lives,
Like many men's. And yet men love to live
As if mere life were worth their living for.
What but perdition will it be to most ?
Life's more than breath and the quick round of blood :
It is a great spirit and a busy heart.
The coward and the small in soul scarce do live.
One generous feeling—one great thought—one deed
Of good, ere night, would make life longer seem
Than if each year might number a thousand days,—
Spent as is this by nations of mankind."
                          Philip James Bailey.

"What is married life ? An occasional meeting, a kiss here and a caress there ? or is it the sacred union of the twain who walk together side by side, knowing each other's joys and sorrows, and going heavenward hand in hand ?"
                          Elizabeth Prentiss.

"Love and its reciprocations develop the full form of life. A man's life is rich just in the measure in which he loves and is loved.   *Rev. J. Baldwin Brown.*

" If we would but look upon every improvement in our lives and hearts, as on the seal and mark of God's presence within us, how little room would there be for that lonely feeling with which some measure, as it were, the distance from earth to Heaven, and think that since Jesus ascended up on high, they are left here as if to weep over the grave where He is to be found no longer."

Thomas Arnold, D.D.

" There are moments in the life both of men and of nations, both of the world and of the Church, when vast blessings are gained, vast dangers averted, through our own exertions—by the sword of the conqueror, by the genius of the statesman, by the holiness of the saint.''

Dean Stanley, D.D.

" A mistake in youth creeps after us through life with the gloomy shadow of a crime. Cæsar crossed but one Rubicon : but for us there often are countless Rubicons in daily life of rash words, hasty impulses, unwise plans, which are but the work of a moment, yet cut our lives in two, and make a wide gulf between a happy past and a clouded future."

Bishop Thorold.

" Life is greater than intelligence ; sympathy is profounder than obedience."

Joseph Parker, D.D.

" Peculiar glory and peculiar peril go together. Human nature is an unspeakable entrustment ; but for that very reason it is exposed to awful abuse. Man may sacrifice his princely heirship to his lowest craving. The simple beast, having no organ for the life of the Divine understanding, is quite innocent in its perfect abandonment to animal life. It is no reproach to the horse and the mule to live exclusively the horse and the mule-life. But the wondrous creature man, whose animal nature is the tabernacle of his celestial nature, cannot give himself over to intensify and aggrandize the life of his senses, and be innocent."

Rev. John Pulsford.

" Life is in fruitfulness which brings content to others, and which brings that content to us which makes us happy in our work, and, therefore, fit to do it well."

Rev. Stopford A. Brooke.

" Always the memory
Of overwhelming perils or great joys,
Avoided or enjoyed, writes its own trace
With such deep characters upon our lives,
That all the rest are blotted."

Lewis Morris.

" Life without love does but fade."

Matthew Arnold.

" The heart strikes its own hours, and has its own great risings
and settings, often measuring out a lifetime of feeling in a single
hour by the clock." *Ellice Hopkins.*

" Who can foretell what shall be said of us, when this, our busy
day, is over? We are always affecting other men with a power
which, could we fully know it, would make us tremble. Our
thoughtless actions, random words, unguarded hints, our very
tones, even our gestures, in our most relaxed hours, leave impressions on other men such as we neither design nor imagine.
We may learn it in ourselves. Who is there but can trace back
thoughts, wishes, imaginations, habits, or even the bias of a whole
life to some act or word of another?"

Cardinal Manning, D.D.

" O stream !
Whose source is inaccessibly profound,
Whither do thy mysterious waters tend ?
Thou imagest my life. Thy darksome stillness,
Thy dazzling waves, thy loud and hollow gulphs,
Thy searchless fountain, and invisible course,
Have each their type in me : and the wide sky
And measureless ocean may declare as soon
What oozy cavern or what wandering cloud
Contains thy waters, as the universe
Tell where these living thoughts reside, when stretched
Upon thy flowers my bloodless limbs shall waste
I' the passing wind ! " *P. B. Shelley.*

" The beginning of life comes from the partaking of God."

Edward B. Pusey, D.D.

" Life would not be worth having if a man had no sort of credit from the society in which he moved, if he stood low in the esteem of every soul which formed his little circle. To be respected by others who know us, to have some influence with them, to carry some weight—this is in itself a form of life. Says St. Francis of Sales, ' We live three lives : a corporal life, which stands in the union of soul and body ; a spiritual life, which stands in the grace of God ; and a civil life, which stands in our reputation. The corporal life is stifled by murder ; the spiritual life is stifled by sin ; and the civil life is stifled by slander, which is a species of murder, inasmuch as it destroys a species of life."

Dean Goulburn, D.D.

" Life is its own discipline.

" Every sorrow of life is the consequence of sin. It is the reminder of what we are and what we need. And when we have learned to recognise it thus, it ceases to be a hardship, and becomes an act of mercy. And as the Christian spirit grows within our subdued and softened hearts, we thank God that He hath not left us without chastisement, but that, by the visitation of a Father's rod, He reminds us that, despite our stubbornness, He regards us as children still, and would fain break us till the child-spirit blossoms over all our life. Life's discipline, about which we often talk, means just this : that we are in God's school, not simply under law, as a revelation of duty, but likewise under government, a system involving consequences and results of moral deportment ; an economy under which obedience is happiness, ' and every transgression and disobedience receives its just recompense of reward.' " *Rev. Arthur Mursell.*

" Some people's lives did seem to become like shells, incapable of expanding as of perishing ; fixed in a fair mould, not without colour or beauty, but unvarying, the same from year to year ; specimens classified in the great museum of humanity, not human individualities tossed hither and thither on the common sea of life." *Elizabeth Charles.*

" So soon as there is a suspicion that there is not an eternal goodness behind and under life, it changes colour, and grows cheap and poor." *Rev. Theodore T. Munger.*

"Each man is sent into the world to work out, by his acts or words, some particular truth which he alone possesses ; and the inimitable speciality of each man's experience must present things to him in an aspect which can be exactly the same for no other."   *Rev. Hugh Macmillan.*

"A new day is as a new life. Every day is a little life by itself. This little life is like our greater one in many ways. We little think at its commencement what shall happen before its close, we little think of what we shall become ready to do, and what we shall be compelled to bear. We think not of sorrows, changes, and unfaithfulness. Our great life and our little one are also alike in this, that the character of their advance and ending depends very much upon that of their commencement. The way in which we spend our morning will influence greatly the way in which we spend our day, as the character of our youth will affect that of our after-life. Waste early hours or early years, and who shall ensure the security of later ones? Sin away early strength, and cast away early opportunities, and who can tell whether strength shall be repaired or opportunities renewed?"
                                        Rev. T. T. Lynch.

"A life of beauty lends to all it sees
        The beauty of its thought ;
And fairest forms and sweetest harmonies
        Make glad its way, unsought.

In sweet accordancy of praise and love,
        The singing waters run ;
And sunset mountains wear in light above
        The smile of duty done ;

Sure stands the promise—ever to the meek
        A heritage is given ;
Nor lose they earth who, single-hearted, seek
        The righteousness of Heaven!"
                                        J. G. Whittier.

"Human life should indeed be sacred, on account of the Divine Spirit enshrined in it."   *Archdeacon Julius C. Hare.*

" There's a deal in a man's inward life as you can't measure by the square, and say, ' Do this, and that'll follow,' and ' Do that, and this'll follow.' There's things go on in the soul, and times when feelings come into you like a rushing mighty wind, as the Scripture says, and part your life in two a'most, so as you look back on yourself as if you was somebody else."

George Eliot.

" There is a sphere in the life of every one, except the child, in which he is appointed to rule, and to exercise some functions by the methods of his own will." *James Martineau, D.D.*

" For ah ! the weariness and weight of tears,
   The crying out to God, the wish for slumber,
   They lay so deep, so deep ! God heard them all ;
   He set them into music of His own ;
   But easier far the task to sing of kings,
   Or weave weird ballads where the moon-dew glistens,
   Than body forth this life in beauteous sound."

Robert Buchanan.

" The web of life is complex to an unparalleled degree. Well is the living frame called a microcosm ; it contains in itself a representation of all the powers of nature. It cannot be paralleled by any single order of forces ; it exhibits the interworking of them all. And these processes of decomposition which generate functional activity are so mixed up with other vital processes, that no experiment can disentangle them." *James Hinton.*

" Nothing done by independent human effort can have the nature of spiritual life ; it is out of the spiritual order ; therefore it is that the Scriptures sometimes seem to speak more of what God has done for grafting man again into the vine, than of what is required from man as duty." *Thomas Erskine.*

" A sacred burden is this life ye bear,
   Look on it, lift it, bear it solemnly,
   Stand up, and walk beneath it steadfastly.
   Fail not for sorrow, falter not for sin,
   But onward, upward, till the goal ye win."

Frances A. Kemble.

" The decline of life can never know again the freshness of the
spring, but it may have its Indian summer, even more delicious
in its deep calm, its magical colouring, and its mysterious loveliness."   *Bishop Connop Thirlwall.*

> " Death !   There is not any Death ; only infinite change,
> Only a place of life which is novel and strange.
> Change !   There is nought but change and renewal of strife,
> Which make up the infinite changes we sum up in life.
> Life !   What is life, that it ceases with ceasing of breath ?
> Death !   What were Life without change, but an infinite
>   Death ? "   *Lewis Morris.*

" Growth in Christian life involves *changes ;* it is growth through
change."   *Rev. R. Tuck.*

" The law of life is renewal, not repetition ; development, not
invariableness."   *Rev. Alexander Mackennal.*

> " Spiritual life is great and clear,
> And self-continuous as the changeless sea,
> Rolling the same in every age as now ;
> Whether o'er mountain-tops, where only snow
> Dwells, and the sunbeam hurries coldly by ;
> Or o'er the vales, as now, of some old world,
> Older than ancient man's.   As is the sea's,
> So is the life of spirit, and the kind.
> And then with natures raised, refined, and freed
> From these poor forms, our days shall pass in peace
> And love ; no thought of human littleness
> Shall cross our high calm souls, shining and pure
> As the gold gates of Heaven.   Like some deep lake
> Upon a mountain Summit they shall rest,
> High above cloud and storm of life like this,
> All peace and power, and passionless purity ;
> Or if a thought of other troubled times
> Ruffle it for a moment, it shall pass
> Like a chance raindrop on its heavenward face.

       *   *   *   *

This life, this world is not enough for us ;
They are nothing to the measure of our mind.
For place we must have space ; for time we must have
Eternity ; and for a spirit, godhood.

      *   *   *   *   *

True bliss is to be found in holy life ;
In charity to man—in love to God.
Why should such duties cease, such powers decay ?
Are they not worthy of a deathless state—
A boundless scope—a high uplifted life ?
Man, like the air-born eagle, who remains
On earth only to feed, and sleep, and die,
But whose delight is on his lonely wing,
Wide sweeping as a mind, to force the skies
High as the lightfall, ere, begirt with clouds,
It dash this nether world—immortal man
Rushes aloft, right upwards, into Heaven,
O faith of Christ, sole honour of the world ! "

Philip James Bailey

" There is no state in life hath all the ' ands,'
  Nor any all the ' buts.' "   *S. W. Partridge.*

" A human life, I think, should be well rooted in some spot of
a native land, where it may get the love of tender kinship for
the face of earth, for the labours men go forth to, for the sounds
and accents that haunt it, for whatever will give that early home
a familiar unmistakable difference amidst the future widening of
knowledge ; a spot where the definiteness of early memories may
be inwrought with affection, and kindly acquaintance with all neighbours, even to the dogs and donkeys, may spread not by senti-
mental effort and reflection, but as a sweet habit of the blood.
At five years old mortals are not prepared to be citizens of the
world, to be stimulated by abstract nouns, to soar above prefer-
ence into impartiality ; and that prejudice in favour of milk with
which we blindly begin, is a type of the way body and soul must
get nourished, at least for a time. The best introduction to
astronomy is to think of the mighty heavens as a little lot of stars
belonging to one's own homestead."   *George Eliot.*

"Sorrow is life with an honest face. It is life looking what it is. Nevertheless there is the truest, the heavenliest of all joys in sorrow, because it detaches us from the world, and draws us with such quiet, persuasive, irresistible authority to God."

F. W. Faber, D.D.

"It is a wonderful thing—Life, ever growing old, yet ever young; ever dying, ever being born ; cut down and destroyed by accident, by violence, by pestilence, by famine ; preying remorselessly and insatiably upon itself, yet multiplying and extending still, and filling every spot of earth on which it once obtains a footing; so delicate, so feeble, so dependent upon fostering circumstances and the kindly care of nature, yet so invincible ; endowed as if with supernatural powers, like spirits of the air, which yield to every touch, and seem to elude our force ; subsisting by means impalpable to our grosser sense, yet wielding powers which the mightiest agencies obey. Weakest, and strongest, of the things that God has made, Life is the heir of Death, and yet his conqueror. Victim at once and victor. All living things succumb to Death's assault ; Life smiles at his impotence, and makes the grave her cradle."

James Hinton.

"Life is a fire, yet not to blast and reduce to ashes, but to fuse. It takes a vast assemblage of qualities and faculties most unlike and often discordant, and reduces them first to harmony and then to oneness."

Rev. Theodore T. Munger.

"Life in every shape should be precious to us, for the same reason that the Turks carefully collect every scrap of paper that comes in their way, because the name of God may be written upon it."

Jean Paul Richter.

"He is blessed over all mortals who loses no moment of the passing life in remembering the past."

H. D. Thoreau.

"With many life is but a continuous endeavour to forget and keep out of sight of their true selves—a vain eluding and outstripping of a reality which is still ever with them, and to the consciousness of which they must one day awake."

John Caird, D.D.

" Our whole happiness and power of energetic action depend upon our being able to breathe and live in the cloud ; content to see it opening here, and closing there ; rejoicing to catch through the thinnest films of it, glimpses of stable and substantial things ; but yet perceiving a nobleness even in the concealment, and rejoicing that the kindly veil is spread where the untempered light might have scorched us, or the infinite clearness wearied."

John Ruskin.

"The true way to begin life is not to look off upon it to see what it offers, but to take a good look at self. Find out what you are, how you are made up, your capacities and lacks, and then determine to get the most out of yourself possible. Your faculties are avenues between the good of the world and yourself; the larger and more open they are, the more of it you will get. Your object should be to get all the riches and sweetness of life into yourself; the method is through trained faculties."

Rev. Theodore T. Munger.

" Life goes best with those who take it best."

Jean Ingelow.

" To dignify the day with deeds of good,
And constellate the eve with holy thoughts :
This is to live, and let our lives narrate,
In a new version, solemn and sublime,
The grand old legend of Humanity."

Philip James Bailey.

" Life would be no better than candle-light tinsel and day-light rubbish if our spirits were not touched by what has been, to issues of longing and constancy." *George Eliot.*

" We are all born to fill a certain sphere, to play a part in life, and, if that part be carelessly done, slurred over, or spoiled, we at once do an injury which no one else can repair."

J. H. Friswell.

" Though we cannot create life, we can starve it ; though the new man can be born only of God, he can be hurt, and dwarfed, and ruined by man." *Rev. John S. B. Monsell, LL.D.*

"The man who delights in regarding this life as a stage cannot attach an overwhelming importance to any incident; he observes life as a spectator, and does not engage in it as an actor."

John Inglesant.

"Life does not suspend the chemical or any other laws; they are operative still, and evidence of their action is everywhere to be met with; but in living structures force is employed in opposing chemical affinity, so that the chemical changes which go on in them take place under peculiar conditions, and manifest, accordingly, peculiar characteristics."

James Hinton.

"He who habituates himself in his daily life to seek for the stern facts in whatever he hears or sees, will have these facts again brought before him by the involuntary imaginative power in their noblest associations; and he who seeks for frivolities and fallacies, will have frivolities and fallacies again presented to him in his dreams."

John Ruskin.

"Daily, customary life is a dark and mean abode for man. Unless he often opens the door and windows, and looks out into a freer world beyond, the dust and cobwebs soon thicken over every entrance of light; and in the perfect gloom he forgets that beyond and above there is an open air."

John Sterling.

"Our life from a two-fold root
　　Springs upwards to the sky,
　　One, surface only, shared with tree and brute,
　　And one, as deep and strong as heaven is high.
　　Spirit and sense,
　　Each bears its part and dwells in innocence,
　　Yet only grown together can they bear
　　The one consummate fruit."

Lewis Morris.

"The blessedness of life depends far more on its interests than upon its comfort."

George MacDonald, LL.D.

"The life of the flesh is only possible, on the condition that the glory of the Eternal Kingdom is strongly shut out."

Rev. John Pulsford.

"A man's life is not worth much if it ceases to be capable of enlargement." *Alexander Raleigh, D.D.*

"If life can start at the point of mere existence, and thence grow up into likeness to God, it is worth living. And if life reaches so far, we may be sure it will go on. If it gets to the point of laying hold of God, and begins to feel and act like God, it will never relax its hold, it will never cease from action so essentially and eternally valuable. There is the same reason for the continued existence of such a being as of God Himself ; that which is like the Best must, for that very reason, live on with the Best. . . . Life of itself may not reach its proper fulness, but One is in humanity who is redeeming it from its failures, and filling its cup even to overflow." *Rev. Theodore T. Munger.*

"Luxurious and polished life, without a true sense for the beautiful, the good, and the great, is far more barren and sad to see, than that of the ignorant and brutalized. Even as a mere wilderness would be less dreary to traverse, than a succession of farms and gardens diligently and expensively cultivated to produce no crops but weeds." *John Sterling.*

"In whatever is an object of life, in whatever may be infinitely and for itself desired, we may be sure there is something of divine, for God will not make anything an object of life to His creatures which does not point to, or partake of, Himself."
John Ruskin.

"A life framed after the Divine idea participates in the Divine reality. If we live in harmony with the will that made and rules the world, the issue of our life must be good. Our part is, to be and do our best in the present ; God's part is, to make our future correspond to the present out of which it grows."
A. M. Fairbairn, D.D.

"He who lives for heaven, lives for the Divine union of right heart and right conditions." *Rev. T. T. Lynch.*

"Our spiritual life begins with distant glimpses, erroneous conceptions, broken and imperfect lights of God."
Henry Allon, D.D.

" By fair dealing, justice, kindness, self-control, and the great work of helping others while you help yourself, let your life prove a worship. Criticise the world not by censure only, but by the example of a great life." *Rev. Theodore Parker.*

" We know not what Thou art, and yet we love;
We know not where Thou dwell'st, yet still above
We turn our eyes to Thee, knowing Thou wilt take
Our yearnings and wilt treasure them, and make
Our little lives fulfil themselves and Thee :
And in this trust we bear to be.

Oh, Light, so white and pure,
Oft clouded, and yet sure !
Oh, inner Radiance of the heart,
That drawest all men, whatsoe'er Thou art !
Spring of the soul, that dost remove
Winter with rays of love,
And dost dispel of Thy far-working might
The clouds of Ill and Night,
For every soul which cometh to the earth ;
That beamest on us at our birth,
And paling somewhat in life's grosser day,
Lightest, a pillar of fire, our evening way ;
What matter by what Name
We call Thee ?—Still art Thou the same,
God call we Thee, or Good,—still through the strife
Unchangeable alone, of all our changeful life,
With awe-struck souls we seek Thee, we adore
Thy greatness ever more and more,
We turn to Thee with worship, till at last,
Our journey well-nigh past,
When now our day of Life draws to its end,
Looking, with less of awe and more of love,
To Thy high throne above,
We see no dazzling brightness as of old,
No kingly splendours cold,
But the sweet Presence of a heavenly Friend."
Lewis Morris.

" True life begins when the purpose of life begins. All things are made for purposes higher than themselves. Thus vegetable life is for animal life, and animal life for human life, and human life for the Divine life. Everything looks up for its end to a kind of life superior to itself." *Rev. Benjamin Kent.*

" Every man is bound to develop his individuality, to endeavour to find the right way of life, and to walk in it. He has the will to do so ; he has the power to be himself, and not the echo of somebody else, nor the reflection of lower conditions, nor the spirit of current conventions." *Samuel Smiles.*

" Every moment carries the threads to and fro in the loom of life, and fills in our destiny. The mark of God or of Cain is slowly coming out on our forehead day by day. Life is the building-yard, Eternity the ocean ; and as the ribs, and plates, and girders determine, so will the voyage be." *J. Cunningham Geikie, D.D.*

" Life—a continual building up, a ceaseless fortifying, and enlargement, and multiplication of the treasures of the spirit." *John Morley.*

" What is life but a continual growing, or a continual decaying? " *Canon Kingsley.*

" It's well we should feel as life's a reckoning we can't make twice over ; there's no real making amends in this world, any more nor you can mend a wrong subtraction by doing your addition right." *George Eliot.*

" A particular appointment, ordering the life of individual men, appears to be inseparable from the idea of God's providential government over the world. As that government is carried on upon a perfect general scheme, so it must necessarily involve an ordering and disposal of particular agents." *Cardinal Manning, D.D.*

" Salvation is the healing of spiritual disease, and eternal life is the communication of the life of God to the Soul. Eternal life is not given as a premium for knowing God ; the knowledge of God, as revealed in Christ, *is eternal life.*" *Thomas Erskine.*

" Our life begins in the senses. Men walk upon the ground; but above it God has sprung the blue arch of heaven, and they live by breathing the air. So it is with our interior life. The material of the world is the foundation, the grand workshop for our faculties; but if this be all,—if there hangs not above it God's invisible realm of truth, in which we breathe,—there can be no healthy living. That a plant may grow, we put manure into the soil; but when the roots have taken hold upon it, and it has shot up into stem, and leaves, and flowers, we do not pour manure into the white blossom. It holds up its cup, and says, ' O Heaven ! send Thy light, and drop down Thy dew.' And the light glows, and the dew falls, and the flower expands by feeding upon the air. So man's life must begin in the material. He must first learn how to live as an animal, and must employ all those forces which will contribute to his development; but when he comes to the blossoms of faith, and hope, and courage, he needs other aliment. They must unfold, and be nourished in God's upper air."   *Henry Ward Beecher, D.D.*

" All true life and success are from within. God so made the world and all things in it,—' seed within itself' is the eternal law. No one can row against the stream all his life and make a success of it.   *Rev. Theodore T. Munger.*

" Whatever is lofty and noble in life and history, whatever lifts us by some celestial attraction above the downward gravitation of self, it has been the function of suffering to create. All that is vast and majestic, even in our material and mechanical life, the successes of engineering on land and water, is the result of labouring thought coming down upon the theatre of creation, grappling with its mightiest energies, and chaining the captive Titans of the rock, the storm, the ocean, to the triumphal car of human improvement. And whenever anything morally great arrests our eye, it is always that conscience or love has been summoned to the field, and has not declined the war; that obstructions, of condition or of opinion, have beset some felt obligation, and the mind has yet burst through the entanglement, and determined to be free; that, for example, the arts of tyrants, or the ignoble sleep of a people's better mind, have threatened the higher franchise of a nation's thought, or speech, or action, and some one has been content to stand alone and perish with expostulating death ; or that in private the inquisition of some dreadful torture has vainly tried to crush forth a querulous confession, or some deep grief been hid beneath the silent and cheerful toil of duty. All the pure brilliants of history stand forth from the night of darkest necessity, and make a heaven of what else were the dreariest abyss. Whatever is higher than happiness is revealed to us only in the loss of happiness ; and that which is highest of all, the life of religion, the sense of sanctity, the allegiance to God, find no place within us, till we are cast down in true affliction." *James Martineau, D.D.*

. " Self's dark shadow is that which saddens all life, sours all sweets, darkens all joy." *Rev. J. S. B. Monsell, LL.D.*

" Every state of life is ordered by the same Divine Governor. Even our unmarked and homely life may be the scene of as direct a variance of our will with the will of God, as the life of Pharaoh or of Saul." *Cardinal Manning.*

" We sleep, but the loom of life never stops ; and the pattern which was weaving when the sun went down is weaving when it comes up to-morrow." *Henry Ward Beecher, D.D.*

" Life of any kind is a confounding mystery ; nay, that which we commonly do not call life, the principle of existence in a stone or a drop of water, is an inscrutable wonder. That in the infinity of Time and Space anything should be, should have a distinct existence, should be more than nothing ! The thought of an immense abysmal Nothing is awful, only less so than that of All and God ; and thus a grain of sand, being a fact, a reality, rises before us into something prodigious, immeasurable,—a fact that opposes and counterbalances the immensity of non-existence. And if this be so, what a thing is the life of man, which not only is, but knows that it is; and not only is wondrous, but wonders !" *John Sterling.*

" There is no possibility of getting the Omega and omitting the Alpha in life." *Rev. George Dawson.*

"Truth gives to life interpretation and hope; life gives to truth new reality and impressiveness." *Rev. T. T. Lynch.*

"A life spent amidst holy things may be intensely secular; a life the most of which is passed in the thick and throng of the world, may be holy and divine." *John Caird, D.D.*

"My children, ere it be too late, be warn'd!
The pathway of obedience and of life
Is one and narrow and of steep ascent,
But leads to limitless felicity.
Not so the tracks of disobedience stretch
On all sides, open, downward, to the Deep
Which underlies the kingdom of My love.
Good, evil; life and death : here is your choice.
From this great trial of your fealty,
This shadow of all limited free will,
It is not Mine, albeit Omnipotent,
To save you. Ye yourselves must choose to live.
But only supplicate My ready aid,
And My Good Spirit within you will repel
Temptation from the threshold of your heart
Unscathed, or if conversed with heretofore
Will soon disperse the transitory film,
And fortify your soul with new resolve."
  Bishop E. H. Bickersteth.

"It is not love received
That maketh man to know the inner life
Of them that love him; his own love bestowed
Shall do it. Love thy Father, and no more
His doings shall be strange. Thou shalt not fret
At any counsel, then, that He will send,—
No, nor rebel, albeit He have with thee
Great reservations. Know, to Be is more
Than to have acted." *Jean Ingelow.*

"We paint our lives in fresco. The soft and fusile plaster of the moment hardens under every stroke of the brush into eternal rock." *John Sterling.*

" Mere matter is the only thing which is permanent here. Forms of matter, which have *life* in them, are not permanent. All living forms, whether in the vegetable, animal, or human world, wax old, dissolve, and are no more. Living forms owe their continuance in the material universe to ceaseless reproduction. All the forms of beautiful and of active life, which are now flourishing in the light of the sun, are very recent. The forms which *were*, are not ; the forms which now are, cannot continue. An inevitable doom bears everything to destruction. If the generation of ever new forms were interrupted, there would soon be no such thing as a single living plant or creature in the whole world. The dead matter of the globe would still be here, but without one solitary instance of life. Again and again the whole living world has fallen into the jaws of death ;—the matter of the globe still remaining, as the material and platform of future organizations. All we know of life, at present, is from its works and manifestations in death's dominions. We have innumerable forms in which life resides ; but no living forms. Life's own forms would be eternal. Life lodges like a foreigner in a material vessel. Life to the vessel is a foreigner, and the vessel is a foreigner to life. Life will be ever and ever touching, and working, and playing on these shores, but no organization belonging to the material universe can retain the mysterious presence. Life is the phœnix of the world, always leaving us in order to be always here. Life is destructive of the material vessel, and yet it will tabernacle in the vessel." *Rev. John Pulsford.*

" Life will have its load for each one of us, whether in God's vineyard or out of it. The cares of life, the toils of life, the sorrows of life, are not lightened by living to ourselves. The scorching sirocco will beat upon us equally—the sudden access of calamity, inward or outward ; the cruel blast of calumny, or the withering breath of disappointment—whether we be keeping close to Christ, or living without God in the world. The only difference will be, shall we have a Friend with us in all, a Friend constant in love and changeless as eternity ? or shall we live alone in spirit, and *die to ourselves ?* "

Dean Vaughan, D.D.

" Toil is the law of life, and its best fruit ;
   This from the uncaring brute
   Divides ;—this and the prescient mind whose store
   Grows daily more and more.
   Toil is the mother of wealth,
   The nurse of health ;
   Toil 'tis that gives the zest
   To well-earned rest ;
   The law of life laid broad and deep
   As are the fixed foundations of the sea,
   The medicine of grief, the remedy,
   Wherefrom Life giveth his beloved sleep."

Lewis Morris.

" Life cannot be made up of recreations, they must be garden spots in well-farmed land."   *Ann Gilbert.*

" A false choice often costs a man half his life. No greatness of intellectual powers, no scholastic attainments, no worldly advantages, will compensate for a rash step at the outset. Even those that best recover themselves are not what they would have been. Many never recover themselves at all ; one false choice leads to another ; when they attempt to begin over again, they cannot find the place from which they set out ; they have lost the point of sight. They pass from one wrong path to another, and a succession of changes is generally a succession of mistakes."

Cardinal Manning.

" So live that when thy summons comes to join
   The innumerable caravan which moves
   To that mysterious realm where each shall take
   His chamber in the silent halls of death,
   Thou go not, like the quarry-slave at night,
   Scourged to his dungeon ; but, sustained and soothed
   By an unfaltering trust, approach thy grave,
   Like one that wraps the drapery of his couch
   About him, and lies down to pleasant dreams."

William Cullen Bryant.

" Preparations are good in life, prologues ruinous."
Margaret Fuller Ossoli.

" We struggle with all natural laws, and make
Our life a strange disorder."   *Letitia E. Landon.*

" This circulating principle of life,
That vivifies the outside of the earth
And permeates the sea ; that here and there,
Awakening up a particle of matter,
Informs it, organizes, gives it power
To gather and associate to itself,
Transmute, incorporate other, for a term
Sustains the congruous fabric, and then quits it ;
This vagrant principle so multiform,
Ebullient here and undetected there,
Is not unauthorized, nor increate,
Though indestructible ? life never dies ;
Matter dies off it, and it lives elsewhere,
Or else how circumstanced and shaped ? it goes ;
At every instant we may say 'tis gone,
But never it hath ceased ; the type is changed,
Is ever in transition, for life's law
To its eternal essence doth prescribe
Eternal mutability—and thus
To say I live—says I partake of that
Which never dies.   But how far I may hold
An interest indivisible from life
Through change (and whether it be mortal change,
Change of senescence, or of gradual growth,
Or other whatsoever 'tis alike),
Is question, not of argument, but fact.
In all men some such interest inheres ;
In most 'tis posthumous ; the more expand
Our thoughts and feelings past the very present,
The more that interest overtakes of change,
And comprehends, till what it comprehends
Is comprehended in eternity,
And in no less a span."   *Sir Henry Taylor.*

" We are part of an Infinite Scheme,
    All we that are ;
    Man the high crest and crown of things that be,
    The fiery-hearted earth, the cold, unfathomed sea,
    The central sun, the intermittent star,
    Things great and small,
    We are but parts of the Eternal All
    We live not in a barren, baseless dream
    No endless, ineffectual chain
    Of chance successions launched in vain ;
    But every beat of Time,
    Each sun that shines or fails to shine,
    Each animate life that comes to throb or cease,
    Each life of herb or tree
    Which springs aloft and then has ceased to be,
    Each change of strife and peace,
    Each soaring thought sublime,
    Each deed of wrong and blood,
    Each impulse towards an unattainèd good,—
    All with a sure, unfaltering working tend
    To one Ineffable, Beatific End.
    Oh, hidden Scheme, perfect Thyself, and take
    Our petty lives, and mould them as Thou wilt !
    All things that are, are only for Thy sake,
    And not to obey Thee is our only guilt !
    Perfect Thyself, and be fulfilled, O great
    Unfathomable Will, who art our Life and Fate ! "

Lewis Morris.

" Sleeping or waking, we hear not the airy footsteps of the strange things that almost happen. Does it not argue a superintending Providence, that, while viewless and unexpected events thrust themselves continually athwart our path, there should still be regularity enough in mortal life, to render foresight even partially available ? "   *Nathaniel Hawthorne.*

" He who has never wondered has never *lived*. Life has lost its heart when it ceases to present the grand and the marvellous." *Rev. Benjamin Kent.*

" In the life of every man there are sudden transitions of feel
ing, which seem almost miraculous. At once, as if some magician
had touched the heavens and the earth, the dark clouds melt into
the air, the wind falls, and serenity succeeds the storm. The
causes which produce these sudden changes may have been long
at work within us ; but the changes themselves are instantaneous
and apparently without sufficient cause."

Henry W. Longfellow.

" Life is full of voices of God, only we lack the spiritual faculty
which discerns them." *Henry Allon, D.D.*

" The highest and first law of the universe—and the other
name of life, is, . . . ' help.' " *John Ruskin.*

" I long for other life more full, more keen,
And yearn to change with such as well have run—
Yet reason mocks me—nay, the soul, I ween,
Granted her choice, would dare to change with none."

Jean Ingelow.

" No one, of or by himself, can enter into the springs of his
own being. . . . No one ever yet entered into, or found out
the resources, either of his thoughts or feelings, until that
particular person appeared, who had the particular keys by which
to unlock his resources. The bell cannot reveal to itself the
sound of its metal, the friendly hammer must do that. My friend,
wherever he is, must put me in possession of myself. Many are
quite conscious that the person has never yet appeared who
can unlock for them their own nature, and lead their way into
its depths and hiding-places. Others are quite conscious that
the presence of certain individuals gives them a totally new and
different possession of their being. With most persons, they live
only on the ground-floor of their nature, and, for the time being,
are neither conscious of the higher floors, nor of the inner
apartments. With other persons they ascend a story, and look
out at other windows, and see another class of objects. With a
very few, they ascend to higher stories, where the windows open
inwards and *upwards*, whence the look-out is to high heavens
and deep eternities." *Rev. John Pulsford.*

"A meek heart, in which the altar-fire of love to God is burning, will lay hold of the commonest, rudest things in life, and transmute them, like coarse fuel at the touch of fire, into a pure and holy flame. Religion in the soul will make all the work and toil of life—its gains and losses, friendships, rivalries, competitions—its manifold incidents and events—the means of religious advancement. Marble or coarse clay, it matters not much with which of these the artist works, the touch of genius transforms the coarser material into beauty, and lends to the finer a value it never had before. Lofty or lowly, rude or refined as our earthly work may be, it will become to a holy mind only the material for an infinitely nobler than all the creations of genius—a pure and God-like life."

John Caird, D.D.

" Life's troubles stir life's waters all too much,
　　Passions chase fancies, and though still we dream,
　　The colouring is from reality."　　*Letitia E. Landon.*

"At last, life will be a broken series of unfinished enterprises."
Rev. F. W. Robertson.

" In real life, which of us has made a divine sacrifice, without undoing it twenty times in the thoughts of our hearts? Which of us has left our costly gift on the altar, without at dead of night returning in the secret desires of our hearts to fetch it away? Well for us that we are in the hands of a strong Father, who takes us at our word, and keeps the precious gift we gave, laying it up for us in His treasure, where our wild cries, and sobs, and recalcitrant desires can never come at it again."

Ellice Hopkins.

"The green of the spring-tide is the emerald of God's life, the gold of the autumn is the sheen of God's smile."
Rev. Arthur Mursell.

" Marvel not at thy life!—patience shall see
　　The perfect work of wisdom to her given;
　　Hold fast thy soul through this high mystery,
　　And it shall lead thee to the gates of heaven."
Frances A. Kemble.

" The life of action is nobler than the life of thought."

Dinah M. Muloch.

" Man is no better than a leaf driven by the wind until he has completely mastered his great, lonely duties. If he has no habit of retiring from all that is *world*, and of conversing face to face with his inner man ; if he does not, alone, invite the gaze of God ; if he does not draw down upon his soul ' the powers of the world to come,'—then he is no man yet ; he has not found the life of man, nor the strength of man ; he is a poor, unhappy man, sporting only with shadows, and affrighted before the real and the eternal. He owns a great house, a wonderful house, but it is shut up, and he lives outside with his fellow cattle ; the inside is wholly unknown to him, and he has lived outside so long, that he is afraid of the inside."

Rev. John Pulsford.

" Alas ! it is not till time, with reckless hand, has torn out half the leaves from the Book of Human Life to light the fires of passion with, from day to day, that man begins to see that the leaves which remain are few in number, and to remember, faintly at first, and then more clearly, that upon the earlier pages of that book was written a story of happy innocence, which he would fain read over again. Then come listless irresolution, and the inevitable inaction of despair ; or else the firm resolve to record upon the leaves that still remain a more noble history than the child's story with which the book began."

Henry W. Longfellow.

" Every moment of a working life may be a decisive victory."

Samuel Smiles.

" There are some days, even moments, in our lives, *upon which the burden of the whole seems laid*, which, as in a parable, condense within them the mystery, the contradiction of our existence, and *perhaps hint at its solution*. After such times, life grows clearer before and after. These seasons are set apart from the rest by a solemn consecration. We feel that we are anointed above our fellows ; it may be for the joy of the bridal, for the wrestler's struggle, *or against the day of our burial*, we know not which."

Dora Greenwell.

" Oh, Life, without thy chequered scene,
  Of right and wrong, of weal and woe,
  Success and failure, could a ground
  For magnanimity be found ? "

William Wordsworth.

" Suspended life cannot flow again without great pain."

Edward B. Pusey, D.D.

" The object of human existence is not to be as comfortable
as possible in every stage of its progress, but to make every
advantage possible of the circumstances, whether pleasing or
unpleasing, into which the path of life may successively bring
you. . . . A School is the image of life ; schoolboys do but show
what the natural man is, before he has been worn smooth in some
degree by the world's rough billows ; or, what is not only higher
and better, but alone efficient, before the discipline of the cross
of Christ, received by a free and willing spirit, has subdued the
native powers of hatred and selfishness, which lead the natural
man to delight in giving pain rather than pleasure, because he
looks upon everything desirable which another enjoys, as stolen
from himself. The advantage, however, and an inestimable one,
of the foretaste of the world which is experienced in a school,
is the being habituated to a steady course of conduct, with
responsibility to your own conscience alone."

Frances Baroness Bunsen.

" There is an intermediate moment between life and death
when, as it seems to me, the sweetness and sacredness of both
is distilled into one exquisite drop of suffering—triumph—a crystal
tear, as we may call it when it is leaving its fount, and has not
yet fallen on the page of being to blot the writing there. Death
and life—we cannot separate them even in thought, any more
than we can divide between the shadow and the light when a
body comes between, and the one melts into the other.

The two are to each other as the Dawn and the Day in ancient
fable. Dawn flees from Day, Daphne from the pursuit of
Phœbus, and dies at last under his hot embrace."

Rev. J. B. Heard.

" No life is waste in the great worker's hand.
The gem too poor to polish in itself
Is ground to brighten others."

Philip James Bailey.

" The city of life can only be entered through the gates of death. There is first the sharp education of earth, and then the full freedom of the Father's house."

Hubert Bower.

" Humble life, that is to say, proposing to itself no future exaltation, but only a sweet continuance ; not excluding the idea of foresight, but wholly of fore-sorrow, and taking no troublous thought for coming days ; so also not excluding the idea of providence or provision, but wholly of accumulation ;—the life of domestic affection and domestic peace, full of sensitiveness to all elements of costless and kind pleasure ;—therefore chiefly to the loveliness of the natural world."

John Ruskin.

" Is it not certain that a life of high earnest purpose will die outright, if it is permitted to sink into the placid reverie of perpetual retrospect, if the man of action becomes the mere ' laudator temporis acti '? "   *Canon Liddon, D.D.*

" If we are organs of our own life,—that is, of our own measure of truth and love,—our experience will be subject to the limits and qualities of our own life. If we become the organs of God's life we shall be greatly emancipated from ourselves."

Rev. John Pulsford.

" The soul is faithless which, when it is stung by severities and bowed by afflictions, tries to choke its sympathies and bring a frost upon its mellow seasons. It is not by reducing life to less, but by expanding it to more, not by muffling its stern tones, but by ringing its sweetness clearly out, that a serene harmony can be obtained. When duty is severe, we must be more reverently dutiful; if love brings sorrow, we must love more and better; when thought chills us with doubt and fear, we must think again with fuller soul and deeper trust."

James Martineau, D.D.

" Like coral insects multitudinous
The minutes are whereof our life is made.
They build it up as in the deep's blue shade
It grows, it comes to light, and then, and thus
For both there is an end."

Jean Ingelow.

"There are moments in life, when the heart is full of emotion,
That if by chance it be shaken, or into its depths like a pebble
Drops some careless word, it overflows, and its secret,
Spilt on the ground like water, can never be gathered together."

Henry W. Longfellow.

" A man's life is where the kingdom of heaven is—within him."

George MacDonald, LL.D.

" The highest or inmost degree of man's life lies next to the Lord, or to the purest vital forces which perpetually flow from Him, and fill, and give life to all beings, and perpetual creation to all things. This inmost degree of his spiritual organization is brooded over and pressed upon by Divine influences, as the outer surface of the material body, which lies next to the material world, is pressed on all sides by the atmosphere, the ether, and the various material forces."

Chauncey Giles.

" That which you shall discern and enjoy to-day in the sphere of Divine realities is determined for you by the life you have been living. You cannot at any moment separate yourself from its influence, or understand and appreciate in defiance of it. It infallibly pursues you to affect your vision. You cannot make yourself wings and fly to the height of the Delectable Mountains when you choose. To stand upon their summits, you must need have been living on high. A low life shuts you up to a low view, and the heart is betrayed by what the eye sees."

Rev. S. A. Tipple.

" The clouds are dark, but the raindrops which fall from them are bright and glistering like diamonds. So are life's troubles and pains—very dark when you view them in the mass; but look at them singly, and you will find some light of heaven sparkling in every one." *Bishop W. Boyd Carpenter.*

" Where should the scholar live ? In solitude, or in society ?
In the green stillness of the country, where he can hear the heart
of Nature beat ; or in the dark, grey town ? Oh ! they do greatly
err who think that the stars are all the poetry which cities have ;
and, therefore, that the poet's only dwelling should be in sylvan
solitudes, under the green roof of trees. Beautiful, no doubt,
are all the forms of Nature, when transfigured by the miraculous
power of poetry ; hamlets, and harvest-fields, and nut-brown
waters, flowing ever under the forest, vast and shadowy, with all
the sights and sounds of rural life. But, after all, what are these
but the decorations and painted scenery in the great theatre of
human life ? What are they but the coarse materials of the poet's
song ? Glorious indeed is the world of God around us, but more
glorious the world of God within us. There lies the Land of
Song ; there lies the poet's native land. The river of life, that
flows through streets tumultuous, bearing along so many gallant
hearts, so many wrecks of humanity ; the many homes and
households, each a little world in itself, revolving round its fire-
side, as a central sun ; all forms of human joy and suffering,
brought into that narrow compass ;—and to be in this, and be a
part of this ; acting, thinking, rejoicing, sorrowing with his fellow-
men ; such, such should be the poet's life."

Henry W. Longfellow.

" ' The thing that might have been
Is called, and questioned why it hath not been ;
And can it give good reason, it is set
Beside the actual, and reckoned in
To fill the empty gaps of life.' Ah ! so
The possible stands by us ever fresh,
Fairer than aught which any life hath owned,
And makes divine amends.

*　　*　　*　　*　　*

Oh, yet to taste the whole, to understand
The grandeur of the story, not to feel
Satiate with good possessed, but evermore
A healthful hunger for the great idea,
The beauty and the blessedness of life ! "

Jean Ingelow.

" I cannot choose but marvel at the way
  In which our lives pass on from day to day,
  Learning strange lessons in the human heart,
  And yet, like shadows, letting them departed.
  Is misery so familiar that we bring
  Ourselves to view it as a usual thing?
  Thus is it; how regardless pass we by
  The cheek to paleness worn, the heavy eye!
  We do too little feel each other's pain;
  We do relax too much the social chain
  That binds us to each other; slight the care
  There is for grief in which we have no share."

Letitia E. Landon.

"The steps to greatness take a life to climb,
  And he who dreams its morning at the base,
  How shall he hope to gain the pinnacle?
  Alas! how many vainly strive to weave
  Great patterns on the self-edge of a life,
  And crowd a world of enterprise and work
  In the brief space of its scant afternoon!
  The leaf in autumn scarce becomes the tree,
  When men are seeking fruit.   The bud, the flower,
  Pleasant in spring, are then poor substitutes
  For the ripe growth of full maturity.
  Not the seed-basket, but the sickle, then,
  Becomes the autumn-field.   Alas, alas!
  There is too much to be, too much t' achieve,
  In this short life, for any to delay,
  Or waste its hours in meaningless resolves.
  'There will be time to-morrow,' saith the fool:
  There *may* be time, and opportunity;
  But he who hath no willingness to-day,
  Will he have more to-morrow?
                  Life fast wanes;
  And all its glorious possibilities
  Grow daily less and less."

S. W. Partridge.

"There is not a moment of a man's active life in which he may not be indirectly preaching; and throughout a great part of his life he ought to be *directly* preaching, and teaching both strangers and friends." *John Ruskin.*

"Life is one and universal; its forms many and individual. Throughout this beautiful and wonderful creation there is never-ceasing motion, without rest by night or day, ever weaving to and fro. Swifter than a weaver's shuttle it flies from Birth to Death, from Death to Birth; from the beginning seeks the end, and finds it not, for the seeming end is only a dim beginning of a new out-going and endeavour after the end. As the ice upon the mountain, when the warm breath of the summer sun breathes upon it, melts, and divides into drops, each of which reflects an image of the sun; so life, in the smile of God's love, divides itself into separate forms, each bearing in it and reflecting an image of God's love. Of all these forms the highest and most perfect in its God-likeness is the human soul. The vast cathedral of Nature is full of holy scriptures, and shapes of deep, mysterious meaning; but all is solitary and silent there: no bending knee, no uplifted eye, no lip adoring, praying. Into this vast cathedral comes the human soul, seeking its Creator; and the universal silence is changed to sound, and the sound is harmonious, and has a meaning, and is comprehended and felt. It was an ancient saying of the Persians, that the waters rush from the mountains and hurry forth into all the lands to find the Lord of the Earth; and the flame of the fire, when it awakes, gazes no more upon the ground, but mounts heavenward to seek the Lord of Heaven; and here and there the Earth has built the great watch towers of the mountains, and they lift their heads far up into the sky, and gaze ever upward and around, to see if the Judge of the World comes not! Thus in Nature herself, without man, there lies a waiting and hoping, a looking and yearning, after an unknown somewhat. Yes; when, above there, where the mountain lifts its head over all others, that it may be alone with the clouds and storms of heaven, the lonely eagle looks forth into the grey dawn, to see if the day comes not; when, by the mountain torrent, the brooding raven listens to hear if the chamois is returning from his nightly pasture in the valley ; and when the soon uprising sun calls out the spicy odours of the thousand flowers, the Alpine flowers, with heaven's deep blue and the blush of sunset on their leaves—then there awake in Nature, and the soul of man can see and comprehend them, an expectation and a longing for a future revelation of God's majesty. They awake, also, when, in the fulness of life, field and forest rest at noon, and through the stillness are heard only the song of the grass-hopper and the hum of the bee ; and when at evening the singing lark up from the sweet-smelling vineyards rises, or in the later hours of night Orion puts on his shining armour, to walk forth into the fields of heaven. But in the soul of man alone is this longing changed to certainty, and fulfilled. For, lo ! the light of the sun and the stars shines through the air, and is nowhere visible and seen ; the planets hasten with more than the speed of the storm through infinite space, and their footsteps are not heard ; but where the sunlight strikes the firm surface of the planets, where the storm-wind smites the wall of the mountain cliff, there is the one seen and the other heard. Thus is the glory of God made visible, and may be seen, where, in the soul of man, it meets its likeness changeless and firm-standing. Thus, then, stands Man,—a mountain on the boundary between two worlds,—its foot in one, its summit far-rising into the other. From this summit the manifold landscape of life is visible, the way of the Past and Perishable, which we have left behind us ; and as we evermore ascend, bright glimpses of the daybreak of Eternity beyond us !" *Henry W. Longfellow.*

> " The cloud is cold,
> Although ablaze with lightning—though it shine
> At all points like a constellation ; so
> We live not to ourselves, our work is life ;
> In bright and ceaseless labour as a star
> Which shineth unto all worlds but itself."
>
> *Philip James Bailey.*

" The world is full of Woodmen who expel
Love's gentle Dryads from the haunts of life,
And vex the nightingales in every dell."

P. B. Shelley.

" A life of great excitement will, after the effervescence has passed off, leave a sad residuum." *J. Hain Friswell.*

" The ' Life hid with Christ in God ' . . . a life which in the midst of outward change can remain immovable, ever strengthening, enlarging, and deepening—a life which may not be affected by the things of the body, but which may gradually mould and fashion all things to itself. It is, in fact, the beginning of that transformation by which the mortal is to be clothed with immortality." *Maria Hare.*

" In everything we do there may be a whole world of inward life." *Edward B. Pusey, D.D.*

" Though each human life is, in a sense, complete to itself, and must work itself out independently, clinging to no other, still there is a great and beautiful mystery in the way one life seems to influence another ; sometimes for ill, but far, far oftener for good." *Dinah M. Muloch.*

" From every life—nay, from every event in every life—there is distilled an essence—a medicine or a poison, to be the blessing or the bane of the lives or the events which follow. And while some leave the precious legacy of their life's wine poured out in loving service, and others the strange bequest of their life's wine turned to vinegar by its reservation for themselves, there are yet others who drop a strange and subtle poison, which, falling often into the most generous wine poured out by their contemporaries, chills and impoverishes it, and even gives it a taint which may prove deadly to some." *Edward Garrett.*

" The true nobility of life is to be ever helping and serving." *Rev. W. G. Blaikie, LL.D.*

" Life is the brief disunion of that nature
Which hath been one and same in heaven ere now,
And shall be yet again, renewed by death."
Philip James Bailey.

" Waste and supply are the necessary conditions of life." *Rev. George Dawson.*

" We must go in contemplation *out of life*, ere we can see how its troubles subside and are lost, like evanescent waves, in the deeps of eternity and the immensity of God. A mind that can make this migration from the scene by which it is surrounded is removed from all vain strife of will, and gains its tranquillity without an effort ; feels no difficulty in being gentle and serene, but rather wonders that it could ever be tempted from its pure repose. How welcome would it often be to many a child of anxiety and toil to be suddenly transferred from the heat and din of the city, the restlessness and worry of the mart, to the midnight garden or the mountain top ! And like refreshment does a high faith, with its infinite prospects, ever open to the heart, afford to the worn and weary : no laborious travels are needed for the devout mind ; for it carries within it Alpine heights and starlit skies, which it may reach with a moment's thought, and feel at once the loneliness of nature, and the magnificence of God." *James Martineau, D.D.*

" Love is Youth,
And still the world is young.   Still shall I reign
Within the hearts of men, while Time shall last
And Life renews itself.   All Life that is,
From the weak things of earth, or sea, or air,
Which creep or float for an hour ; to godlike man—
All know me and are mine.   I am the source
And mother of all, both gods and men ; the spring
Of Force and Joy, which, penetrating all
Within the hidden depths of the Unknown,
Sets the blind seed of Being, and from the bond
Of incomplete and dual Essences
Evolves the harmony which is Life.   The world
Were dead without my rays, who am the Light
Which vivifies the world.   Nay, but for me,
The universal order which attracts
Sphere unto sphere, and keeps them in their paths
For ever, were no more.   All things are bound
Within my golden chain, whose name is Love."

Lewis Morris.

" If you desire to see the dead heart put forth the energies of spiritual life, and the dark heart illumined by the fair colours of spiritual grace, throw wide open the passage of communication between Christ and it, and allow the Life which is in Him, and the Light which is in Him, to circulate freely through it."

Dean Goulburn, D.D.

"A life which stimulates the imagination, and introduces the mind to the knowledge of things which can be safely read only with pure eyes, and understood by clean hearts, has dangers peculiar to itself." *Cardinal Manning.*

" The religious life is thoughtful, but thought is not alone its nature. It is full of affection, but it has more than mere feeling ; it abounds in grand moral impulses. Effervescent experiences are not its characteristic. It is the soul of a man made wondrously rich, moving to the touch of Divine influence, in every way to which so facile and elaborate a creature as man can move. There is no end to its combinations. It shapes itself beyond all enumeration of shapes. It thinks in vast and fathomless streams. It wills with all attitudes of authority and decision. It feels with all moods and variations of social affection. It rises by the wings of faith into the invisible, and fashions for itself a life there, glowing with every imaginable ecstasy. And neither one of these is religion more than another. It is the whole soul's life that is religion. When the sun rose on Memnon, it was fabled to have uttered melodious noises ; but what were the rude twangings of that huge, grotesque statue, compared with the soul's response when God rises upon it, and every part, like a vibrating chord, sounds forth to His touch, its joy and worship ? "

Henry Ward Beecher, D.D.

" From the Lord all good expect,
Who many mercies strews below,
Who in life's narrow garden-strip   ·
Has bid delights unnumbered blow."

Archbishop Trench.

" Every deepening of life creates a chasm which needs a deepening of faith to fill it." *Elizabeth Charles.*

" The time will come when the soul of man shall return again childlike and trustful, to its faith in God, and look God in the face and die ; for it is an old saying, full of deep mysterious meaning, that he must die who hath looked upon a God. And this is the fate of the soul, that it should die continually. No sooner here on earth does it awake to its peculiar being, than it struggles to behold and comprehend the Spirit of Life. In the first dim twilight of its existence it beholds this spirit, is pervaded by its energies, is quick and creative like the spirit itself, and yet slumbers away into death after having seen it. But the image it has seen remains ; in the eternal procreation, as a homogeneal existence, is again renewed ; and the seeming death, from moment to moment, becomes the source of kind after kind of existences in ever-ascending series. The soul aspires ever onward to love and to behold. It sees the image more perfect in the brightening twilight of the dawn, in the ever higher-rising sun. It sleeps again, dying in the clearer vision ; but the image seen remains as a permanent kind ; and the slumberer awakes anew and ever higher after its own image, till at length, in the full blaze of noonday, a being comes forth, which, like the eagle, can behold the sun and die not. Then both live on, even when this bodily element, the mist and vapour through which the young eagle gazed, dissolves and falls to earth."

Henry W. Longfellow.

" The higher a man rises in spiritual as in intellectual life, the more lonely he becomes. There is always, as it has been often said, a degree of solitude about a great man ; and this is especially true of the Christian, whose greatness is reflected upon him by the contemplation of the things unseen and eternal."

Rev. Hugh Macmillan.

" Life is no pastoral ; the earnest live,
    And they alone. It is a solemn game ;
    Heaven, hell, are struggling for the precious pool.
    'Tis no parade, but a stern battle-field ;
    No playground, but a schoolroom ; no calm port,
    But a fierce open sea."

S. W. Partridge.

"Imperfection is in some sort essential to all that we know of life. It is the sign of life in a mortal body—that is to say, of a state of progress and change. Nothing that lives is, or can be, rigidly perfect; part of it is decaying, part nascent. The foxglove blossom—a third part bud, a third part past, a third part in full bloom—is a type of the life of this world. And in all things that live there are certain irregularities and deficiencies which are not only signs of life, but sources of beauty. . . . All things are literally better, lovelier, and more beloved for the imperfections which have been divinely appointed, that the law of human life may be Effort, and the law of human judgment Mercy."

John Ruskin.

"The spirit out-acts the life,
But MUCH is seldom theirs who can perceive THE WHOLE."

Jean Ingelow.

"All our life, as it reaches its higher stages,—as it speaks a more refined language and exchanges richer thought,—necessarily becomes more reflective, communes more with itself, and takes the eternal Universe more into the colours of the Atmosphere within."

James Martineau, D.D.

"Sanctity is not the work of a day, but of a life."

Dean Goulburn, D.D.

"Knowledge is a steep which few may climb,
While Duty is a path which all may tread.
And if the Soul of Life and Thought be this,
How best to speed the mighty scheme, which still
Fares onward day by day—the Life of the World,
Which is the sum of petty lives, that live
And die so this may live—how then shall each
Of that great multitude of faithful souls
Who walk not on the heights, fulfil himself,
But by the duteous Life which looks not forth
Beyond its narrow sphere, and finds its work;
And works it out; content, this done, to fall
And perish, if Fate will, so the great Scheme
Goes onward?"

Lewis Morris.

" Half the misery of human life consists in our making a wrong estimate of it, and in being disappointed when we find out our fault.   We do not often begin it at the right end.   We put a much higher figure in the sum than it will bear, and we cry like a schoolboy when the addition is wrong."

J. Hain Friswell.

" However wise and analytical we may be, we want some power to take us as a whole, to inspire the instinctive movements of desire and affection ; and so to mould directly the grand evolution of increasing purpose by which a Life is built up."

J. Allanson Picton.

" The various forms of life do not differ in their inherent capacity for spiritual progress, but in the opportunities for its manifestation."   *Canon B. F. Westcott, D.D.*

" Exalt the motive of daily life, and you refine the manner of daily duty."   *Rev. T. T. Lynch.*

" The great object of a great man's life, is to make the uncommon into the commonplace ; until angels' visits shall no longer be accounted visits, because they shall be continuous."

Rev. George Dawson.

" How much of old material goes to make up the freshest novelty of human life.   Hence, . . . might be drawn a weighty lesson from the little-regarded truth, that the act of the passing generation is the germ which may and must produce good or evil fruit, in a far distant time ; that, together with the seed of the merely temporary crop, which mortals term expediency, they inevitably sow the acorns of a more enduring growth, which may darkly overshadow their posterity."

Nathaniel Hawthorne.

" Life is not marked off in so many inches and done with ; it is full of reference, allusion, collateral and incidental bearing, so that an act done is not self-complete, but may be the beginning of endless other acts nobler than itself."

Joseph Parker, D.D.

" Life is nothing but one vast series of dependencies. So subtle and so persuasive is this law of association, that it is influential, even when we are hardly conscious of its existence. The chance word from the lips of a friend, falling upon some nascent desire like a spark upon tinder ; the vision of some grave or wise one, held up to the glance of fancy so often, that it has become the ideal model of the heart's aspiring ; the music of some old word greeting the ear with a strange melody, have fixed the tone of a spirit, and have fashioned the direction of a life The world is just one unbroken chain of these actions and reactions. We are bound by them ; we are compassed by them ; and we can no more escape from them than we can fling ourselves beyond the influence of the law of gravitation, or refuse to be trammelled by the all-embracing air."

W. Morley Punshon, D.D.

" True life converges upon Christ, revolves round Christ, draws power from Christ, goes out from Christ, flows back to Christ. We can't help living, but we can help that which gives its tone to life." *Rev. Arthur Mursell.*

" What do we live for, if it is not to make life less difficult to each other ? " *George Eliot.*

" There is a Life which taketh not its hues
From Earth or earthly things ; and so grows pure,
And higher than the petty cares of men,
And is a blessed Life and glorified."
Lewis Morris.

" The life of Christ upon earth is the revelation of the beauty of God that can be upon us." *Rev. George Dawson.*

" Men call the shadow, thrown upon the universe where their own dusky souls come between it and the eternal sun, life, and then mourn that it should be less bright than the hopes of their childhood. Keep thou thy soul translucent, that thou mayest never see its shadow ; at least, never abuse thyself with the philosophy which calls that shadow life. Or, rather would I say, become thou pure in heart, and thou shalt see God, whose vision alone is life." *George MacDonald, LL.D.*

"The grain cannot mature without a sky. There can be no perfect morality without some chemistry of the heavens in it. Every life needs some sky. Every man . . . has a larger life to live than that part of it which is turned towards this world or one's fellow-men." *Rev. Newman Smyth.*

" Life—'tis the plastic stuff the wise man moulds
 To great and good results ; the priceless wine
 The sleeping fool allows to flow away.
 'Tis the rough pregnant ore, from which with sweat
 The earnest smelts the gold of endless life ;
 The sparkling stone the gaping trifler hugs,
 Proud of the bauble. 'Tis the smooth descent
 Down which the wicked to their ruin slide ;
 'Tis the ringed ladder good men climb to heaven.
 'Tis the sky-kissing pyramid, all built
 Out of minutest thoughts and actions—all
 Ranged by thyself, and piled by thine own hand.
 Thou standest just where thou hast climbed or fall'n ;
 And if the credit be not all thine own,
 Thine own assuredly is all the blame."
 S. W. Partridge.

" There is no romance like that of real life, and nothing can be fancied so extraordinary as what happens."
 Frances Baroness Bunsen.

" The life of this world is one of probation, but not necessarily of gloom or melancholy." *J. Hain Friswell.*

" Our life should feed the springs of fame
 With a perennial wave,
 As ocean feeds the babbling founts
 Which find in it their grave."
 Henry D. Thoreau.

"The happy day will be when mind, heart, and hands shall be alive together, and shall work in concert ; when there shall be a harmony between God's munificence and man's delight in it."
 Madame Sand.

" In proportion as the different stages of life have sprung naturally and spontaneously out of each other, without any abrupt revulsion, each serves as a foundation on which the other may stand ; each makes the foundation of the whole more sure and stable.   In proportion as our own foundation is thus stable, and as our own minds and hearts have grown up gradually and firmly, without any violent disturbance or wrench to one side or to the other, in that proportion is it the more possible to view with calmness and moderation the difficulties and differences of others—to avail ourselves of the new methods and new characters that the advance of time throws in our way—to return from present perplexities to the pure and untroubled well of our early years—to preserve and to communicate the childlike faith, changed, doubtless, in form, but the same in spirit, in which we first knelt in humble prayer for ourselves and others, and drank in the first impressions of God and of Heaven."

Dean Stanley, D.D.

" Life is a search after power ; and this is an element with which the world is so saturated,—there is no chink or crevice in which it is not lodged,—that no honest seeking goes unrewarded.'

Ralph Waldo Emerson.

" That which is deemed the *happiest* period of life must pass away, before we can sink into the deep secrets of faith and hope. The primitive gladness of childhood is that of a bounded and limited existence, which earnestly wishes for nothing that exceeds the dimensions of possibility ;—of a human Paradise, about whose enclosure-line no inquiry is made ; and through sorrow and the sense of sin we must issue from those peaceful gates, and make pilgrimage amid the thistle and the thorn instead of the blossom and the rose, and lie panting on the dust, instead of sleeping on the greensward of life, before we learn through mortal weakness our immortal strength, and feel in the exile of the earth the shelter of the skies."   *James Martineau, D.D.*

" A man may do wrong, and his will may rise clear out of it, though he can't get his life clear."

George Eliot.

"The battle of life is generally fought under difficulties, with the sun in our faces, uphill, without aid, and with a strong foe pressing us just as we are spent. Troubles, opposition, crosses, and disappointments are the ladders by which the true man rises."

J. Hain Friswell.

"Man's life is a ruin despoiled and defaced by sin. We cannot build upon the old foundation and with the old materials, for the structure to be erected is a "Palace Beautiful," a habitation of God through the Spirit. The rubbish must be cleared away; the dark, opaque, worthless stones of our own good works encumbering the ground must be removed; and the Stone which the builders rejected—disallowed, indeed, of men, but chosen of God and precious, the sapphire-stone of Christ's finished work—must become the head-stone of the corner. And the foundation being thus laid, we must remember that we have not materials for the construction of a palace of our own and for a spiritual building. We cannot, like Solomon, build the temple of the Lord and the house of the forest of Lebanon. If we build the earthly house, it will be at the expense of the heavenly; and if we build the heavenly, we must sacrifice the earthly. Let us not build on this foundation, therefore, wood, hay, stubble, lest our work be burnt, and we suffer loss, and we ourselves 'be saved as by fire.' But let us build a glorious structure of gold, silver, precious stones,—faith, hope, and charity,—the three things that abide. Let us learn, too, in our spiritual architecture, a lesson from the pearly nautilus. As it grows older, it forms a series of new and larger chambers in its spiral shell, until at last it lives only in the uppermost and largest compartment. So let us go on to perfection, not laying again the foundation of repentance from dead works and of faith toward God, but building, in the advancing work of sanctification, nobler and heavenlier mansions for our spirits, until at last the narrow earthly house of this tabernacle is exchanged for the city which hath foundations, garnished with all manner of precious stones, whose Builder and Maker is God."

Rev. Hugh Macmillan.

"Religion is a life; and if it be not found a life, it cannot be successfully pursued as a study."

Rev. T. T. Lynch.

"When the veil is lifted, and we see things as they really are, nothing will so much amaze us as the blindness and perversity that marked our life among our fellow-men. Surely the lofty life is hard, . . . but the very effort itself is gain."

John Inglesant.

"If there be no sense of duty in us, governing our whole lives and actions, we shall never perceive the true beauty and glory of Christ's character, who sacrificed Himself for His duty, which was to do His Father's will." *Canon Kingsley.*

"No man can order his life, for it comes flowing over him from behind. But if it lay before us, and we could watch its current approaching from a long distance, what could we do with it before it had reached the now? In like wise a man thinks foolishly who imagines he could have done this and that with his own character and development, if he had but known this and that in time. Were he as good as he thinks himself wise, he could but at best have produced a fine cameo in very low relief; with a work in the round, which he is meant to be, he could have done nothing. The one secret of life and development is not to devise and plan, but to fall in with the forces at work—to do every moment's duty aright—that being the part in the process allotted to us ; and let come—not what will, for there is no such thing, but what the eternal Thought wills for each of us, has intended in each of us from the first. If men would but believe that they are in process of creation, and consent to be made, let the Maker handle them as the potter his clay, yielding themselves in respondent motion and submissive, hopeful action with the turning of his wheel, they would ere long find themselves able to welcome every pressure of that hand upon them, even when it was felt in pain, and sometimes not only to believe, but to recognize, the Divine end in view, the bringing of a son into glory ; whereas, behaving like children who struggle and scream while their mother washes and dresses them, they find they have to be washed and dressed, notwithstanding, and with the more discomfort ; they may even have to find themselves set half-naked, and but half-dried, in a corner, to come to their right minds, and ask to be finished." *George Macdonald, LL.D.*

"Heaven methinks—
So awful is eternal life, so vast
Its lights and shadows—heaven itself would seem
Too solemn and severe without its choirs
Of infants revelling in innocence,
Who never knew a touch of sinful grief,
But live in joy, and joy because they live."

Bishop E. H. Bickersteth.

"There is no constituent of our human life that the experience of God's great love does not transfigure."

Henry Allon, D.D.

"The great object of life should be to make our immediate aims and our highest interests coincident."

W. B. Clulow.

"Life should be active. In order to be kept pure and wholesome, it ought, like the waters of the lake, to be always flowing. Each one of us should have our inlets and outlets."

J. R. Macduff, D.D.

"Life is not a dazzling romance; life is not one continual funeral; nor is it one continual wedding-feast. Life is made up of *ordinary* duties, *average* occupation, faithful, diligent continuance in the vocation wherewith we are called, and we have to establish our life in patience and in well-doing, rather than to glorify it by ecstasies which perish because of their very violence."

Joseph Parker, D.D.

"When we consider the incidents of former days, and perceive, while reviewing the long line of causes, how the most important events of our lives originated in the most trifling circumstances, how the beginning of our greatest happiness or greatest misery is to be attributed to a delay, to an accident, to a mistake; we learn a lesson of profound humility. This is the irony of life."

Sir Arthur Helps.

"Think nought a trifle, though it small appear,
Small sands the mountain, moments make the year,
And trifles life." *Edward Young.*

"There lies the 'fine gold' beneath all the dimness and the rust of the humblest and rudest life ; and all the powers, passions, possibilities of *a soul* may be found in each."

Alexander Raleigh, D.D.

"The refuge you are needing from personal trouble is the higher, the religious life, which holds an enthusiasm for something more than our own appetites and vanities. The few may find themselves in it simply by an elevation of feeling; but for us who have to struggle for our wisdom, the higher life must be a region in which the affections are clad with knowledge."

George Eliot.

"Grudge not the living sacrifice
　　Of a life fashion'd to His will ;
　Its own reward within it lies ;
　　But, should He ask for greater still,

Break at His feet, if He require,
　　Life's alabaster casket fair ;
　And every thought and fond desire
　　Pour out in adoration there.

Nothing too costly to lay down
　　For Him, whose smile pays every loss ;
　Could we but see it, there's a crown
　　Hangs halo-like round every cross."

Rev. J. S. B. Monsell, LL.D.

"Jesus' human life was 'an ephod on which was inscribed the one word God.' Written on His inmost spirit, written in His most trivial experiences, written in sunbeams, written in the light of stars, He read everywhere His Father's name."

Archdeacon Farrar, D.D.

"True Worship and True Life are blent together. Life without Worship is hard of outline, colourless, cold of temperature. Worship without life is a gaudy idolatry. One is of marble, the other of wax." *Archbishop Benson, D.D.*

"Life is gladness; it is the death in it that makes the misery."

George MacDonald, LL.D.

"The weaknesses, the littlenesses, the incoherences of daily life, so long as they are felt and struggled with, are evidences of victory yet to come. They bear witness to us that we cannot rest till we rise to the level of Him in whom we live."

Canon B. F. Westcott, D.D.

" A life without love, even if it be a life of strictest morality, or of ascetic struggles after Divine communion, will never bring us really into His inner temple. Each step we gain thitherward, we shall lose again by the jar of hard or unkind feelings, and at the end of years be further away than at first. To cast out of our hearts all bitterness once and for ever ; to cultivate, by gentle thoughts and self-sacrificing deeds, the power of sympathy ; to ask God to pour the spirit of love into our souls ;—these are the means He has appointed whereby we may come nearer to Him with unerring certainty. ' He that dwelleth in love dwelleth in God, and God in him.' Our virtue, and rectitude, and sacrifices will avail nothing. We may give our bodies to be burned, and if we have not charity it profiteth nothing. We may hold the purest theologic creed, and dwell in the loftiest regions of thought, and yet find God never the nearer. It is not the marble-palace mind of the philosopher which He will visit, but the humble heart which lies sheltered from the storms of passion, and all trailed over by the fragrant blossoms of sweet human affections."

Frances P. Cobbe.

" Our slender life runs rippling by, and glides
    Into the silent hollow of the past ;
      What is there that abides
    To make the next age better for the last ?
      Is earth too poor to give us
Something to live for here that shall outlive us ?
      Some more substantial boon
Than such as flows and ebbs with Fortune's fickle moon?
      The little that we see
      From doubt is never free ;
      The little that we do
      Is but half-nobly true ;
      With our laborious hiving

What men call treasure, and the gods call dross,
  Life seems a jest of Fate's contriving,
  Only secure in every one's conniving,
A long account of nothings paid with loss,
Where we poor puppets, jerked by unseen wires,
  After our little hour of strut and rave,
With all our pasteboard passions and desires,
Loves, hates, ambitions, and immortal fires,
  Are tossed pell-mell together in the grave.
But stay ! no age was e'er degenerate,
Unless men held it at too cheap a rate,
For in our likeness still we shape our fate.
    ▪ Ah ! there is something here
  Unfathomed by the cynic's sneer,
  Something that gives our feeble light
  A high immunity from Night,
  Something that leaps life's narrow bars
To claim its birthright with the hosts of heaven ;
  A seed of sunshine that doth leaven
Our earthly dulness with the beams of Stars,
      And glorify our clay
With light from fountains elder than the Day ;
  A conscience more divine than we,
  A gladness fed with secret tears,
  A vexing, forward-reaching sense
  Of some more noble permanence ;
    A light across the sea,
Which haunts the soul, and will not let it be,
Still glimmering from the heights of undegenerate years."
                              J. Russell Lowell.

" To believe and know that everything shall have a higher end
and issue than we can see,—this is to see life, to feel it in and
around us."   *James Hinton.*

"Nothing in life has any meaning, except as it draws us
farther into God, and presses us more closely to Him."
                              F. W. Faber, D.D.

" To live consists not in enjoying the day and forgetting in
the night; but in a waking conscience, a self-forgetful heart, an
ungrudging hand, a thought ever earnest for the truth; in a perpetual outlook of hope from our lower point upon an upper and
infinite glory."   *James Martineau, D.D.*

" As, in a narrow isle, whatever path we follow it soon ends in
the pathless sea, and all movements have one destiny; so in our
narrow life thought never travels far before it looks out on that
which it cannot measure or define; which was, and is, and is to
come.   This, the Everlasting, is the only Substance, of which all
things are phenomena.   This is the abiding Power of which the
recurrent sequences of natural law are fragmentary manifestations.
This is the all-pervading life which makes the heavens to smile,
and the twinkling leaves to dance, and the clouds to frown, and
the winds and the waves to sing their ' song which is wild and
slow.' "   *J. Allanson Picton.*

" 'Tis the good acting, rather than great part,
    Ennobles life's poor play.   The tawdry robe,
    The tinsel crown, distinguish for the hour
    Its wearer from his fellows.   But the power,
    The thorough, the whole-hearted energy,
    With which the player plays his special part,
    However mean it be—'tis this alone
    That constitutes true greatness."

                                          S. W. Partridge.

" Everywhere the birth of the spiritual requires the death of the
carnal.   Everywhere the husk must drop away, in order that the
germ may spring out of it.   Everywhere, according to our Lord's
declaration, that which would save its life loses it, and that which
loses its life preserves it.   And the highest glory of the highest
life is to be offered up a living sacrifice to God for the sake of our
brethren.   This is the principle of life which circulates through
the universe, and whereby all things minister to each other, the
lowest to the highest, the highest to the lowest.   This is the
golden chain of love, whereby the whole creation is bound to the
throne of the Creator."   *Archdeacon Julius C. Hare.*

" Lord, when in silent hours I muse
  Upon myself and Thee,
I seem to hear the stream of life
  That runs invisibly.

*   *   *   *   *

And I would live in such a course,
  That men to me may say,
' Oh, whence hast thou thy joy and force,
  What is thy secret stay ? '

My joy, when truest joy I have,
  It comes to me from heaven ;
My strength, when I from weakness rise,
  Is by Thy Spirit given.

And while He shines as He has shone,
  Whom Thou hast made my stay,
Life can but gently float me on,
  Not hurry me away."

Rev. T. T. Lynch.

" It is one great advantage of a gregarious mode of life, that each person rectifies his mind by other minds, and squares his conduct to that of his neighbours, so as seldom to be lost in eccentricity."   *Nathaniel Hawthorne.*

" Life is composed of few things indefinitely diversified, and is like the ringing of a great many changes on a small number of bells ; or as the ever new appearances from the shifting of the same materials in a kaleidoscope."

W. B. Clulow.

" Many parts of our lives that seemed unmarked by any conspicuous Divine help while passing, flash up into clearness when seen through the revealing light of memory, and gleam in purple in the sunset, though they seemed but grey bare rock while we stumbled among them."

Alexander Maclaren, D.D.

" No man does much with life who does not plant his foot firmly down on some one ' to-day,' and strive with his whole energy to impress himself upon it."   *Rev. W. Dorling.*

6

" The events of our life become clear in their significance and meaning in proportion as we travel away from them. We discover, too, that not only do the events of our life become clearer in their significance, but more influential in our lives, the further we travel from them."   *Rev. H. Simon.*

" Happy the man whose life is one long Te Deum ! He will save his soul, but he will not save it alone, but many others also. Joy is not a solitary thing, and he will come at last to His Master's feet, bringing many others rejoicing with him, the resplendent trophies of his grateful love."   *F. W. Faber, D.D.*

"There is no hour that has not its births of gladness and despair, no morning brightness that does not bring new sickness to desolation as well as new forces to genius and love. There are so many of us, and our lots are so different : what wonder that Nature's mood is often in harsh contrast with the great crisis of our lives ? We are children of a large family, and must learn, as such children do, not to expect that our hurts will be made much of—to be content with little nurture and caressing, and help each other the more."   *George Eliot.*

" There is a public life, there is a life that the neighbours can see, and read, and comment upon ; but there is a within life, an interstitial life, that fills up all the open lines and broken places, and only God sees that interior and solemn existence."

Joseph Parker, D.D.

" Christian life must be individual, as the natural character is."

Elizabeth Prentiss.

" In the autumn season of life character comes out, like the leaves, in its true colours, beautiful or repulsive. There is an accent in a true life that all men can recognise."

J. W. Blore.

" The hardest parts of life—the most bitter things in it—are written by our own hands,—the upbraidings of conscience, the stings of memory, the reproach of wasted opportunities, and the falsity and folly which make our life often seem so mean to ourselves.'   *Rev. John Ker.*

"' What joy to live beneath the eyes
    Which look'd the spirit ' through and through,'
Which penetrated each disguise,
    And would not let us be untrue ;

Yet through the thickest veil descried
    The little spring of good below,
And pierced the icy crust of pride,
    That happy, humble tears might flow ;

Rending each soft disguise, which spares
    The evil thing by gentle name,—
For sinners, founts of melting tears,
    But for the sin unquenchèd flame ;

That saw the very spot within
    On which to lay the healing touch ;
That had no pity for the sin,
    Because for those who sinn'd so much ;

    *   *   *   *   *

Those eyes still watch us, not from far,
    Still pitying, ' look us through and through,'
And through the broken sketch we are,
    Foresee the heavenly likeness true ;

Through all its soft and silken dress
    The creature of the dust descry,
Yet 'neath the shapeless chrysalis
    The Psyche moulding for the sky."

                        Elizabeth Charles.

       " Would'st truly live ?
Regret not yesterday, scorn not to-day,
Nor trust too much to-morrow. But live so
That earth shall be to thee heaven's corridor,
The ante-room of bliss. Ah ! trifle not
With life's young hours, but while thou livest, live.
The palette, colour-filled, is on thine hand,
The virgin canvas wooeth thy design ;
What picture wilt thou paint ? "

                        S. W. Partridge.

"Of each individual among us it may be said with truth, at any given moment, that he is either rising to, or declining from, the prime of life and the maturity of his physical powers. And the mind, no less than the body, is in a continual flux. It, too, has its moral element, the society in which it lives; it, too, has its nourishment, which it is constantly imbibing,—the influences of the world and the lower nature, or those of the Spirit of God."

Dean Goulburn.

"In the fields of thought, feeling, speculation, faith—wherever there are any outputtings of life, there will the living soul be found more or less in conflict. It is impossible to have an inner life without its asserting itself." *Rev. P. B. Power.*

"Life is made up of marble and mud. And without all the deeper trust in a comprehensive sympathy above us, we might hence be led to suspect the insult of a sneer, as well as an immitigable frown, on the iron countenance of fate. What is called poetic insight is the gift of discerning, in this sphere of strangely-mingled elements, the beauty and the majesty which are compelled to assume a garb so sordid."

Nathaniel Hawthorne.

"Temptation is the condition of human life, and to try to flee from it in one shape, is often only to provoke it in another. Every period of life, every class in society, every occupation and calling, duties as well as pleasures, work as well as rest, contain within them the elements of an incessant temptation, which it is at once our folly to ignore, our discipline to encounter, and our glory to overcome." *Bishop Thorold.*

"It is a line of death that marks the track of life."

Rev. T. T. Lynch.

"Remember that some of the brightest drops in the chalice of life may still remain for us in old age. The last draught which a kind Providence gives us to drink, though near the bottom of the cup, may, as is said of the draught of the Roman of old, have at that very bottom, instead of dregs, most costly pearls."

W. Abiah Newman.

" The conception is at least in close kindred with a noble truth ;—*that a soul occupied with great ideas best performs small duties ;* that the divinest views of life penetrate most clearly into the meanest emergencies ; that so far from petty principles being best proportioned to petty trials, a heavenly spirit taking up its abode with us can alone sustain well the daily toils, and tranquilly pass the humiliations, of our condition ; and that, to keep the house of the soul in order due and pure, a god must come down and dwell within, as its servant of all work."

James Martineau, D.D.

" The life of a holy Christian should be one perpetual Sacrament. Every moment of his daily life may unite him by faith with Christ, so that his clothing, food, home, friends, work, and leisure may all nourish and feed the life within, and bring into his storehouse things new and old to enrich the mind of the spirit from without. By thus receiving Christ in His providences and His creation, by His outward no less than His inward teachings, we shall be fashioned after His likeness, and grow to manhood in His kingdom." *Maria Hare.*

"You have been speaking, . . . of very high and wonderful things, into which, it would seem, even the angels dare not look ; for we are, as would appear, taught in Scripture that it is in man's history that they see the workings of Divine Glory. And indeed, . . . when you have lived to the limit of my many years, you will not stumble at this ; nor think this life a low and poor place in which to seek the Divine Master, walking to and fro. These high matters of which you speak, and this heavenly life, is not to be disbelieved, only it seems to me—more and more— that the soul or spirit of every man in passing through life among familiar things is among supernatural things always, and many things seem to me miraculous, which men think nothing of, such as memory, by which we live again in place and time . . . and the love of one another, by which we are led out of ourselves, and made to act against our own nature by that of another, or, rather, by a higher nature than that of any of us ; and a thousand fancies and feelings which have no adequate cause among outward things." *John Inglesant.*

" Upon the banks of Life's deep streams
Full many a flower groweth,
Which with a wondrous fragrance teems,.
And in the silent water gleams,
And trembles as the water floweth.
Many a one the wave upteareth,
Washing ever the roots away,
And far upon its bosom beareth,
To bloom no more in Youth's glad May ;.
As farther on the river runs,
Flowing more deep and strong,
Only a few pale scattered ones
Are seen the dreary banks along ;
And, where those flowers do not grow,
The river floweth dark and chill,
Its voice is sad, and with its flow
Mingles ever a sense of ill ;
Then, Poet, thou who gather dost
Of Life's blest flowers the brightest,
Oh, take good heed they be not lost
While with the angry flood thou fightest !
In the cool grottoes of the soul,
Whence flows thought's crystal river,
Whence songs of joy for ever roll
To Him who is the Giver,—
There store thou them, where fresh and green
Their leaves and blossoms may be seen,
A spring of joy that faileth never ;
There store thou them, and they shall be
A blessing and a peace to thee,
And in their youth and purity
Thou shalt be young for ever ;
Then, with their fragrance rich and rare,
Thy living shall be rife,
Strength shall be thine thy cross to bear,
And they shall be a chaplet fair,
Breathing a pure and holy air,
To crown thy holy life." *J. Russell Lowell.*

" If one advances confidently in the direction of his dreams, and endeavours to live the life which he has imagined, he will meet with a success unexpected in common hours. He will put some things behind, will pass an invisible boundary ; the old laws will be expanded, and interpreted in his favour in a more liberal sense. In proportion as he simplifies his life, the laws of the universe will appear less complex, and solitude will not be solitude, nor poverty poverty, nor weakness weakness. If you have built castles in the air, your work need not be lost ; that is where they should be. Now put the foundations under them."

Henry D. Thoreau.

" The boundless blue sky of Christ's love bends over us, comprehends our little life within it, as the horizon embraces the landscape ; wherever we move, we are within that blue circular tent, but can never touch its edges ; it folds about with equal serenity and adaptability the lofty mountain and the lowly vale, the foaming torrent and the placid lake ; the bold, rugged, aspiring nature, and the quiet, retiring disposition, the man of action and the man of thought, the impetuous Peter and the loving John ; it softens the sharp extremes of things, and connects the highest and lowest by its subtle, invisible bond, and yet stretches far aloft beyond the reach of sight or sense into the fathomless abyss of infinity. Or, to take the sea as the comparison, the sea touches the shore along one narrow line, and all the beauty and fertility of that shore are owing to its life-giving dews and rains ; but it stretches away from the shore, beyond the horizon, into regions which man's eye has never seen, and the further it recedes, the deeper and the bluer its waters become. And so the love of Christ touches us along the whole line of our life, imparts all the beauty and fruitfulness to that life, but it stretches away from the point of contact into the unsearchable riches of Christ, the measureless fulness of the Godhead,—that ocean of inconceivable, incommunicable love which no plummet can sound, or eye of angel or saint ever scan ; and the love that we cannot comprehend, that is beyond our reach, is as much love as that whose blessed influences and effects we feel."

Rev. Hugh Macmillan.

" There comes a time to us all, when the sense of responsibility starts up and rebukes our anxiety for ease ; tells us that we are living fast, and once for all, a life that enlarges to the scale of eternity, and is embosomed everywhere in God ; bids us spring from our collapse of selfishness and sleep, take up the full dimensions of our strength, and go forth to do much, if it be possible, and at least to do worthily and well."

James Martineau, D.D.

" The Increate alone is self-sustain'd,
  Life in Himself possessing, and all other
  His creatures, from the burning seraphim
  That sing around His everlasting throne,
  Even to the moth which, floating in the light,
  Wings in an hour its little life away,
  Feed on the bounty of a Father's love,
  Who opens wide His hand and satisfies
  All living things with life-sustaining food."

Bishop E. H. Bickersteth.

" In every man there is a loneliness, an inner chamber of peculiar life into which God only can enter."

George MacDonald, LL.D.

" Does your life tell what God's intention is with it ? "

Thomas Jones.

" The Christian life is conflict all the way,
  An onward pressing through a deadly fray ;
  No Reverend status, rest, or respite claims,
  Dangers but thicken round distinguished names ;
  And while enamoured audiences conclude
  All ghostly strife in such a soul subdued,
  It may be, faith and prayer sustain a brunt
  In the heart's field, as in the battle's front.
  How hard, how hopeless, save as helped of heaven,
  To keep all motive pure from earthly leaven."

Ann Gilbert.

" To make popularity a guide is to come into middle life weak, and into age crippled." *Rev. Theodore T. Munger.*

"Life is deeper than it seems ; and it may well check our petty cavils and censorious judgments to remember, that he who sees and loves according to the truth of things may have his ·place and dear abode in the inner mind of the very neighbour we criticise and the heretic we shun ; may think nothing at all of the small matters we derisively apprehend, and gently love the greater ones we blindly overlook ; and find not only many a precious thing concealed from us, but gracious affection and pure thought that do not even see themselves. Nay ; have you never known among your own friends, one whom you would completely misjudge, if you looked no farther than the outward ways and words through which he intentionally speaks ; who lightly plays with the surface of experience, and elastically throws off its severer incidents ; who is reticent of his own troubles and calm towards those of others, as if both were matters of course, to be quickly dismissed into the past and cleared out of the way ; but who, within this smooth and hard activity, hides quite another nature unsuspected by the common eye ; a pathetic thought betrayed only in the flash of humour that tries to suppress it ; a fire of enthusiasm which never reports itself as heat, but simply in the steadfast tension of a noble life ;—a religious depth, un- revealed unless in the books he loves, and in the simple dignity of his presence ? Were you blind to these things, how different and how mistaken would your affection for him be ! What folly, then, there is in our cynic mood, which either heeds not these inner secrets of the soul, or replaces them by mean conjectures of our own ! There is no human life so poor and small as not to hold many a divine possibility,—its 'angel that always beholds the face of the Father who is in Heaven.' "

James Martineau, D.D.

"There is no organic life without growth in nature, and there is no spiritual life without growth in grace. I say, no spiritual life,—no *continuous state of life*. Spiritual impulses there may be many. Impulses, however, are not life, though they may originate or restore life." *Dean Goulburn.*

"Life is strong, because it is dependent ; immortal, because it draws its being from a perennial source." *James Hinton.*

" Life may change, but it may fly not ;
  Hope may vanish, but can die not ;
  Truth be veiled, but still it burneth ;
  Love repulsed,—but it returneth !

Yet were Life a charnel where
  Hope lay coffined with Despair ;
  Yet were truth a sacred lie,
  Love were lust—if Liberty

Sent not life its soul of light,
  Hope its iris of delight,
  Truth its prophet's robe to wear,
  Love its power to give and bear."

P. B. Shelley.

" Religion is not just one of the many duties of life ; it is
itself the life, through which alone all duty can be done."

Thomas Erskine.

" I can judge
Of others but by outward show, and that
Is falser than the actor's studied part.
We dress our words and looks in borrow'd robes ;
The mind is as the face,—for who goes forth
In public walks without a veil at least ?
'Tis this constraint makes half life's misery.
'Tis a false rule : we do too much regard
Others' opinions, but neglect their feelings ;
Thrice happy if such order were revers'd.
Oh, why do we make sorrow for ourselves,
And, not content with the great wretchedness
Which is our native heritage,—those ills
We have no mastery over,—sickness, toil,
Death, and the natural grief which comrades death,—
Are not all these enough, that we must add
Mutual and moral torment, and inflict
Ingenious tortures we must first contrive ? "

Letitia E. Landon.

"Let your daily life be an unuttered yet perpetual pleading
with man for God."   *John Caird, D.D.*

" Only in the sacredness of inward silence does the soul truly meet the secret, hiding God. The strength of resolve which afterwards shapes life and mixes itself with action, is the fruit of those sacred, solitary moments. There is a Divine depth in silence." *Rev. F. W. Robertson.*

" The secret . . . of a cheerful life is involved in a true doctrine as to the end of life. According to the end will be the way; and so far as we make exertions answering to the dignity of the end, and choose and cultivate pleasures like those we expect at the end, we are secure from the canker of ignoble unhappiness." *Rev. T. T. Lynch.*

" Life is to Act, and not to Do is Death."
Lewis Morris.

" Oh, may I join the choir invisible
Of those immortal dead who live again
In lives made better by their presence : live
In pulses stirred to generosity,
In deeds of daring rectitude, in scorn
For miserable aims that end with self,
In thoughts sublime that pierce the night like stars,
And with their mild persistence urge man's search
To vaster issues.
So to live is heaven :
To make undying music in the world,
Breathing a beauteous order that controls
With growing sway the growing life of man.

*　　*　　*　　*　　*

May I reach
That purest heaven, and be to other souls
That cup of strength in some great agony,
Enkindle generous ardour, feed pure love,
Beget the smiles that have no cruelty—
Be the sweet presence of a good diffused,
And in diffusion ever more intense.
So shall I join that choir invisible
Whose music is the gladness of the world."
George Eliot.

"We sit beside the Sphinx of Life,
We gaze into its void, unanswering eyes,
   And spend ourselves in idle strife
To read the riddle of their mysteries.

   *   *   *   *   *

   The meaning of all things in us,—
Yea, in the lives we give our souls,—doth lie ;
   Make, then, their meaning glorious
By such a life as need not fear to die !

   There is no heart-beat in the day,
Which bears a record of the smallest deed,
   But holds within its faith alway
That which in doubt we vainly strive to read.

   One seed contains another seed,
And that a third, and so for evermore ;
   And promise of as great a deed
Lies folded in the deed that went before.

   So ask not fitting space or time ;
Ye could not dream of things which could not be ;
   Each day shall make the next sublime,
And Time be swallowed in Eternity.

   God bless the Present ! it is All ;
It has been Future, and it shall be Past !
   Awake and live ! thy strength recall,
And in one trinity unite them fast.

   Action and Life,—lo ! here the key
Of all on earth that seemeth dark and wrong !
   Win this,—and, with it, freely ye
May enter that bright realm for which ye long."
                        J. Russell Lowell.

"Nothing but the infinite pity is sufficient for the infinite pathos of human life."   *John Inglesant.*

"There is nothing more real, more important to us in daily life than 'not'; we must bring our intellect into accordance with it."   *James Hinton.*

"Oftentimes in life we may seem as those who struggle in a wide storm-sea, knowing their strength only by the greatness of their ineffectual efforts. Yet are we safe. For though we may feel as if rather drifting in a slight skiff over boisterous waters, than making way over them in a strong vessel—yet if, after many days, Columbus found the land which reason taught him to hope for, much more shall we reach the country promised to the faithful."

Rev. T. T. Lynch.

"'The secret of the Lord is with them that fear Him.' Surely in words of inspiration like these there is an endless germinative power to fill with spiritual life the widest horizon of knowledge. For what is the secret of the Lord but this—that all life is a communion with the heavenly Father, all beauty a glimpse of His light, all joy a share in His bliss, all struggle and sorrow but a hint of the ineffable burden that He bears 'in bringing many sons into glory'? He, then, who has this blessed secret, knows why he lives, and why creation enspheres his life, and why the whole world groans and travails in pain until now. Such an experience, when bright and clear, is heaven begun on earth; it is a draught from that 'river of God's pleasures,' which some day we shall follow up to its source behind the veil. And he with whom is this secret of the Lord can look, if with painful longing, yet without despair, on all the darkness of the world's mystery of sin. For his own experience tells him that God is not very far from every one of us. His own communion with God he values, not as a personal or sectarian peculiarity, but as a token of the Divine kinship of all mankind. Indeed, herein often lies the distinction between genuine religious experience and mere sectarian fanaticism. For the one makes us more human than before, brings us down from our personal isolation into the deeper region of life, which, though beneath the surface of consciousness in many, is nevertheless, we feel, a generic attribute of man. The other shuts us up in self or sect, and makes us feel as the detestable Calvinistic sentiment has it,—

'A garden walled around,
Chosen and made peculiar ground.'"

J. Allanson Picton.

"If life were but a brief reality, that fleetly passed into a shadow and nothingness, the point of vanishing would not be without its solemn grandeur. But with how profound a reverence must we look on its last stage, as entering the margin of God's eternity ; as the landmark of earth's boundary ocean, fanned already by the winds, and feeling the spray, of the infinite!"

James Martineau, D.D.

"When the love of God has taken possession of the soul, and the whole man is consecrated to His service, life loses its fragmentary character, and one guiding stream seems to run through it. . . . Many a little rock or eddy that early in its course would turn it aside, is, as it becomes more powerful, swept away or passed over."

Maria Hare.

"Who can know how much of his most inward life is made up of the thoughts he believes other men to have about him, until that fabric of opinion is threatened with ruin?"

George Eliot.

"'Twas a lovely thought to mark the hours,
    As they floated in light away,
By the opening and the folding flowers,
    That laugh to the summer's day.

Thus had each moment its own rich hue,
    And its graceful cup and bell,
In whose colour'd vase might sleep the dew,
    Like a pearl in an ocean-shell.

*   *   *   *

Yet is not life, in its real flight,
    Mark'd thus—even thus—on earth,
By the closing of one hope's delight,
    And another's gentle birth?

Oh! let us live so that flower by flower,
    Shutting in turn, may leave
A lingerer still for the sunset hour,
    A charm for the shaded eve."

Felicia Hemans.

"We must live *in the eternity of God* if we would be quiet amid all the storm and stress of life."

Joseph Parker, D.D.

"The secrets of life are not shown except to sympathy and likeness."   *Ralph Waldo Emerson.*

"How graphically the varied aspects of the leaf picture the various seasons of man's life! The tenderness of its budding and blooming in spring, when that rich golden-green glints on it, that comes only once a year, represents the bright beauty and innocence of youth, when every sunrise brings its fresh glad hopes, and every night its holy, trustful calm. The dark greenness and lush vigour of the summer leaf portray the strength and self-reliance of manhood; while its fading hues on the tree, and its rustling heaps on the ground, typify the decay and feebleness of old age, and that strange, mysterious passing away which is the doom of every mortal. The autumn leaf is gorgeous in colour, but it lacks the balmy scent and the dewy freshness of hopeful spring; and life is rich and bright in its meridian splendour;— deep are the hues of maturity, and noble is the beauty of success, but who would not give it all for the tender sweetness and promise of life's morning hours? Happy they who keep the child's heart warm and soft over the sad experiences of old age, whose life declines as these last September days go out, with the rich tints of autumn and the blue sunny skies of June!"

Rev. Hugh Macmillan.

"The fragment of a life, however typical, is not the sample of an even web; promises may not be kept, and an ardent outset may be followed by declension; latent powers may find their long-waited opportunity; a past error may urge a grand retrieval."

George Eliot.

"The noblest things in life are mixed with the most ignoble, great pretence with infinite substance, vain-glory with solidness. . . . A man has mistaken the secret of human life who does not look for greatness in the midst of folly, for sparks of nobility in the midst of meanness; and the well-poised mind distributes with impartiality the praise and the blame."

John Inglesant.

"Life is never barren or impotent; words, theories, controversies may be, but not life—whatever its character or quality. The meanest, vilest, most erring life does something, and not merely in an evil and harmful way; it goes also to serve for something in connection with the great Divine purpose of human education and development. It is used up without observation, and secretly, in aid thereof. But an honest and dutiful life, though ever so dumb, and ever so lowly—that is sure to be beautifully productive; and the grace of it will be surviving among us, and contributing to the growing health and soundness of the world, long after it has passed away."

Rev. S. A. Tipple.

"We must rise from our ideals, however beautiful, and by effort that will not be conquered, by effort that lifts its hand to heaven for a blessing on the struggle before it grasps the sword for conflict, make the ideals real in our lives."

James McCann, D.D.

"Who doubts, that as in every breathing the life of the body is retained within us through the secret operation of Almighty God, so for every healthful function of our soul's life we need the continual, forecoming, accompanying, sealing grace of God, in Whom it lives and breathes?"

Edward B. Pusey, D.D.

"All draw their life from one deep fountain, all take their goodness and their beauty from Him whose joy is co-eternal with His holiness." *Rev. Stopford A. Brooke.*

"Oh! there are times whose pressure doth efface
Earth's vain distinctions!—when the storm beats loud,
When the strong towers are tottering to their base,
And the streets rock. Who mingle in the crowd?—
Peasant and chief, the lowly and the proud,
Are in that throng! Yes, life hath many an hour
Which makes us kindred, by one chast'ning bow'd,
And feeling but, as from the storm we cower,
What shrinking weakness feels before unbounded power!"

Felicia Hemans.

" Ah ! sweet and strange,
The cycle of a life which turns and turns
Round to the self-same spot, changed yet the same ;
The same but for the mystic beat of Time ;
The same but for the ineffable change of Being,
Which in the same life, grown another, works
Infinite depths of change."   *Lewis Morris.*

" When life begins to be true, it announces itself as an eternal
thing to the mind ; as a caged bird when let loose into the sky
might say : Now I know that my wings are made to beat the air
in flight ; and no logic could ever persuade the bird that it was not
designed to fly ; but when caged, it might have doubted, at times,
as it beat the bars of its prison with unavailing stroke, if its wings
were made for flight.   So it is not until a man begins to use his
soul aright that he knows for what it is made.   When he puts his
life into harmony with God's laws ; when he begins to pray ; when
he clothes himself with the graces of Christian faith and conduct—
love, humility, self-denial, service ; when he begins to live out of,
and unto, his spiritual nature, he. begins to realize what life is,—
a reality that death and time cannot touch."

                              Rev. Theodore T. Munger.

" Many a man the foliage of whose character had been turning
brown and seared and dry, rattling rather than rustling in the
faint hot wind of even fortunes, has come out of the winter of a
weary illness with the fresh delicate buds of a new life bursting
from the sun-dried bark."   *George Macdonald, LL.D.*

" Pentecost after Pentecost comes in our life ; successive
revelations of new and creative thoughts, deeper and clearer
views of truth, uplift and strengthen us ; brighter and truer is our
sight of God, more earnest and more stern, yet more divinely
beautiful, the face of duty ; more loving and more inspiring the
call of Christ to follow Him through life and death to higher life ;
till at last, in the passion of death, we hear the rushing wind of
eternity, and the final earthly Pentecost takes place in the release
of the spirit to find itself at one, in nearer blessedness, with the
Spirit of Eternal Love."   *Rev. Stopford A. Brooke.*

"There is no 'death' worthy to be so called, that does not stretch out its hand and grasp the skirts of a higher life ; save indeed that utter death wherein he lives who lives in pleasure."

James Hinton.

"The severest trials, the happiest privileges of our lives, come to us through our being members one of another."

Rev. J. Llewelyn Davies.

"The higher life begins for us, . . . when we renounce our own will to bow before a Divine law."

George Eliot.

"The lowliest life that faith has freed
Bears witness still that Christ is life,
And that the Life is risen indeed."

Elizabeth Charles.

"Eternal life is holy life,—the exercise of *love* to God and all beings."

W. E. Channing, D.D.

"How often, in the stifling heat and press of life, when trivial cares rise with dry and dusty cloud to shut us in, do we wholly lose our place in the great calm of God, and fret as if there were no infinite Reason embracing the vortex of the world."

James Martineau, D.D.

"Why should we ever weary of this life ?
Our souls should widen ever, not contract,
Grow stronger, and not harden, in the strife,
Filling each moment with a noble act."

James Russell Lowell.

"Our senses are avenues to the inner man ; they ought never to be made independent centres of life. They were given us at once to invite and facilitate the development of the inward nature. When they are confined to this mission, their gratification never palls upon us, nor degenerates into the fierceness of passion. For as they feed the whole man, the glow of healthful life reacts upon them gratefully, with a never-failing sense of pleasure. . . . Social pleasures have a happy place in the by-play of our lives."

J. Allanson Picton.

" The shadows of the mind are like those of the body. In the morning of life they all lie behind us ; at noon we trample them under foot ; and in the evening they stretch long, broad, and deepening before us. Are not, then, the sorrows of childhood as dark as those of age ? Are not the morning shadows of life as deep and broad as those of its evening? Yes; but morning shadows soon fade away, while those of evening reach forward into the night, and mingle with the coming darkness. Man is begotten in delight and born in pain ; and in these are the rapture and labour of his life foreshadowed from the beginning. But the life of man upon this fair earth is made up, for the most part, of little pains and little pleasures. The great wonder-flowers bloom but once in a lifetime."   *Henry W. Longfellow.*

" Thoughts are life's great human links,
    And mingle with our feelings."
                    Letitia E. Landon.

" To create anything in reality is to put life into it."
                    John Ruskin.

" The real is but the half of life ; it needs
    The ideal to make a perfect whole ;
    The sphere of sense is incomplete, and pleads
        For closer union with the sphere of soul."
                    Rev. Hugh Macmillan.

" Between earth and man arose the leaf. Between the heaven and man came the cloud. His life being partly as the falling leaf, and partly as the flying vapour."   *John Ruskin.*

" Unity with duality ; . . . this in every region is the condition of all the higher developments of life."
                    Rev. J. Baldwin Brown.

" We live each of us two lives, an outward and an inward life. And it is only our outward lives which come into frequent contact."   *Montagu Butler, D.D.*

" Life is a book which lasts one's lifetime, but it requires wisdom to understand its difficult pages."   *Samuel Smiles.*

"Spiritual life, . . . is the sum total of the functions which resist sin. The soul's atmosphere is the daily trial, circumstance, and temptation of the world. And as it is life alone which gives the plant power to utilize the elements, and as, without it, they utilize it, so it is the spiritual life alone which gives the soul power to utilize temptation and trial; and without it they destroy the soul."   *Professor Henry Drummond.*

"The Stelvio is more wonderful, and more grand, too. It is a narrow cleft in the mountain, through which the river Inn gushes on its way to Innsbruck. The cliffs on each side rise steep and precipitous, leaving only room for the stream and the road by its side. The descent to it from Nauders is very rapid, which adds to the grandeur. The Inn roars and thunders through it, and I took pleasure in watching the fir-tree stumps, which are cut by the woodmen above in certain lengths, and then committed to the stream to be carried down to the valleys. Some pieces stemmed all falls and projecting points gallantly; others sunk for a time, and then you saw them emerging below, conquerors out of trial. Some were stranded, and left high and dry upon the bank, or on rocks in the centre of the stream: others had got out of the current, and were carried round a projecting point into still water, either stationary, or floating slowly back instead of on, as if there had been a destiny before them, and that destiny unfulfilled; while others beside them, not their superiors in activity or strength, were steadily buffeting their way forwards and home. What an image of life!"

Rev. F. W. Robertson.

"'Tis this which makes
The best assurance of our promised heaven:
This triumph intellect has over death,—
Our words yet live on others' lips; our thoughts
Actuate others. Can that man be dead
Whose spiritual influence is upon his kind?
He lives in glory; and such speaking dust
Has more of life than half its breathing moulds."

Letitia E. Landon.

" Life is the state in which Christ makes Himself known to us, and through which we must make ourselves known to Him."

Dean Stanley.

" We walk here, as it were, in the crypts of life ; at times, from the great cathedral above us, we can hear the organ and the chanting of the choir : we see the light stream through the open door, when some friend goes up before us ; and shall we fear to mount the narrow staircase of the grave, that leads us out of this uncertain twilight into the serene mansions of the life eternal ? "

Henry W. Longfellow.

" The life of a wise man is most of all extemporaneous, for he lives out of an eternity which includes all time."

H. D. Thoreau.

" Too long have I, methought, with tearful eye
　　Pored o'er this tangled work of mine, and mused
Above each stitch awry, and thread confused ;
Now will I think on what in years gone by
I heard of them that weave rare tapestry
At Royal loom, and how they constant use
To work on the rough side, and still peruse
The pictured pattern set above them high :
So will I set MY COPY high above,
　　And gaze and gaze till on my spirit grows
It gracious impress ; till some line of love,
　　Transferred upon my canvas, faintly glows ;
Nor look too much on warp or woof, provide
He whom I work for sees their fairer side ! "

Dora Greenwell.

" Life, like the fountain of Ammon, overflows only at dawn and early morning."　　　　　*J. Cunningham Geikie, D.D.*

" A religious life is not a thing which spends itself like a bright bubble on the river's surface. It is rather like the river itself, which widens continually, and is never so broad or so deep as at its mouth, where it rolls into the ocean of eternity."

Henry Ward Beecher, D.D.

"Through wood, and stream, and field, and hill, and Ocean,
   A quickening life from the Earth's heart has burst,
   As it has ever done, with change and motion,
   From the great morning of the world when first
   God dawned on Chaos ; in its stream immersed
   The lamps of Heaven flashed with a softer light ;
   All baser things pant with life's sacred thirst ;
   Diffuse themselves; and spend in love's delight
   The beauty and the joy of their renewèd might.
   The leprous corpse touched by this spirit tender   ·
   Exhales itself in flowers of gentle breath ;
   Like incarnations of the stars, when splendour
   Is changed to fragrance, they illumine death,
   And mock the merry worm that wakes beneath ;
   Nought, we know, dies."   *P. B. Shelley.*

" Our moments are, so to speak, the gold-dust of life—each a
very small particle by itself, but all golden, and when put together
making a great total, and mounting up to a very high value."
                                        James Culross, D.D.

"The secret of true life is to live according to Nature. But
what Nature—of body, mind, or spirit? Of all three! No one
side of Nature can be exclusively cultivated without harm to the
other. This might be illustrated at length, and the cultivation
of each in proper subordination, the lower to the higher, might
then be duly urged. But how, and in what proportion? The
family, the social, the political pressure without, provides the
solution. We do not live for ourselves. The world needs our
bodies, our minds, our affections, our spiritual nature. We must
cultivate each, not according to whim, but according to individual
endowment, and the social demand ; unselfishly remembering
that because we belong to the Head of Humanity—Christ—we
are members one of another."
                                        Rev. H. R. Haweis.

" The whole course of the life of God in the soul, from first to
last, shows a co-operation of the Divine and the human."
                                        J. Cunningham Geikie, D.D.

" 'Tis a vile life that, like a garden pool,
  Lies stagnant in the round of personal loves ;
  That has no ear save for the tickling lute
  Set to small measures—deaf to all the beats
  Of that large music rolling o'er the world :
  A miserable, petty, low-roofed life,
  That knows the mighty orbits of the skies   .
  Through nought save light or dark in its own cabin.
  The very brutes will feel the force of kind
  And move together, gathering a new soul—
  The soul of multitudes. . . .
  The crane with outspread wing that heads the file
  Pauses not, feels no backward impulses :
  Behind it summer was, and is no more ;
  Before it lies the summer it will reach
  Or perish in mid-ocean.   You no less
  Must feel the force sublime of growing life.
  New thoughts are urgent as the growth of wings ;
  The widening vision is imperious
  As higher members bursting the worm's sheath.
  You cannot grovel in the worm's delights :
  You must take wingèd pleasures, wingèd pains."
                                    George Eliot.

" The Christian life is the only life that will ever be completed. Apart from Christ the life of man is a broken pillar, the race of men an unfinished pyramid.   One by one in sight of Eternity all human Ideals fall short. one by one before the open grave all human hopes dissolve."   *Professor Henry Drummond.*

" Life is based upon caution, unless it be founded in God, and then it is lifted up above all danger, or the dangers that affect it themselves fall away before its supreme strength and immovable confidence."   *Joseph Parker, D.D.*

" Is there any other greater, more satisfying, more majestic thought of life than this—the scaffolding by which souls are built up into the Temple of God? "
                                Alexander Maclaren, D.D.

" Nothing that altogether dies
Suffices man's just destinies.

So should we live, that every Hour
May die as dies the natural flower,—
A self-reviving thing of power ;

That every Thought and every Deed
May hold within itself the seed
Of future good and future need ;

Esteeming Sorrow, whose employ
Is to develop, not destroy,
Far better than a barren Joy."

Lord Houghton.

" Each man's orbit in the world is in reality so circumscribed that we are sure to encounter our own doings, and beings, and havings again and again, and 'ring the changes upon our individuality.' Life is a maelström, in which things converge strongly and swiftly to one centre, and meeting once must meet repeatedly."

Rev. Hugh Macmillan.

" Wouldst thou the life of souls discern ?
Nor human wisdom nor divine
Helps thee by aught beside to learn ;
Love is life's only sign.
The spring of the regenerate heart,
The pulse, the glow of every part,
Is the true love of Christ our Lord,
As man embrac'd, as God ador'd.

But he whose heart will bound to mark
The full bright burst of summer morn,
Loves, too, each little dewy spark
By leaf or flow'ret worn :
Cheap forms, and common hues, 'tis true,
Through the bright shower-drop meet his view ;
The colouring may be of this earth ;
The lustre comes of heavenly birth."

John Keble.

" The life that lives for another, in so doing bursts into flower, and shows its brightest hues, and yields its sweetest fragrance. As the common coarse green leaf changes into the delicately formed and brilliantly coloured petal in the conversion of leaf buds into flower buds ; so in the conversion of lovers of pleasure into lovers of God—the common things of life, the gifts and attainments of the natural man, are taken up into a higher experience, and beautified and ennobled. Nothing is lost in the transference, but all is changed and enriched. All is given to Christ, and all is received back an hundredfold."

Rev. Hugh Macmillan.

" The epochs of our life are not in the visible facts of our choice of a calling, our marriage, our acquisition of an office, and the like, but in a silent thought by the wayside as we walk ; in a thought which revises our entire manner of life, and says : ' Thus hast thou done, but it were better thus.' And all our after years, like menials, serve and wait on this, and, according to their ability, execute its will. This revisal or correction is a constant force, which, as a tendency, reaches through our lifetime. The object of the man, the aim of these moments, is to make daylight shine through him, to suffer the law to traverse his whole being without obstruction, so that, on what point soever of his doing your eye falls, it shall report truly of his character, whether it be his diet, his house, his religious forms, his society, his mirth, his vote, his opposition. Now he is not homogeneous, but heterogeneous, and the ray does not traverse : there are no thorough lights : but the eye of the beholder is puzzled, detecting many unlike tendencies, and a life not yet at one."

Ralph Waldo Emerson.

" Two streams circulate through the universe,—the stream of Life, and the stream of Death. Each feeds, and feeds upon the other. For they are perpetually crossing, like the serpents round Mercury's Caduceus, wherewith *animas ille evocat Orco Pallentes, alias sub Tartara tristia mittit.* They began almost together ; and they will terminate together, in the same unfathomable ocean ; after which they will separate, and take contrary directions, and never meet again."

Archdeacon Julius C. Hare.

"Such is *the nobility of man's spirit*, that no influence, no occupation, no fascination, nor any reward, can induce him to live, exclusively, in the world to which he seems to be restricted.'

Rev. John Pulsford.

"The world's life may be compared to a coat of chain armour, and every one of us is a mesh or link in it."

Archbishop Benson.

"Life is passion controlled.

"We are parts of Nature, and share her perfection. To a man who thus acts with Nature, failure is not nor can be. He does not succeed in life; his life is success.

"This is success, to find, in all events, my Life.

"Life is no mystery; it is an axiom; it all lies in a definition. The mystery is, not life, but *death*—not that Nature lives, but that man refuses to live."

James Hinton.

"Life glides away in many a bend,
In chapters which begin and end;
Each has its trial, each its grace,
Each in life's whole its proper place.
Life has its joinings and its breaks,
But each transition swiftly takes
Us nearer to or further from
The Threshold of our heavenly home."

F. W. Faber, D.D.

"Every man's work, pursued steadily, tends . . . to become an end in itself, and so to bridge over the loveless chasms of his life."

George Eliot.

"The life of heaven, illumined and quickened continually by the immediate presence and power of the infinite Jehovah, shall flow on an unebbing tide, higher, stronger, farther on with every heave of the restless wave, never pausing to recover strength, never turning back to gain increased momentum, but with resistless, uninterrupted, undiminished volume, filling all eternity with the beauty and the gladness of its perfection."

Rev. Hugh Macmillan.

"Life exists, to our experience, in an almost endless variety of forms; but there is one note which is common to them all, and that is the impression which they make of spontaneous energy.

"Life is never so much life to us as when it most intensely realizes that it is spontaneous or free. This does not imply arbitrariness, or caprice, or self-will; rather the reverse. For never do we feel our energy so spontaneous, and never do we so keenly realize life, as when we are possessed by some noble passion, which bears us, as we say, beyond ourselves; which makes us, in fact, the centre of a power that is far grander than self-will, and that radiates from us with as little effort as heat from burning flames. When we love with self-forgetful devotion, or hate with righteous indignation, we have no feeling of labour, and just as little suspicion of compulsion. Life flows like an impetuous river, with no thought of the heights from which it falls, nor of the broad levels that it seeks. Our moral ideas also modify the sense in which we speak of life. For selfishness seems self-consumed by introverted energies, like a decaying corpse; and so we liken it to death. While generosity and loyalty seem to live the more intensely through their self-expenditure, just as exercise imparts a glow of health." *J. Allanson Picton.*

"Dear to us are those who love us; the swift moments we spend with them are a compensation for a great deal of misery; they enlarge our life;—but dearer are those who reject us as unworthy, for they add another life; they build a heaven before us whereof we had not dreamed, and thereby supply to us new powers out of the recesses of the spirit, and urge us to new and unattempted performances."

Ralph Waldo Emerson.

"The crystal river of eternal life
Flows ever deeper on."
Bishop E. H. Bickersteth.

"All through life there are wayside inns, where man may refresh his soul with love;
Even the lowest may quench his thirst at rivulets fed by springs from above." *Henry W. Longfellow.*

" There are swift hours in life—strong, rushing hours,
  That do the work of tempests in their might !
  They shake down things that stood as rocks and towers
  Unto th' undoubting mind ;—they pour in light
  Where it but startles—like a burst of day
  For which the uprooting of an oak makes way ;—
  They sweep the colouring mists from off our sight,
  They touch with fire thought's graven page, the roll
  Stamp'd with past years—and lo ! it shrivels as a scroll ! "

Felicia Hemans.

" In proportion as our desire to enter into a life altogether
worthy, and so altogether happy, is sincere and earnest, the
entrance into such a life ⁴ ministered to us ' will be abundant.
Christ came that we might have this life, and that we might have
it abundantly. And though we can attain to the sweetness of
life only by overcoming the sharpness of death ; though, only by
a tension of endeavour that seems to tighten ' the strings of life '
till they must snap, can we tune the heavenly harp for its music,—
yet all we *need* do, be assured we *can* do, through Christ who
strengtheneth us."   *Rev. T. T. Lynch.*

" So long as life is young, a perpetual stream of wonder pours
on the mind and bathes it with exhaustless admirations : even
were no lines of unexpected order, no new regions of knowledge
opened, the rapid ripening of the faculties themselves would alter
the apparent lights on every scene, and dissolve the outlines of
each prior experience. And in this training of constant change
there is a marvellous tendency to drive us upon faith in the
Unchangeable. Finite things can be discerned only against the
background of the Infinite. The visible body that glides before
the eye is an island in the Space that has no bounding shore.
The passing event that marks the moment is but a point of
contact where the curve of our being meets the tangent of
Eternity. No appearance emerges and arrests our thought,
without raising questions of Causation, and speaking to us as
from a hidden Mind that meditates in beauty and speaks in
law. To the pure and unspoiled heart, all phenomena that

present no deformity, and all experience clear of sin, open a
way for the consciousness of God ; gleams of Him will frequently
break through ; and a certain tacit sense of His reality and
nearness will linger around even common hours and daily tasks.
Where the first lessons of life, the first stirrings of the soul, are
hindered by no hardening and ungenial culture, its features of
earthly gladsomeness will have a certain modest setting of heavenly
reverence. But the cycle of young experience soon completes
itself. At each return its repetitions become more and more
familiar. Change itself becomes customary, and visits the mind
with monotony rather than variety. The spring seems to burst
with a fainter verdure, and the winter hearth to burn with a less
vivid glow. The morning breeze of young enthusiasm, so fragrant
of the night, so fresh from heaven, grows drowsy with the steady
heat, and sinks to rest ; and the mental and moral life which had
been nursed in vicissitude threatens to perish under the opiate
of usage. Not that Providence abandons us in our maturity, or
omits to ply us with awakening appeals. No sooner has life
ceased to be a *constant* flow of novelty, than it enters on a series
of grand crises, which intersect its even course : its current orbit
has become as a beaten track; but there are nodes it cannot
pass without a spark and thrill. When life-long ties are contracted,
and the green path is entered at one end at whose other the
death-shadow waits in ambush ; when first the home of marriage
is set in order; when the child is born ; when the parent dies ;
when the friend deserts, or the business fails, or the sickness
prostrates,—the Angel of Change looks in again, through her veil
of light, or her curtain of shadows, and reminds us of Him who
abideth in the midst for ever. All these are epochs of natural
devotion ; and only the most insensible heart can pass them with
the neutral heedlessness of instinct, and without any enriching
hue of awful thought. The incidents of the great mortal drama
are so prepared as never to permit the interest to flag ; and even
in its quietest development, where the plot seems most evenly
to act itself out, we cannot be long without some scene whose
pathos touches us, or whose misery appals. These times, moreover, are irregularly scattered on our way, that they may the
better surprise our insensibility, and that we may not kill them

by anticipation ere they come. They are not like the steadily-recurring hours that announce the stated duty and find us mechanically prepared. With whatever wonder we watch the dial-plate of life, we cannot find them there. The deeper crises are marked in invisible characters there, legible only to the Omiscient eye; and as the index traverses, we know not what birth, what death, what sudden hope, what blighted joy, lies just upon its touch. When these hours strike, neither matin nor vesper has such a holy sound : it is God Himself that tolls us in to prayer, and calls us to listen to His great Sermon on the Mount; and whether we are in the field or on the sea, we must throw down the common implements of our work, and go and stand before His face. As one crisis after another is brought upon our lot, it gives us the means of moral admeasurement and deeper self-knowledge ; it reads off the reckoning of our spirits, and tells us whether we more deeply live, or more begin to die. Each newest sorrow revives the thought of those before, and spreads out the past in tender colours before the eye; the pictures of other years, the scenes once pressed by our more elastic feet, the dear forms that were with us there, and held us by the hand, stand out in the clear and silent light : and their very looks may tell us whether any grosser film has gathered on our soul ; whether we can meet their calm and holy face ; whether, as we are further from them in one direction, we are nearer to them in another ; and whether the same atmosphere of God seems to enfold us both and make us one with them and Him. The emergencies that reveal things to our sight are a discipline which, however grievous, we can ill spare ; and, to those that give them worthy welcome, they have a trust nobler than security, and a wisdom better than any joy. The men who most escape them, who most completely realize the false elysium of an easy life ; whose heritage saves them the rough battle with difficulty, to win an honourable footing in the world ; whose health is never shaken by disease, and whose home is invaded by no anxiety,—are rarely those who most penetrate to the moral significance of life, and are alive with the quickest affection and the promptest alacrity of conscience."

James Martineau, D.D.

" How life goes on, its great outline
How noble and ennobling !—but within
How mean, how poor, how pitiful, how mix'd
With base alloy ; how Disappointment tracks
The steps of Hope ; how Envy dogs success ;
How every victor's crown is lined with thorns,
And worn 'mid scoffs !   Trace the young poet's fate :
Fresh from his solitude, the child of dreams,
His heart upon his lips,—he seeks the world,
To find him fame and fortune, as if life
Were like a fairy tale.   His song has led
The way before him ; flatteries fill his ear,
His presence courted, and his words are caught ;
And he seems happy in so many friends.
What marvel if he somewhat overrate
His talents and his state?   These scenes soon change.
The vain, who sought to mix their name with his ;
The curious, who but live for some new sight ;
The idle,—all these have been gratified,
And now neglect stings even more than scorn.
Envy has spoken, felt more bitterly,
For that it was not dreamed of ; worldliness
Has crept upon his spirit unaware ;
Vanity craves for its accustom'd food ;
He has turn'd sceptic to the truth which made
His feelings poetry, and discontent
Hangs heavily on the lute, which wakes no more
Its early music :—social life is fill'd
With doubts and vain aspirings ; solitude,
When the imagination is dethroned,
Is turn'd to weariness."   *Letitia E. Landon.*

" What despair must he feel who, after a whole life passed
in trying to build up himself, resolves that it would have been
far better if he had kept still as the clod of the valley, or yielded
easily as the leaf to every breeze."   *Margaret Fuller Ossoli.*

" Life is a continual miracle.   The bread we eat is always
broken by Divine hands."   *Joseph Parker, D.D.*

"It is a wonderful drama this life of ours, and it is infinitely strange to separate ourselves at times from ourselves and look on as a spectator only at our own little kingdom. It has its beginnings, its rightful kings, its hours of mob-rule, its battles for existence, its revolutions, its reorganizations, its usurpers, its triumphs, and we tremble for its safety as we gaze. Will it get out of all its trouble and change into order and peace at last? At first we cannot tell. We rush back and unite our thought to ourselves again, and it seems that nothing can be done in the darkness and the anarchy of life. It is our hour of depression. The chamber of the soul is 'hung with pain and dreams,' and we ourselves feel like wafts of seaweed swept out to sea on the strong tide of fate into the midnight. But stay;— are we so alone, so unhelped, so forgotten, so feeble, such victims of blind fate? Not so, if a triumphant humanity has lived for us—not so, if Christ has been in our nature bringing into it the order and perfection of Divinity—not so if these words have any value: 'Lo! I am with you always'; for then we are in Him, and to be in Him is to be fated to progress passing into perfection, for we are Christ's and Christ is God's."

Rev. Stopford A. Brooke.

" Bits of gladness and of sorrow,
 Strangely crossed and interlaid;
Bits of cloud-belt and of rainbow,
 In deep alternate braid;
Bits of storm, when winds are warring,
 Bits of calm, when blasts are stayed;
Bits of silence and of uproar,
 Bits of sunlight and of shade;
Bits of forest-smothered hollow,
 And of open sunny glade;
Strips of garden and of moorland,
 Heath and rose together laid;
Serest leaf of brown October,
 April's youngest, greenest blade.
Bits of day-spring and of sunset,
 Of the midnight, of the noon;

Snow and ice of pale December,
　　Living flush of crimson June,
Sands of Egypt, fields of Sharon,
　　Rush of Jordan, sweep of Nile ;
Wells of Marah, shades of Elim,
　　Sinai's frown, and Carmel's smile.
Depths of valley, peaks of mountain,
　　Stretch of verdure-loving plain ;
Barren miles of ocean-shingle,
　　Fertile straths of smiling grain.
Broken shafts of Tyrian columns,
　　Rolled and worn by wave and time ;
Miles of colonnade and grandeur,
　　Luxor's still majestic prime.
Truest music, jarring discord,
　　Voice of trumpet and of lute ;
The thunder-shower's loud lashing,
　　And the dew-fall soft and mute.
Now the garland, now the coffin,
　　Now the wedding, now the tomb ;
Now the festal shout of thousands,
　　Now the churchyard's lonely gloom.
Now the song above the living,
　　Now the chaunt above the dead ;
The smooth smile of infant beauty,
　　Age's wan and furrowed head.
These are the mingled seeds,
Some flowers, some idle weeds,
Some crowded, some alone,
With which man's field is sown,
And from which springs the one
Great harvest of a life that can
Be lived but once by man ! "

H. Bonar, D.D.

" How strangely the comic and the serious are mixed up
together in life, and even in one's own nature."

Dinah M. Muloch.

8

"Our life is hinted, but it is hidden. It gleams out at times;
it flashes in sparks upon us. None has seen the full orb, or
known the full measure of it. We stand before each other as
volumes of books. The binding and lettering are plain enough;
the contents are unknown, or but dimly suspected. We are like
books in which some things are to be hidden from the common
reader as unsafe, and at every few paragraphs the critical things
are expressed in a dead language. So in human life, the simplest
things are read; the interior things are not legible."

Henry Ward Beecher, D.D.

"God means that there should be no parenthesis of famine in
our Christian life. It is not His doing if times of torpor alternate
with seasons of quick energy and joyful fulness of life. So far as
He is concerned the flow is uninterrupted, and if it come to us in
jets and spurts like some intermittent will, it is because our own
evil has put some obstacle to choke the channel and dam out His
Spirit from our spirits. . . . An unbroken continuity of supplies of
His grace—unbroken and bright as a sunbeam reaching in one
golden shaft all the way from the sun to the earth—is His purpose
concerning us."   *Alexander Maclaren, D.D.*

"We might have been! these are but common words,
    And yet they make the sum of life's bewailing;
They are the echo of those finer chords,
    Whose music life deplores when unavailing.
            We might have been!
 *   *   *   *   *   *
Life is made up of miserable hours,
    And all of which we craved a brief possessing,
For which we wasted wishes, hopes, and powers,
    Comes with some fatal drawback on the blessing.
            We might have been!

The future never renders to the past
    The young beliefs entrusted to its keeping;
Inscribe one sentence—life's first truth and last—
    On the pale marble where our dust is sleeping—
            We might have been."

Letitia E. Landon.

" Life is a running shade, with fettered hands,
That chases phantoms over shifting sands ;
Death is a still spectre on a marble seat,
With ever clutching palms and shackled feet ;
The airy shapes that mock life's slender chain,
The flying joys he strives to clasp in vain,
Death only grasps ; to live is to pursue."

Oliver Wendell Holmes.

" It is precisely when we drink in the greatness of the universe, that we least miss the diviner life within ourselves ; precisely at the solemn moment when the stellar circles glide over our head, and the worlds sweep on profuse as spray from the hidden ocean of creative power ; when the stillness of Nature dissolves us away, and we watch the lights and listen to the leaves, scarce knowing that we have eye or ear ; when in space measurement we are not only dwarfed but absolutely quenched, and become a mere point to mark the zero of physical existence ;—then is it that, in the profound repose of sense, we wake up to the grandeur of our moral being, and feel, as if from the transparent air, the infinite purity we are bound to seek ; that the deforming stains of passion, like the village smoke when the fires of day are dying in the hearth, seem wiped away ; that we own ourselves to belong to One who is deeper than the universe ; and opening our heart to Him, become so conscious of a kindred nature, as to be no longer overpowered by the stars. Standing on the threshold of physical extinction, we are in the very position for looking out through the gate into heavenly glory."

James Martineau, D.D.

" Life will be poor and selfish, and unheroic and mean, unless we live in the presence of Him who loved us even unto the death." *James Culross, D.D.*

" From within we must fetch our strength ; for dependence upon aught external to our own souls leaves us strengthless, when its presence is removed or delayed. . . . Our best blessedness can only be shaken to the centre by ourselves. Life is what we make it."

Rev. F. W. Robertson.

"It is on feeling and on realizing a growth of holiness in pro-portion to the growth of responsible labour and duty, that all the nobility of your inner life depends. For life is then harmonious. The more you become a prince with man, the more you become a son of God. The outward life with man and the inward life with God go hand in hand ; the latter adds the element of eternity to the former." *Rev. Stopford A. Brooke.*

"Look on other lives besides your own. See what their troubles are, and how they are borne. Try to care about some-thing in this vast world besides the gratification of small, selfish desires. Try to care for what is best in thought and action—something that is good apart from the accidents of your own lot." *George Eliot.*

"Is our Christian life to be always lived within barriers which at its best it cannot surmount? Am I never to get into a higher region of experience, a purer air, a brighter light, and a more expansive freedom? We all know how to reply to these questions : we can all say, Ye are not straitened in God, ye are straitened only in yourselves ; straitened in your own expectations almost as much as in your own endeavours." *Dean Vaughan, D.D.*

"There is nothing so sweet as duty, and all the best pleasures of life come in the wake of duties done." *Jean Ingelow.*

"The real poetry of life is found where He found it,—in multiplying loaves and fishes ; in descending to things so mean as wine required for a feast ; in collecting a few rude, simple people around Him ; in working the earlier part of His existence humbly at the carpenter's trade ; in a very homely existence." *Rev. F. W. Robertson.*

"We cannot leave society while one clod remains unpervaded by Divine life. We cannot live and grow in consecrated earth alone. Let us rather learn to stand up like the Holy Father, and with extended arms bless the whole world." *Margaret Fuller Ossoli.*

"Methinks life is what the actor is,—
Outside there is the quaint and gibing mask;
Beneath, the pale and careworn countenance."

Letitia E. Landon.

" He liveth long who liveth well!
All other life is short and vain;
He liveth longest who can tell
Of living most for heavenly gain.

He liveth long who liveth well!
All else is being flung away;
He liveth longest who can tell
Of true things truly done each day.

*　　*　　*　　*　　*

Be what thou seemest; live thy creed;
Hold up to earth the torch divine;
Be what thou prayest to be made;
Let the great Master's steps be thine.

Fill up each hour with what will last;
Buy up the moments as they go;
The life above, when this is past,
Is the ripe fruit of life below."

H. Bonar, D.D.

"In the life of every one there has been one trial, one crisis,
to which great issues are attached."

Rev. F. W. Robertson.

"This life is a great schoolhouse. The wise Teacher trains
in us such gifts as, if we graduate honourably, will be of most
service in the perfect manhood and womanhood that come after.
He sees, as we do not, that a power is sometimes best trained by
repression. 'We do not always lose an advantage when we
dispense with it,' Goethe says. But the suffocated lives . . .
make my heart ache sometimes. I take comfort in thinking how
they will bud and blossom up in the air by-and-bye. . . . We tread
them underfoot in our careless stepping now and then, and do
not see that they have not the elasticity to rise from our touch."

Elizabeth S. Phelps.

" Only in heaven shall each human life be freely suspended in
the midst of its circumstances, and take, as it were, the form of
a perfect sphere."   *Rev. Hugh Macmillan.*

" Life's a vast sea
That does its mighty errand without fail,
Panting in unchanged strength though waves are changing."
                                    George Eliot.

" A man's life should be his vindication."
                                    Joseph Parker, D.D.

" Life is not one of the homeless forces which promiscuously
inhabit space, or which can be gathered like electricity from
the clouds and dissipated back again into space.   Life is definite
and resident ; and Spiritual Life is not a visit from a force, but
a resident tenant in the soul."
                                    Professor Henry Drummond.

" In Christian life, every moment and every act is an opportunity for doing the one thing of *becoming* Christ-like.   Every
day is full of a most impressive experience.   Every temptation
to evil temper which can assail us to-day will be an opportunity
to decide the question whether we shall gain the calmness and
the rest of Christ, or whether we shall be tossed by the restlessness and agitation of the world.   Nay, the very vicissitudes of
the seasons, day and night, heat and cold, affecting us variably,
and producing exhilaration or depression, are so contrived as
to conduce towards the being which we become, and decide
whether we shall be master of ourselves, or whether we shall
be swept at the mercy of accident and circumstance, miserably
susceptible of merely outward influences.   Infinite as are the
varieties of life, so manifold are the paths to saintly character ;
and he who has not found out how directly or indirectly to make
everything converge towards his soul's sanctification has as yet
missed the meaning of this life."   *Rev. F. W. Robertson.*

" The temptations of to-day are always more or less the result
of the life of yesterday, the character and actions of the past
reappearing, not only in the good, but in the evil of the present."
                                    G. S. Barrett.

" The little courtesies which form the small change of life, may separately appear of little intrinsic value, but they acquire their importance from repetition and accumulation. They are like the spare minutes, or the groat a day, which proverbially produce such momentous results in the course of a twelvemonth or in a lifetime." *Samuel Smiles.*

" To live thoughtfully is to advance in life, and feel ourselves being laid hold of by the powers of the world to come."
W. Mountford.

" Live for to-day ! to-morrow's light
To-morrow's cares shall bring to sight,
So sleep like closing flowers at night,
And Heaven thy morn will bless."
John Keble.

"All of life is one great warfare. Every thought, word, and deed is a portion of it. *Edward B. Pusey, D.D.*

" Oh, righteous doom, that they who make
Pleasure their only end,
Ordering the whole life for its sake,
Miss that whereto they tend."
Archbishop Trench.

" It is the characteristic of man that he plans and remembers ; he plans to gain an object, he remembers his plan and looks for its fulfilment. Life is based on this idea of a return or reward to be gained : that is, it is not its own reward. It is not enough for man simply to live."
Rev. Theodore T. Munger.

"A man's life is a tower, with a staircase of many steps,
That, as he toileth upward, crumble successively behind him :
No going back; the past is an abyss; no stopping, for the present perisheth :
But ever hasting on, precarious on the foothold of To-day ;
Our cares are all To-day ; our joys are all To-day ;
And in one little word, our life, what is it but—To-day ?"
Martin F. Tupper, D.C.L.

" In the heat and struggle of mid-life, it is a severe but often a purifying retreat to be lifted into the lonely observatory of memory, above the fretful illusions of the moment, and in presence once more of the beauty and the sanctity of life. The voiceless counsels that look through the visionary eyes of our departed, steal into us behind our will, and sweep the clouds away, and direct us on a wiser path than we should know to choose. If age ever gains any higher wisdom, it is chiefly that it sits in a longer gallery of the dead, and sees the noble and saintly faces in further perspective and more various throng. The dim, abstracted look that often settles on the features of the old, what means it? Is it a mere fading of the life? an absence, begun already, from the drama of humanity? a deafness to the cry of its woes and the music of its affections? Not always so : the seeming forgetfulness may be but brightened memory ; and if the mists lie on the outward present, and make it as a gathering Night, the more brilliant is the lamp within that illuminates the figures of the Past, and shows again, by their flitting shadows, the plot in which they moved and fell. It is through such natural experiences—the treasured Sanctities of every true life—that God ' discovereth to us deep things out of darkness, and turneth into light the shadow of Death.' "

James Martineau, D.D.

"Life isa perpetual Advent. The marriage supper is always laid, in some guise or other. There is no day that has not its approaching glory, its light that beckons, its table that groans."

Rev. S. A. Tipple.

" Our life's floor
Is laid upon Eternity ; no crack in it
But shows the underlying heaven."

Canon Kingsley.

"We often live to see the reason of affliction ; how all the events of life hang so wonderfully together, that afterwards we can frequently trace the chain of events, and see in humble faith and awe that out of each one has been evolved the other, and that everything, bad and good, must necessarily have happened exactly as it did." *Dinah M. Muloch.*

" Human life, as a matter of fact, is made up of graver and lighter passages. There is no true portraiture of it which does not present its reliefs and recreations alongside of its burdensome pressure and cares. There is no single waking moment of our life which we can afford to lose." *Dean Goulburn, D.D.*

"Life is in league with universal forces, and subsists by universal law." *James Hinton.*

" Life has two ecstatic moments—one when the spirit catches sight of Truth, the other when it recognizes a kindred spirit. People are for ever groping and prying around Truth ; but the vision is seldom vouchsafed to them. We are daily handling and talking to our fellow-creatures ; but rarely do we behold the revelation of a soul in its naked sincerity and fervid might. Perhaps, also, these two moments generally coincide. In some churches of old, on Christmas Eve, two small lights, typifying the Divine and the Human nature, were seen to approach one another gradually, until they met and blended, and a bright flame was kindled. So likewise it is when the two portions of our spiritual nature meet and blend that the brightest flame is kindled within us. When our feelings are the most vivid, our perceptions are the most piercing; and when we see the furthest, we also feel the most. Perhaps it is only in the land of Truth that Spirits can discern each other ; as it is when they are helping each other on that they may best hope to arrive there."

Archdeacon Julius C. Hare.

" The growth of Christian life is to be measured by the growth of *love ;* and love itself is to be measured in its progressive states by its restfulness, its undisturbed trust, its victory over every form of fear. The state of perfect loving is incompatible with distrust. When the heart is first awakened to affection, it is disturbed and agitated. It fluctuates with every shade of hope and fear alternately. It rushes from one extreme of confidence to the opposite of doubt. But this is only while it is *filling.* The heart beginning to love is like a bay into which the star-drawn tides are rushing. The waters come with violence. They stir up the sand and sediment. They dash and murmur on the edges of the shore. They whirl and chafe about the rocks, and the whole bay is agitated with strife and counterstrife of swirling waters, until they have nearly reached their height. Then, when great depth is gained, when the shores are full, when no more room is found for the floods, the bay begins to tranquillize itself, to clear its surface ; and, effacing every wrinkle, and blowing out every bubble, and hushing every ripple along the shore, it looks up with an open and tranquil face into the sky, and reflects clearly the sun and moon that have drawn it thither. And so does the soul, while filling, whirl with disquiet, and fret its edges with wrinkles and eddies, but when it is filled with love, it rests and looks calmly up, and reflects the image of its God."

Henry Ward Beecher, D.D.

" What is your life ? It is even as a vapour that appeareth for a little time, and then vanisheth away. I suppose few people reach the middle or latter period of their age without having at some moment of change or disappointment felt the truth of these bitter words, and been startled by the fading of the sunshine from the cloud of their life into the sudden agony of the know-ledge that the fabric of it was as fragile as a dream, and the endurance of it as transient as the dew. But it is not always that even at such times of melancholy surprise we can enter into any true perception that the human life shares, in the nature of it, not only the evanescence, but the mystery of the cloud ; that its avenues are wreathed in darkness, and its forms and courses no less fantastic, than spectral and obscure ; so that not only in the vanity which we cannot grasp, but in the shadow which we cannot pierce, it is true of this cloudy life of ours, that 'man walketh in a vain shadow, and disquieteth himself in vain.' And least of all, whatever may have been the eagerness of our passions, or the height of our pride, we are able to understand in its depth the third and most solemn character in which our life is like those clouds of heaven ; that to it belongs not only their transience, not only their mystery, but also their power ; that in the cloud of the human soul there is a fire stronger than the lightning, and a grace more precious than the rain ; and that, though of the good and evil it shall one day be said alike, that the place that knew them knows them no more, there is an infinite separation between those whose brief presence had there been a blessing, like the mist of Eden that went up from the earth to water the garden, and those whose place knew them only as a drifting and changeful shade, of whom the heavenly sentence is, that they are 'wells without water; clouds that are carried with a tempest to whom the mist of darkness is reserved for ever.'

"Let us, for our lives, do the work of men, while we bear the form of them, since those lives are *Not* as a vapour, and do Not vanish away."
John Ruskin.

"When our Saviour told us to live by the day, He meant, I think, a day encompassed by Eternity—a day whose yesterday had gone up to God, to add its little record to the long unforgotten history of the past, whose to-morrow may take us up to God ourselves. We are to live by the day, not as butterflies, which are creatures of a day, but as mortal yet immortal beings belong ing to eternity, whose immortal life may end to-night, whose longest life is but an ephemeral fragment of our immortality."
Elizabeth Charles.

"'Life is before ye'—oh! if ye could look
  Into the secrets of that sealèd book,
  Strong as ye are in youth, and hope, and faith,
  Ye should sink down, and falter, 'Give us death!'
  Could the dread Sphinx's lips but once unclose,
  And utter but a whisper of the woes
  Which must o'ertake ye, in your lifelong doom,
  Well might ye cry, 'Our cradle be our tomb!'
  Could ye foresee your spirit's broken wings,
  Earth's brightest triumphs what despisèd things,
  Friendship how feeble, love how fierce a flame,
  Your joy half sorrow, half your glory shame,
  Hollowness, weariness, and, worst of all,
  Self-scorn that pities not its own deep fall,
  Fast gathering darkness, and fast waning light,—
  Oh! could ye see it all, ye might, ye might
  Cower in the dust, unequal to the strife,
  And die but in beholding what is life!

' Life is before ye '—from the fated road
Ye cannot turn : then take ye up your load,
Not yours to tread, or leave the unknown way,
Ye must go o'er it, meet ye what ye may.
Gird up your souls within ye to the deed,
Angels and fellow-spirits bid ye speed !
What though the brightness dim, the pleasure fade,
The glory wane,—oh ! not of these is made
The awful life that to your trust is given.
Children of God ! inheritors of heaven !
Mourn not the perishing of each fair toy,
Ye were ordained to do, not to enjoy,
To suffer, which is nobler than to dare ;
A sacred burthen is this life ye bear,
Look on it, lift it, bear it solemnly,
Stand up and walk beneath it steadfastly :
Fail not for sorrow, falter not for sin,
But onward, upward, till the goal ye win ;
God guard ye, and God guide ye on your way,
Young pilgrim warriors who set forth to-day."

Frances A. Kemble.

" A Christian man's life is laid in the loom of time to a pattern which he does not see, but God does ; and his heart is a shuttle. On one side of the loom is sorrow, and on the other is joy ; and the shuttle, struck alternately by each, flies back and forth, carrying the thread, which is white or black, as the pattern needs ; and in the end, when God shall lift up the finished garment, and all its changing hues shall glance out, it will then appear that the deep and dark colours were as needful to beauty as the bright and high colours."   *Henry Ward Beecher, D.D.*

" Life, which else were a series of disconnected fragments, is exhibited to us by memory as an organic whole ; and as we plunge into the past, and reconstruct the picture of our acts and sufferings in bygone years, we gain a clear, sharp insight into the fact of our personality, which has created that history from which we are now so far removed."   *Canon Liddon, D.D.*

" Man is free just in so far as he has life." *James Hinton.*

" Henceforth let no man, peering down
Through the dim glittering mine of future years,
Say to himself, ' Too much ! this cannot be ! '
To-day and custom wall up our horizon :
Before the homely miracle of life
Blindfold we stand, and sigh, as though God were not."
Canon Kingsley.

"Alas, Experience ! No other mentor has so wasted and frozen
a face as yours : none wears a robe so black, none bears a rod
so heavy, none with hand so inexorable draws the novice so
sternly to his task, and forces him with authority so resistless
to its acquirement. It is by your instructions alone that man
or woman can ever find a safe track through life's wilds ; without
it, how they stumble, how they stray ! On what forbidden grounds
do they intrude ; down what dread declivities are they hurled ! "
Charlotte Brontë.

" Man liveth only in himself, but the Lord liveth in all things ;
And His pervading unity quickeneth the whole creation."
Martin F. Tupper, D.C.L.

" Life is God's great Drama. It was thought out and composed
in the Eternal mind before the mountains were brought forth, or
ever the earth and the world were made. In time God made a
theatre for it, called the Earth ; and now the great Drama is being
acted thereon. It is on a gigantic scale, this Drama. The scenes
are shifting every hour. One set of characters drops off the stage,
and new ones come on, to play much the same part as the first,
only in new dresses. There seem to be entanglements, perplexities, interruptions, confusions, contradictions without end ;
but you may be sure there is one ruling thought, one master-
design, to which all these are subordinate. Every incident, every
character, however apparently adverse, contributes to work out
that ruling thought. Think you that the Divine Dramatist will
leave anything out of the scope of His plot ? Nay, the circum-
ference of that plot embraces within its vast sweep every incident
which Time ever brought to birth." *Dean Goulburn, D.D.*

" The secret of true living is to have many interests.

" If you are animated by right principles, and have awakened
to the dignity of life, the subject of amusements may be left
to settle itself."　　　　　　　　　*Rev. Theodore T. Munger.*

" It is hard for us to live up to our own eloquence, and keep
pace with our winged words, while we are treading the solid earth
and are liable to heavy dining."　　　　　　　*George Eliot.*

" Bright with unnumbered laughters, and swollen by a thousand
　　tears,
Rushes along, through upland and lowland, the river of life ;
Sometimes foaming and broken, and sometimes silent and
　　slumbrous,
Sometimes through rocky glens, and sometimes through
　　flowery plains.
Sometimes the mountains draw near, and the black depths
　　swirl at their bases,
Sometimes the limitless meads fade on the verge of the sky,
Sometimes the forests stand round, and the great trees cast
　　terrible shadows,
Sometimes the golden wheat waves, and girls fill their pitchers
　　and sing.

Always the same strange flow, through changes and changes
　　unchanging,
Always—in youth and in age, in calm and in tempest the
　　same—
Whether it sparkle transparent and give back the blue like a
　　mirror,
Or sweep on turbid with flood, and black with the garbage of
　　towns—
Whether the silvery scale of the minnow flash on the pebbles,
Or whether the poisonous ooze cling for a shroud round the
　　dead—
Whether it struggle through shoals of white blooms and
　　feathery grasses,
Or bear on its bosom the hulls of ocean-tost navies—the same.

　　*　　*　　*　　*　　*　　*　　*

What is the secret of life, or the painful riddle of death?
Why is it better to be than to cease, to flow on than to
    stagnate?
Why is the river-stream sweet, while the sea is as bitter as
    gall?

Surely we know not at all, but the cycle of Being is eternal,
Life is eternal as death, tears are eternal as joy.
As the stream flowed, it will flow; though 'tis sweet, yet the sea
    will be bitter:
Foul it with filth, yet the deltas grow green and the ocean is
    clear,
Always the sun and the winds will strike its broad surface and
    gather
Some purer drops from its depths, to float in the clouds of the
    sky;—
Soon these shall fall once again, and replenish the full-flowing
    river.
Roll round then, O mystical cycle! flow onward, ineffable
    stream!"

                             Lewis Morris.

" All noble lives—all lives worth living—are expanded from the
small circles of every-day domestic circumstance into portions of
the grand orbits of the worlds. Yet, doubtless, thereby in themselves such lives must often become fragments instead of wholes,
must seem in themselves unfinished, must be in themselves
inexplicable."   *Elizabeth Charles.*

" Our physical nature is a 'saying' or 'representation' of nature ;
all life indeed is so: *i.e.*, of physical nature. And the human
body, as the ultimate development of the physical life, is a complete
representation of nature. When our mental life attains to be a
perfect representation of nature, then will it not have attained to
the stage of manhood ; a perfect 'saying' or 'representation' of
nature?"   *James Hinton.*

" Life without love would not be worth the having; and without
it, though we had a house and that house a palace, we could not
have a home.'   *Thomas Guthrie, D.D.*

" True Christian life is like the march of a conquering army into a fortress which has been breached : men fall by hundreds in the ditch. Was their fall a failure? Nay, for their bodies bridge over the hollow, and over them the rest pass on to victory."

" We must live to God first-hand."

Rev. F. W. Robertson.

" I say to myself, ' My life is like a wind : it blows and will cease.' But something says in reply, ' Wouldst thou not be one of God's winds, content to blow, and scatter the rain and the dew, and shake the plants into fresh life, and then pass away, and know nothing of what thou hast done?' And I answer, ' Yes, Lord.' "

George Macdonald, LL.D.

" Time is life's freightage, wherewith some men trade and make a fortune ; and others suffer it to moulder all away, or waste it in extravagance. Time is life's book, out of which some extract wondrous wisdom ; while others let it lie unconned, and then die as fools. Time is life's tree, from which some gather precious fruit ; while others lie down under its shadow, and perish with hunger. Time is life's ladder, whereby some raise themselves up to honour, and renown, and glory; and some let themselves down into the deeps of shame, degradation, and ignominy."

John Stoughton, D.D.

" As I watched the ploughman ploughing,
　Or the sower sowing in the fields, or the harvester harvesting,
　I saw there too, O life and death, your analogies ;
　(Life, life is the tillage, and Death is the harvest according)."

Walt Whitman.

" A Christless life under the dominion of tyrannous desires."

Alexander Maclaren, D.D.

" The truest life of man is when he lives on every word that comes forth from God, which God has put it into his power to learn ; and never will he attain to any fulness of stature until he can live in unreluctant recognition of everything around him that he believes to be a Fact."

Rev. F. Myers.

" All duty is eloquent of Deity ; and all the occurrences of daily life by which we are environed, cannot but be . . . within the Providence of God. Therefore, if we would think nothing little, we might perhaps often recognize Christ's presence with us, as in Nathanael's case, when, as it were, merely like him, sitting under our fig-tree."
                                                   Rev. Frederick Myers.

" Occasional wavelets or ripples may be seen at times on the surface of our life, which do not all lie in the same direction, and still less in the direction of the main current; but they are nothing more than the ripples you can see on a gusty day upon the surface of a river, which not only do not go very deep, but do not inter- fere with the settled, constant, irresistible movement of the river towards the sea. Our lives have a general tendency and direction which no mere superficial disturbances will ever avail to arrest, and that general tendency or direction indicates what is the *sake* by which our life is controlled."
                                                   Enoch Mellor, D.D.

" Living, thou dost not live,
    If mercy's spring run dry."
                                                   Oliver Wendell Holmes.

" Religion is not the matter of life, that you can spread it out and show it, but the spirit of life that makes it different from mechanism and death : it is not the poem's rhyme and stanzas that you may count and scan, but the soul of beauty that makes it music, and the pulse of thought that makes it throb. It can be understood only by sympathy from the heart outwards, not by induction from the appearances inwards. Though the most powerful commander of action, and the most productive agency in history, it is not defined by what it does: it is a mood, an attitude of soul towards God, that alters the whole aspect of the universe, and affixes quite different and deeper meanings to all its symbols. It is a presence at the very springs of thought, sending them down limpid and sparkling with a vital air, that nurtures the roots of things wherever the current flows, and enriches life with deeper forests and with greener fields."
                                                   James Martineau, D.D.

" Men's lives are as thoroughly blended with each other as the air they breathe ; evil spreads as necessarily as disease. There is no sort of wrong deed of which a man can bear the punishment alone ; you can't isolate yourself, and say that the evil which is in you shall not spread."   *George Eliot.*

"The visible material life is but the scaffolding under which the unseen and eternal life is rearing. With respect to each of us, there has been from the dawn of our existence a mental as well as a material history—a life of the soul, a course of inward progress or retrogression, a series of changes for good or evil in the character of that mysterious dweller beneath every breast, more worthy to be chronicled, fraught, would we believe it, with interest deeper, more momentous far, than the fortunes and vicissitudes of our outward career. We spend our years, it is written, as a tale that is told ; but there is, may we not say, an underplot in the story of every human life ; and however stirring be the narrative of our outward experience, there is ever a deeper pathos, a more awful and absorbing interest, gathered around the history of the soul."

John Caird, D.D.

" An uneventful life is apt to be poor and barren, unless one has the rare gift, like Wordsworth, of turning every sunrise and sunset, every storm, every changing phase of the old landscape, every fresh day of uneventful household life into newness. It is the events of life—marriage, births, sickness, travel, new scenes and relations, the changes that drop from fortune's wheel, the thunderbolts out of clear skies, the sudden lift of dark clouds—that bring new visions of truth."   *Rev. Theodore T. Munger.*

> "Life, I repeat, is energy of love,
>   Divine or human ; exercised in pain,
>   In strife, and tribulation, and ordained,
>   If so approved and sanctified, to pass,
>   Through shades and silent rest, to endless joy."
>   *Henry W. Wordsworth.*

" The sting of our ignorance is the spur of life, and the consciousness of a secret to discover is the flavour of happiness."

Rev. Stopford A. Brooke·

" Our life must be a holocaust, offered with all its activities and with all its powers upon the altar of the Lord.

" We are to ennoble the ordinary things of life; we are to make trade a beautiful thing, and business a beautiful thing, and commerce a beautiful thing, because it is touched, and hued, and toned, and fringed with the love of God, which is in Christ Jesus our Lord." *W. Morley Punshon, D.D.*

" In order to any great attainment in spiritual life, there must be an indomitable resolve to try and try again, and still to begin anew, amidst much failure and discouragement. On warm dewy mornings in the spring vegetation makes a shoot; and when we rise, and throw open the window, we mark that the may is blossoming in the hedgerows. And those periods when a man can say, ' I lost myself sadly yesterday in temper or in talk; but I know that my crucified Lord took upon Him those sins and answered for them, and to-day I will earnestly strive against them in the Strength of His Spirit, invoked into my soul by earnest prayer,'—these are the warm dewy mornings of the soul, when the spiritual life within us sprouts and blossoms apace. He who would form a sound judgment of his spiritual progress must throw his eye over long, not short, intervals of time. He must compare the self of this year with the self of last; not the self of to-day with the self of yesterday. Enough if amid the divers and shifting expe-riences of the world, and the manifold internal self-communings arising thereupon, that delicate plant, spiritual life, has grappled its fibre a little deeper into the soil than it seemed to have done in an earlier stage of our pilgrimage, now fairly past."
Dean Goulburn, D.D.

" There lies no desert in the land of life,
    For e'en that tract that barrenest doth seem,
    Laboured of thee in faith and hope, shall teem
    With heavenly harvests and rich gatherings rife."
Frances A. Kemble.

" Prayer and kindly intercourse with the poor are the two great safeguards of spiritual life; its more than food and raiment."
Thomas Arnold, D.D.

"Life is lovely every way. Even if we look upon it as an isolated thing, existing apart from the rest of nature, and using the inorganic world merely as a dead pedestal on which to sustain itself, it is still beautiful. Not even a narrow thought like this can strip it of its charm. How lovely life were if it were but a revealing ; the bright blossom wherein nature's hidden force comes forth to display itself; the necessary outpouring of the universal life that circulates within her veins, unseen ! How lovely, if life were rooted in nature's inmost being, and expressed to us in the most perfect form the meaning of the mighty laws and impulses which sway her, and which, as written on the seas, and rocks, and stars, is too vast for us to grasp; the bright and merry life, with its ten thousand voices, bursting forth from the dim and silent Law which rules the world, as, in the babbling spring, the stream that has run darkling underground bursts forth and sparkles to the sun."

James Hinton.

"Life is like the summer's day ; and in the first fresh morning we do not realize the noonday heat, and at noon we do not think of the shadows lengthening across the plain, and of the setting sun, and of the advancing night. Yet, to each and all, the sunset comes at last ; and those who have made most of the day are not unlikely to reflect most bitterly how little they have made of it." *Canon Liddon, D.D.*

"Life is a leaf of paper white,
  Whereon each one of us may write
  His word or two, and then comes night.

'Lo, time and space enough,' we cry,
'To write an epic !' so we try
  Our nibs upon the edge, and die.

Muse not which way the pen to hold,
  Luck hates the slow and loves the bold,
  Soon come the darkness and the cold.

Greatly begin ! though thou have time
  But for a line, be that sublime,—
  Not failure, but low aim, is crime."

J. Russell Lowell.

" Every Christ-like life, that is, is made subject to difficulty, and, like salt—difficulty, trial, hardness, do penetrate, purify, freshen, and preserve the new life from stagnation. It is no solitary law which says that trial penetrates our life with strength. The same law rules nature, and men in their daily work. The school of the veteran soldier, of the great artist, of the skilled mechanic, is hardship, not ease ; severe thought, not lazy fancy ; strong labour, not drifting idleness. The school of high morality is fierce repression of passionate desire. Nor is it otherwise in Nature. A cold wind slays the protected flowers ; but the pine, cradled in the mountains, moored by its anchored roots in the rents of granite ; nursed by rough cold and burning suns, strikes its spurs deeper at every blast, and weaves into its trunk and arms the powers of the frost and storm, until it stands for centuries. It is so with our life, when we have sacrificed it to God. We are salted with difficulty, that we may be the veterans of Heaven ; we learn in sorrow, that we may teach in song ; we bear the storm, that we may be wrought into mighty trees, under whose branches many may find shelter." '

Rev. Stopford A. Brooke.

" Beware of losing self-respect through living dramatically— with a daily appearance put on, which is not true to the reality, with the frequent assumption, before spectators, of that which does not belong to you. Beware of losing it through leading an idle, aimless, useless life, a life without any high or worthy purpose. Beware of losing it, especially, through for ever failing to obey your higher promptings, and for ever regretting and bemoaning the failure, while never seriously endeavouring to improve." *Rev. S. A. Tipple.*

" Our lives make a moral tradition for our individual selves, as the life of mankind at large makes a moral tradition for the race ; and to have once acted nobly seems a reason why we should always be noble." *George Eliot.*

" To know that we have authority, and a sufficient one, is more than half the inspiration of our life."

Enoch Mellor D.D.

" Man's life is not lived in the general : it is made up of a vast multitude of little details ; the sum of which *is* the life ; the putting together of all which, and the tracing up of all which to their secret spring in the principle and in the motive, in the mind and in the soul, is the judgment ; is that great reading of hearts, and that great explaining of mysteries, and that great assignment of destinies, for which the world is daily sowing, and in which shall be the grand reaping."

Dean Vaughan, D.D.

" Life, in its full development, is not the earthly heritage of any human being. We all have some powers that are either wholly or partially dormant. The most earnest and energetic have some talents buried in the napkin, which they have not put out to usury, but have left lying useless in their lives. Many have buried nearly all, and only care to use those which are necessary for their pleasure, or worldly profit. But, in so far exactly as our knowledge of God and Christ is defective, in so far as we hide away from daily work these gifts, does death, and not life, rule over us. And in the same proportion as we progress in consciousness of the growth of God within us, does an increasing activity replace the stagnation that before slumbered in the soul, and do we advance by sure degrees into fuller, deeper, truer life."

James McCann, D.D.

" We know by the truth of Pentecost, that though there is in us baseness, sin, feebleness of will, yet that there is also a God within us, whose inspiration kindles into life the nobler side of our being, and sets it in educating battle against the lower. Religious life is not a succession of constantly recurring shocks, nor ought it to render the man incapable of life in the world. It is not a series of incessant spiritual depressions and excitements, nor is it always being invaded by God with special revelations. It is a slow, though broken growth through trial and failure, through success and joy, through struggle which is commonplace enough—but every now and then it reaches some hilltop, when God appears to bring all the results of our past to a point, and to start us afresh upon a new path."

Rev. Stopford A. Brooke.

" Life is but too dear to us, even with all its precarious joys and heavy calamities ; and constituted even as it is, we can hardly keep our minds fixed upon a brighter state with any degree of steadiness." *Felicia Hemans.*

" We are all, in some measure, children to the end of life, without firmness where we ought to be most deliberate, and governed by passion where we ought to follow most resolutely the dictates of reflection." *W. E. Channing, D.D.*

> " Life is like a journey during night.
> We toil through gloomy paths of the unknown ;
> Heavy the footsteps are with pitfalls round ;
> And few and faint the stars that guide our way :
> But, at the last, comes morning ; glorious ·
> Shines forth the light of day, and so will shine
> The heaven which is our future and our home."
> *Letitia E. Landon.*

" Men go an undulating course,—sometimes on the hill, some-times in the valley.   But he only is in the right who in the valley forgets not the hill-prospect, and knows in darkness that the sun will rise again.   That is the real life which is subordinated to, not merged in, the ideal ; he is only wise who can bring the lowest act of his life into sympathy with its highest thought." *Margaret Fuller Ossoli.*

" The summit of Goatfell, the highest peak in the island of Arran, is composed of the same granite which forms its base, and which has been erupted through intermediate rocks of a different kind.   So we are crowned with the deepest and most essential part of our own life.   Our highest summit is our deepest founda-tion.   Our crown of life is that which we ourselves have formed, and which passes through our whole being." *Rev. Hugh Macmillan.*

" Perfect life is not merely the possessing of perfect functions, but of perfect functions perfectly adjusted to each other, and all conspiring to a single result, the perfect working of the whole organism." *Professor Henry Drummond.*

"The spiritual life is not knowing, nor hearing, but doing. We only know so far as we can do; we learn to do by doing, and we learn to know by doing: what we do, truly, rightly, in the way of duty, that, and only that, we are."

Rev. F. W. Robertson.

"The proof of all life is vital motion; death is stagnant passivity." *J. Cunningham Geikie, D.D.*

"Denial has to come into your life *somewhere*. You deny the body or you deny the soul. Deny the body, and the soul comes to the front, and floods your life with sacred light, with heaven's pure splendour. Gratify the body, and the soul retires, and its hot tears fall in the hearing of God. Self-slaughter takes place somewhere; it is for us to say where it shall take place. It can take place in the cutting off of a hand, or in the thrusting of a dagger into the very fountain of life, and it lies within the power of the human will to say where the wound shall be inflicted."

Joseph Parker, D.D.

"Every human soul has a complete and perfect plan cherished for it in the heart of God—a Divine biography marked out, which it enters into life to live. This life, rightly unfolded, will be a complete and beautiful whole, an experience led on by God and unfolded by his secret nurture, as the trees and the flowers by the secret nurture of the world; a drama cast in the mould of a perfect art, with no part wanting; a Divine study for the man himself, and for others; a study that shall for ever unfold, in wondrous beauty, the love and faithfulness of God; great in its conception, great in the Divine skill by which it is shaped; above all, great in the momentous and glorious issues it prepares."

H. Bushnell, D.D.

"Life is ordained to bear, like land,
Some fruit, be fallow as it will:
Evil has force itself to sow,
Where we deny the healthy seed,—
And all our choice is this,—to grow
Pasture and grain or noisome weed."

Lord Houghton.

"It is a great event in a man's life, when he has discovered that inner 'I' which is always giving its character to the perceptions we form of everything about us, and ever pronouncing its judgment on self and on all things ; which rests not when the body rests, which even then busily strings together pictures, and successions of events, and gives to them all the reality of life ; which stretches back into the past, bridges over the chasm that divides that past from the present, bringing together the dead and the living, and often stirring up the dread exclamation—

'To sleep ! Perchance to dream ! Ay, there's the rub ;
For in that sleep of death, what dreams may come
When we have shuffled off this mortal coil ?'"

H. R. Reynolds, D.D.

"Few know of life's beginnings—men behold
The goal achieved ;—the warrior, when his sword
Flashes red triumph in the noonday sun ;
The poet, when his lyre hangs on the palm ;
The statesman, when the crowd proclaim his voice,
And mould opinion on his gifted tongue :
They count not life's first steps, and never think
Upon the many miserable hours
When hope deferred was sickness to the heart.
They reckon not the battle and the march,
The long privations of a wasted youth ;
They never see the banner till unfurled.

  *   *   *   *   *

Hard are life's early steps ; and, but that youth
Is buoyant, confident, and strong in hope,
Men would behold its threshold, and despair."

Letitia E. Landon.

" As, in the intellectual life, it is better to be possessed by one idea than by none, so in the practical it is better certainly to pursue one right end than none ; but as the former is only the beginning of Reason, so the latter goes no further than the rudiments of Conscience. He is not a musician who can play but one tune ; nor is he a pattern of life who is always on one duty."

James Martineau, D.D.

"There is . . . this consolation to the most way-worn traveller, upon the dustiest road, that the path his feet describe is so perfectly symbolical of human life,—now climbing the hills, now descending into the vales. From the summits he beholds the heavens and the horizon, from the vales he looks up to the heights again. He is treading his old lessons still, and though he may be very weary and travel-worn, it is yet sincere experience."

H. D. Thoreau.

"Life cannot remain quiescent ; it has appropriative and distributive functions, and must operate accordingly."

Joseph Parker, D.D.

"The sculptor, with his Psyche's wings half-hewn,
  May close his eyes in weariness, and wake
  To meet the white cold clay of his ideal
  Flushed into beating life, and singing down
  The ways of Paradise.   The husbandman
  May leave the golden fruitage of his groves
  Ungarnered, and upon the Tree of Life
  Will find a richer harvest waiting him.
  The soldier dying thinks upon his bride,
  And knows his arms shall never clasp her more,
  Until he first the face of his unborn child
  Behold in heaven : for each and all of life,
  In every phase of action, love, and joy,
  There is fulfilment only otherwhere."

H. E. Hamilton King.

"The plant stretches down to the dead world beneath it, touches its minerals and gases with its mystery of Life, and brings them up ennobled and transformed to the living sphere. The breath of God, blowing where it listeth, touches with its mystery of life the dead souls of men, bears them across the bridgeless gulf between the natural and the spiritual, between the spiritually inorganic and the spiritually organic, endows them with its own high qualities, and develops within them those new and secret faculties by which those who are born again are said to *see the kingdom of God.*"

Professor Henry Drummond.

"The life is in the blood, and the will is in the life; the rebellious, independent will of man must be shed out, for in it the fall consists, and in the shedding out of it redemption consists."

Thomas Erskine.

"As the great sky is mirrored in the road-side pool as well as in the ocean, and imparts to that shallow pool something of its own depth and extent, so the infinite life of Christ is represented in the finite life of every one who bears His name, and dignifies and ennobles it." *Rev. Hugh Macmillan.*

"It is how much of the invisible we can bring into this life that makes this life rich and valuable."

Henry Ward Beecher, D.D.

"Life eternal does not consist in knowing that there is a God and that there is a Saviour; but in acquaintance with God and with the Saviour. In knowing Him, as a child knows his father, as a friend knows his friend. When man discovers that his Creator, the fountain of eternity, the fountain of his being and of all being—in whom and by whom he lives, and thinks, and feels, who pervades and sustains his soul and his body in all their parts, who ever is, and ever must be essentially present in every faculty and capacity of his nature, without whom nothing lives, nothing happens, nothing is done through all worlds, in whom, as in their one root, all the varieties of things are united, and from whom, as from their one root, they all grow—when he discovers that this great One, this Mystery which contains and binds in and animates the universe, has a love for him passing thought as well as utterance, a love which led Him to take on Himself the human nature, that in it He might reveal Himself to man— when he discovers that this revelation was made that we might live for ever in the knowledge and fellowship of His holy love, dwelt in by Him, and animated by His Spirit, and filled with His fulness,—oh! then the darkness is past, and the true light is come. We have found the pearl of eternity, the pearl of great price, and know the meaning of that word, 'He that hath the Son hath life'; we have found the pearl, and for joy thereof we go and sell all that we have, and buy it."

Thomas Erskine.

> " They are poor
> That have lost nothing; they are poorer far
> Who, losing, have forgotten ; they most poor
> Of all, who lose and wish they MIGHT forget.
> For life is one, and in its warp and woof
> There runs a thread of gold that glitters fair,
> And sometimes in the pattern shows most sweet
> Where there are sombre colours."
>
> *Jean Ingelow.*

> " Have we not all, amid life's petty strife,
> Some pure ideal of a noble life
> That once seemed possible?   Did we not hear
> The flutter of its wings, and feel it near,
> And just within our reach?   It was.   And yet
> We lost it in this daily jar and fret,
> And now live idle in a vague regret.
> But still *our place is kept*, and it will wait,
> Ready for us to fill it, soon or late :
> No star is ever lost we once have seen,
> We always may be what we might have been.
> Since Good, though only thought, has life and breath,
> God's life—can always be redeemed from death ;
> And evil, in its nature, is decay,
> And any hour can blot it all away ;
> The hopes that lost in some far distance seem,
> May be the truer life, and this the dream."
>
> *Adelaide A. Procter.*

" A man's purpose of life should be like a river, which was born of a thousand rills in the mountains; and when at last it has reached its manhood in the plain, though, if you watch it, you shall see little eddies that seem as if they had changed their minds, and were going back again to the mountains, yet all its mighty current flows, changeless, to the sea.   If you build a dam across it, in a few hours it will go over it with a voice of victory.   If tides check it at its mouth, it is only that when they ebb it can sweep on again to the ocean."

Henry Ward Beecher, D.D.

"Life appears to me too short to be spent in nursing animosity, or registering wrongs."   *Charlotte Brontë.*

"Inspiration is the breathing in of God's life into ours. He has made our hungry and thirsty life to be preparative for the breathing in of His own satisfying life."
                                        Rev. T. T. Lynch.

"Woe to the men who see no place for resistance in this generation! I believe in a growth, a passage, and a new unfolding of life whereof the seed is more perfect, more charged with the elements that are pregnant with diviner form. The life of a people grows, it is knit together and yet expanded, in joy and sorrow, in thought and action; it absorbs the thought of other nations into its own form, and gives back the thought as new wealth to the world; it is power, and an organ in the great body of the nations. But there may come a check, an arrest; memories may be stifled, and love may be faint for the lack of them; or memories may shrink into withered relics—the soul of a people, whereby they know themselves to be one, may seem to be dying for want of common action. But who shall say, 'The fountain of their life is dried up, they shall for ever cease to be a nation'? Not he who feels the life of his people stirring within his own. Shall he say, 'That way events are wending, I will not resist'? His very soul is resistance, and is a seed of fire that may enkindle the souls of multitudes, and make a new pathway for events."   *George Eliot.*

"This is life—broken chapters, exhausted affections, buried interests, ghosts that drift and die, things that are uneternal. And our conscious personality would be in much danger were it not for one thing that binds the whole together, . . . it is the uninterrupted growth of the spiritual life in us."
                                    Rev. Stopford A. Brooke.

"Life, all kinds of life, tend to companionship, and rejoice in it, from the fecund larvæ and the buzzing insect cloud, up to the kingly lion and the kinglier man."
                                    W. Morley Punshon, D.D.

"I may not hope from outward forms to win
   The passion and the life, whose fountains are within.

      *   *   *   *   *   *

      We receive but what we give,
And in our life alone does nature live :
Ours is her wedding-garment, ours her shroud !
   And would we aught behold, of higher worth,
Than that inanimate cold world allowed
To the poor loveless ever-anxious crowd,
   Ah ! from the soul itself must issue forth,
A light, a glory, a fair luminous cloud
      Enveloping the Earth—
And from the soul itself must there be sent
   A sweet and potent voice, of its own birth,
Of all sweet sounds the life and element ! "

                           S. T. Coleridge.

" Art thou stricken in life's battle ?   Many wounded round thee
   moan,
Lavish on their wounds thy balsams, and that balm shall heal
   thine own.

      *   *   *   *   *   *

Is the heart a living power ?   Self-entwined, its strength sinks
   low ;
It can only live in loving, and by serving love will grow."

                           Elizabeth Charles.

" There is a sense in which our faith—*i.e.*, our religious life—
never can be ' finished.'   It will remain a perennial growth, with
and in ourselves for ever."

                         Alexander Raleigh, D.D.

" The most exulting moments of life are those when, after a
conflict of strong passion with the sense of duty, we come off
conquerors, and are conscious that we have risen in spiritual
existence."   *W. E. Channing, D.D.*

" Life can be reared only by life."

                         Joseph Parker, D.D.

" It is an awful hour—let him who has passed through it say how awful—when this life has lost its meaning, and seems shrivelled into a span; when the grave appears to be the end of all, human goodness nothing but a name, and the sky above this universe a dead expanse, black with the void from which God Himself has disappeared. In that fearful loneliness of spirit, when those who should have been his friends and counsellors only frown upon his misgivings, and profanely bid him stifle doubts, which for aught he knows may arise from the fountain of truth itself; to extinguish, as a glare from hell, that which for aught he knows may be light from heaven, and everything seemed wrapped in hideous uncertainty,—I know but one way in which a man may come forth from his agony scathless; it is by holding fast to those things which are certain still—the grand, simple landmarks of morality. In the darkest hour through which a human soul can pass, whatever else is doubtful, this at least is certain. If there be no God, and no future state, yet, even then, it is better to be generous than selfish, better to be chaste than licentious, better to be true than false, better to be brave than to be a coward. Blessed beyond all earthly blessedness is the man, who, in the tempestuous darkness of the soul, has dared to hold fast to these venerable landmarks. Thrice blessed is he who— when all is drear and cheerless within and without, when his teachers terrify him, and his friends shrink from him—has obstinately clung to moral good. Thrice blessed, because *his* night shall pass into clear, bright day."

Rev. F. W. Robertson.

" The influences which co-operate to maintain the spiritual life of the world and to accomplish its progression are all indefinite. Most of the great works done on earth have not been done by any definite Mechanism, or by any Order of men who have had visible ordination thereto. They have been the effects of individual, invisible Inspiration."

Rev. Frederick Myers.

"We can conceive of no future life which is not a continuation of this : to anticipate in that *future* life *another* life, a *different* life ; what is it but to call in doubt our individual identity ? "

Anna Jameson.

" Life is no merry march, or holiday pastime for any of us ; but the true agony of life must be with those who are without God and without hope in the world."

Rev. J. Baldwin Brown.

" Death takes us by surprise,
    And stays our hurrying feet ;
The great design unfinish'd lies,
    Our lives are incomplete.

" But in the dark unknown,
    Perfect their circles seem,
Even as a bridge's arch of stone
    Is rounded in the stream.

" Alike are life and death
    When life in death survives,
And the interrupted breath
    Inspires a thousand lives."

Henry W. Longfellow.

" Life should be the same as love. There is no life worth having which does not give as much as it can give—that is, as much as it receives, or rather, as much as it can receive."

Rev. Stopford A. Brooke.

" Life should be a web of piety, custom makes it a web of impiety."

Rev. Edward Irving.

" We must have an inward life of heavenly thought, and purpose, and hope, in order guiltlessly and relishingly to partake of diversified natural joys."

Rev. T. T. Lynch.

" Every man has two lives—the life of motive, and the life of behaviour, into the first of which none can enter but the Spirit of spirits."

Joseph Parker, D.D.

" The life that is strongest and most secure is that which is a law unto itself, which has the franchise of the creatures of God, and which, guided only by its own holiness and love, ' proves all things, and holds fast that which is good.' "

Henry Allon, D.D.

" Life has always action ; it is our own fault if it ever be dull :
youth has its enterprise, manhood its schemes ; and even if
infirmity creep upon age, the mind still triumphs over the mortal
clay, and in the quiet hermitage, among books, and from thoughts,
keeps the great wheel within everlastingly in motion."

Bulwer Lytton.

"We are so bound up together in society—the human race
constitutes such a compact and sensitive brotherhood—that the
power which men insensibly exert over one another must spread
and widen, like the ripples from a stone thrown into a pool, until
all feel it. The ownership of sins is a very solemn question,
which in this view of the matter comes home to every human
bosom. ' I ask the mountain,' says the author of ' Thorndale,'
' Why art thou suddenly so dark ? and the mountain answers,
Ask the passing cloud that overshadows me. I ask the ocean, Why
art thou so changeable ? and the sea answers, Ask the sky above,
that showers down now sunshine and now gloom ; sends now calm
and now stormy winds. I ask again, Why, O sky, dost thou wrap
thyself in gloomy clouds ? and the sky answers, Ask the valleys of
the earth ; they send these vapours up to me—they are not
mine.' Every particle of dust comes from a mine long wrought :
storms, earthquakes, many geological revolutions, have been
concerned in its origin. And thus is it in human life. No
man stands isolated and circumscribed within himself—full-
orbed and self-contained. None of us liveth to himself. The
career of every single soul is wrought out, and its moral
elements are mingled by its immersion in the social atmosphere,
and its giving and taking with other persons. And thus, in
judging every single soul, it is the whole world we judge ; for
every individuality is but the power of the whole manifesting itself
in this particular form." *Rev. Hugh Macmillan.*

"The fault that saps the life
Is doubt half-crushed, half-veiled ; the lip-assent
Which finds no echo in the heart of hearts ;
The secret lie, which, conscious of its guilt,
Atones for falsehood by intenser zeal."

Dean E. H. Plumptre, D.D.

10

" What a thing is life and being, when a soul has become but the room in which ghosts hold their revel ; when the man is no longer master of himself, can no more say to this or that thought, thou shalt come, and thou shalt go, but is a slave to his own existence, can neither cease to be, nor order his being—able only in fruitless rebellion to entangle himself yet more in the net he has knotted around him ! Such is every one parted from the essential life, who has not the power by which he lives one with him, holding pure, and free, and true the soul he sent forth from the depths of his being."   *George MacDonald, LL.D.*

" To live with God is to be perpetually rising above the world ; to live without Him is to be perpetually sinking into it, and with it, and below it."   *Bishop Temple, D.D.*

" Love and creativeness are dynamic forces, out of which we, individually, as creatures, go forth bearing His image, that is, having within our being the same dynamic forces, by which we also add constantly to the total sum of existence, and shaking off ignorance, and its effects, and by becoming more ourselves,—*i.e.,* more Divine,—destroying sin in its principle, we attain to absolute freedom, we return to God, conscious like Himself, and, as His friends, giving, as well as receiving, felicity for evermore. In short, we become gods, and able to give the life which we now feel ourselves able only to receive."

Margaret Fuller Ossoli.

" There are times, even on the stormy sea, when a gentle whisper breathes softly as of heaven, and sends into the soul a dream of ecstasy which can never again wholly die, even amidst the jar and whirl of waking life. How such whispers make the blood stop and the very flesh creep with a sense of mysterious communion ! How singularly such moments are the epochs of life—the few points that stand out prominently in the recollection after the flood of years has buried all the rest, as all the low shore disappears, having only a few rock-points visible at high-tide ! "   *Rev. F. W. Robertson.*

" Principles do not give life, they only bind up life into a consistent whole."   *Anna Jameson.*

"Only by the will is another life produced. It is the opener of all evil or good in the creature. As we love, we live."

Rev. Andrew Jukes.

"Life is to be reckoned not only extensively, but also intensively; not merely by the number of its days, but also by the amount of thought and energy which we infuse into them."

John Caird, D.D.

"We grow like those with whom we daily blend;
To yield is to resemble."

Letitia E. Landon.

" The food of hope
Is meditated action ; robbed of this,
Her sole support, she languishes and dies.
We perish also; for we live by hope
And by desire ; we see by the glad light,
And breathe the sweet air of futurity ;
And so we live, or else we have no life."

William Wordsworth.

"We exist here only in the small, that God may have us in a state of flexibility, and bend or fashion us, at the best advantage, to the model of His own great life and character."

"In God's sight we are all under obligation continually to undertake and do what is above our power, and to have this as the acknowledged rule of our life. He requires of us to be doing what we shall feel, to be carrying loads of duty, and responsibility, and sacrifice, under which, as men, we must tremble and faint ; and so to be proving always that, 'to them that have no might, He increaseth strength.'" *H. Bushnell, D.D.*

"There is no such thing as a level in the spiritual life. All is ascent or descent, advance or retreat."

F. W. Faber, D.D.

" Life is only bright when it proceedeth
Towards a truer, deeper Life above."

Adelaide A. Procter.

" Eternal life is a hope, a divine, abounding, purifying hope, which holds all heaven in its arms."

H. R. Reynolds, D.D.

" Human Spirit, bravely hold thy course,
Let virtue teach thee firmly to pursue
The gradual paths of an aspiring change :
For birth, and life, and death, and that strange state
Before the naked soul has found its home,
All tend to perfect happiness, and urge
The restless wheels of being on their way,
Whose flashing spokes, instinct with infinite life,
Bicker and burn to gain their destined goal :
For birth but wakes the spirit to the sense
Of outward shows, whose unexperienced shape
New modes of passion to its frame may lend ;
Life is its stage of action, and the store
Of all events is aggregated there
That variegate the eternal universe ;
Death is a gate of dreariness and gloom,
That leads to azure isles and beaming skies,
And happy regions of eternal hope."

P. B. Shelley.

"All the world reposes in beauty to him who preserves equipoise in his life, and moves serenely on his path without secret violence ; as he who sails down a stream, he has only to steer, keeping his bark in the middle, and carry it round the falls."

H. D. Thoreau.

" The reality of life is manifested by nothing so much as by the endless variety of its outward developments. Every herb of the field has its own individuality of form ; every acorn enfolds a different oak. Attempt to construct some outward framework of uniformity for nature, and the latitudinarian oaks and elms, the informal lilies of the field and fowls of the air, will breathe forth their protest in beauty, and sound it out in song. And how shall the nobler life of the soul be constrained into uniformity ? "

John Caird, D.D.

"As life advances, impressions of all kinds become less rapturous owing to their repetition." *John Ruskin.*

"The tenor
Which my life holds, he readily may conceive
Whoe'er hath stood to watch a mountain brook
In some still passage of its course, and seen
Within the depths of its capacious breast
Inverted trees, and rocks, and azure sky ;
And, on its glassy surface, specks of foam
And conglobated bubbles undissolved,
Numerous as stars ; that, by their onward lapse,
Betray to sight the motion of the stream,
Else imperceptible ; meanwhile, is heard
Perchance a roar or murmur ; and the sound,
Though soothing, and the little floating isles,
Though beautiful, are both by Nature charged
With the same pensive office ; and make known
Through what perplexing labyrinths, abrupt
Precipitations, and untoward straits,
The earth-born wanderer hath pass'd, and quickly,
That respite o'er, like traverses and toils
Must be again encounter'd. Such a stream
Is human life ; and so the spirit fares
In the best quiet to its course allow'd."
William Wordsworth.

"Every man's life, practically speaking, is shaped by his love. If it is a downward, earthly love, then his actions will be tinged by it, all his life will be as his reigning love. This love . . . is not a mere sentiment, or casual emotion, but is the man's settled affinity ; it is that which is to his character, what the magnetic force is to the needle, the power that adjusts all his aims and works, and practically determines the man. It only must be either a downward love or an upward love ; for, being the last love and deepest of the man, there cannot be two last and deepest, it must be one or the other. And then, as this love changes, it works a general revolution of the man."
H. Bushnell, D.D.

"Why should not spiritual life be the counterpart of natural? Both are of God, and there is nothing to hinder both from being equally steadfast in their development."

J. Cunningham Geikie, D.D.

"The old leaf will fall, and the leaf-sheath,
The young spread glad and green,
And gaze on the sun in his beauty
Without a veil between.

For the Lord of Life is working,
And His strongest force is *life ;*
Ever with death it wageth
Silent, victorious strife.

Ever with death it weaveth
The warp and woof of the world,
The nights when the forces are gathered,
The dawns with their banners unfurled."

Elizabeth Charles.

"Every vital process in the world is subject to pause, and blight, and hindrance. Buds are nipped with frost; green leaves are shrivelled with the east wind; young creatures pine and sicken, and for a while cease to grow. And the *highest* vital process is subject to the same vicissitudes. The *Divine* life in a man has times of pause and uncertainty, even of apparent retro-gression, when all that is past seems quite in vain, and the so-called progress has circled round, almost to the very beginning, once more." *Alexander Raleigh, D.D.*

"There is a hope in God that is merely despair of the world but there is a hope that comes of having lived wisely; and that is the experience of a man who has seen on the tree of his life, as one after another its blossoms opened, how there was on them the dew of God's grace; and so when the tree begins to be bared in autumn, early or late, he does not fear but that it will live and be beautiful again, in that great spring-time that will be followed by no winter."

William Mountford, M.A.

A life that waits on man, sinks itself to the level of a brute's."
Rev. J. Baldwin Brown.

" Live truly, and thy life shall be
A great and noble creed."
H. Bonar, D.D.

" With Him that is the Life man's life shall blend ;
E'en now the sacred heavens do help his strife,
There do they knead his bread and mix his cup,
And all the stars have leave to bear him up.

Yet must he sink and fall away to a sleep,
As did his Lord, His Life, his worshippèd
Religion, Life.   The silence may be deep,
Life listening, watching, waiting by His dead,
Till at the end of days they wake full fain
Because their King, the Life, doth love and reign."
Jean Ingelow.

" Life is for service true,
Life is for battle too,
Life is for song."
H. Bonar, D.D.

" The life of contemplation and the life of practice, so hard to
harmonise in our experience, perfectly meet in Christ."
Alexander Maclaren, D.D.

" Life is not divided into religions and secular parts ; all should
be religious, because it is a spirit and not a mere letter which God
has bestowed on us in Christ.   The world is a temple, or ought
to be, and the business of life ought to be the services of a
temple."
Thomas Erskine.

" Life always creates its form . . . it cannot remain without
shaping itself into an outer image of itself. . . . All life has the
passion of the artist in it, and all art is life passing into form."
Rev. Stopford A. Brooke.

" Life . . . depends upon contact with life."
Professor Henry Drummond.

" The light is ever silent ;
   Its sparkles on morn's million gems of dew,
   It flings itself into the shower of noon,
   It weaves its gold into the cloud of sunset,—
   Yet not a sound is heard ; it dashes full
   On yon broad rock, yet not an echo answers :
   It lights in myriad drops upon the flower,
   Yet not a blossom stirs ; it does not move
   The slightest film of floating gossamer,
   Which the faint touch of insect's wing would shiver.

The light is ever silent ;
   Most silent of all heavenly silences ;
   Not even the darkness stiller, nor so still ;
   Too swift for sound or speech, it rushes on
   Right through the yielding skies, a massive flood
   Of multitudinous beams ; an endless sea,
   That flows but ebbs not, breaking on the shore
   Of this dark earth, with never-ceasing wave,
   Yet in its swiftest flow, or fullest spring-tide,
   Giving less sound than does one falling blossom,
   Which the May breeze lays lightly on the sward.

Such let my life be here ;
   Not marked by noise, but by success alone ;
   Not known by bustle, but by useful deeds,
   Quiet and gentle, clear and fair as light ;
   Yet full of its all-penetrating power,
   Its silent but resistless influence ;
   Making no needless sound, yet ever working,
   Hour after hour, upon a needy world !"

H. Bonar, D.D.

" We need to have some one Life, which shall sum up the influence of love, past, present, and to come, and which shall be to lesser lives what the sun is to the myriad reflections of its rays."

E. A. Abbot, D.D.

" Our best light must be made life, and our best thought action."

Samuel Smiles.

" That which is our real life can be seen only by its effects ; never in itself. The reality of our life, the fulness of our being, the richness of God's gift to us, divine, immortal, glorious, is invisible. No one has ever seen the man that is in man."

Henry Ward Beecher, D.D.

" In the Christian life there must be concentration of effort, conservation of force. . . . The great fault of the Christian life of the present day is diffusion."

Rev. Hugh Macmillan.

" Life lies in embryo,—never free
    Till Nature yields her breath ;
Till Time becomes Eternity,
    And Man is born in Death."

James Montgomery.

" The ' soul ' is man's *higher life ;* the life not of the body, nor even of the intellect, but of the feelings, the affections, the aspirations. A man may ignore this higher life, and do his best to drown and stifle it ; but he cannot divest himself of it. It is part of himself. Willingly or unwillingly, worthily or unworthily, he must carry it about with him till death and through death. There is a *for ever* stamped visibly upon it. He can ennoble, or he can degrade, but he cannot destroy. To ' lose the soul ' in scriptural language is to spoil this higher life; to quench the Divine Spirit by whose fire alone it burns ; to lose the capacity of caring for God and for all those lofty things which we believe to be dear to God and the natural heritage of man."

Montagu Butler, D.D.

" We are ourselves
Our heaven and hell, the joy, the penalty,
The yearning, the fruition. Earth is hell
Or heaven, and yet not only earth ; but still,
After the swift soul leaves the gates of death,
The pain grows deeper and less mixed, the joy
Purer and less alloyed, and we are damned
Or blest, as we have lived."

Lewis Morris.

" The hidden wealth of man's spirit by far exceeds the whole appearance and work of his life.

" Every man is another unknown world. He is not what you think he is. He is not where you see him. You may shut him up, but after all he is not shut up. He is living in the world of his own imagination. You cannot hinder him from living in that world. Nor can you set any limits to that world, wherein his spirit roams and rests. You think that he is walking in the street, by your side, but you are mistaken ; he is in the midst of a group of angels, looking upon the face of God. You may live in your own spirit-world, but you cannot live in his, nor can you imagine it."   *Rev. John Pulsford.*

" If it is true, that the reason we see not God is the grossness of this tabernacle wherein the Soul is encased, then the more and the oftener we recognise the supernatural in our ordinary life, and not only expect but find it in those rare and short moments of devotion and prayer, the more, surely, the rays of the Divine Light will shine through the dark glass of this outward form of life, and the more our own spirit will be enlightened and purified by it, until we come to that likeness to the Divine Nature, and that purity of heart to which a share of the Beatific Vision is promised."   *John Inglesant.*

"Our life is determined for us ; and it makes the mind very free when we give up wishing, and only think of bearing what is laid upon us, and doing what is given us to do."
                                                        George Eliot.

" Dissipation in any form is the great drain of life. Life is the most precious thing which God has given or can give us. What shall a man give in exchange for his life ? You have only a certain amount in you of life. You may spend it quickly or slowly. You may expend or husband it ; but when it is gone, there is an end. No agony of effort or prayer can bring you a new store. ' A short life and a merry one ' is the cry of dissipation. ' A noble life and an eternal one ' is the creed of the man who has learned the secret of life from God."
                                                        Rev. J. Baldwin Brown.

" Where'er a human Spirit strives
After a life more true and fair,
There is the true man's birthplace grand,
His is a world-wide fatherland ! "

J. Russell Lowell.

"Our life on earth is formative, combines, for its own purpose, things dissimilar, enters into relations false and true according to its will, has the power to assume the appearance without possessing the reality, to hide what is true and exhibit what is false. The outward history of all this passes away, but nothing is lost, or forgotten, or unproductive. The inner life treasures up the results of the outward history. The spirit makes faithful record in its nature of all that takes place, and is the living witness of whatever has happened. Just as the deposits which compose the crust of the earth, the water-marks on the rock that was once yielding sand, the footprints of creatures which no longer exist, reveal to us a world that has passed away, and also a world brought into existence, so in our souls will be found the history and results of the life we have lived. The most fleeting and trivial things, the very shadows of our passing days, leave their records behind them. In our hidden life, time and eternity meet, the infinite awakens and characterizes the infinite, and every experience has its influence in the formation of the character of our souls." *William Pulsford, D.D.*

"Great art is nothing else than the type of strong and noble life ; for as the ignoble person, in his dealings with all that occurs in the world about him, first sees nothing clearly, looks nothing fairly in the face, and then allows himself to be swept away by the trampling torrent and unescapable force of the things that he would not foresee, and could not understand, so the noble person, looking the facts of the world full in the face, and fathoming them with deep faculty, then deals with them in unalarmed intelligence and unhurried strength, and becomes, with his human intellect and will, no unconscious nor insignificant agent in consummating their good and restraining their evil."

John Ruskin.

> " He only lives with the world's life,
> Who hath renounced his own."
> *Matthew Arnold.*

" Man lives *from* the unseen, and therefore cannot rest in the seen." *Rev. John Pulsford.*

" Life is an outliving of world after world."
William Mountford.

" Life is not mean. It spreads itself in aspiration, it has possession through its hope. It inhabits all remoteness that the eye can reach ; it inherits all sweetness that the ear can prove ; always bereaved of the whole, it yet looks for a whole ; always clasping its little part, it believes in the remainder. Sometimes, too often, like a bird, it gets tangled in a net, which notwithstanding it knew of. It must fly with broken wings ever after. Or, worse, it is tempted to descend, as the genii into the vase, for a little while, when sealed down at once unaware, it must lie in the dark so long that it perhaps denies the light in heaven for lack of seeing. If those who have the most satisfying lot that life can give are to breathe freely, they must get through, and on, and out of it.

> " This is God !
> He moves me so to take of Him what lacks ;
> My want is God's desire to give ; He yearns
> To add Himself to life, and so for aye
> Make it enough." *Jean Ingelow.*

> " ' Time flies too fast, too fast our life decays.'
> Ah, faithless ! in the present lies our being ;
> And not in lingering love for vanished days !
> .*   *   *   *   *   *
> ' Live for what is : future and past are nought.'
> Ah, blind ! a flash, and what shall be, has been,
> Where, then, is that for which thou takest thought ?
>
> Not in what has been, is, or is to be,
> The wise soul lives, but in a wider time,
> Which is not any, but contains the three."
> *Lewis Morris.*

" The energy of life may be
Kept on after the grave, but not begun."
Matthew Arnold.

" Every calling of life has its serious side, if it be not sinful."
Thomas Arnold, D.D.

" Our life is an apprenticeship to the truth, that around every circle another can be drawn ; that there is no end in nature, but every end is a beginning ; that there is always another dawn risen on mid-noon, and under every deep a lower deep opens."
Ralph Waldo Emerson.

" Sad things in this life of breath
Are truest, sweetest, deepest."
Robert Buchanan.

" There is more in human life of the song than the sigh, if we only know how to draw out the notes and make the harmony. And in every life there are special mercies."
Alexander Raleigh, D.D.

" Pleasure is a component part of human life, without which life cannot be healthy. What you have got to do is, not to crush it, and not to abuse it, but to use it. . . . In Christ's life do you suppose there were no flowers springing up by the wayside ? There were. There were quiet moments at Bethany, quiet moments in the olive garden often and often before the night of the bloody sweat ; also when He walked by the way, or by the sea, enjoying social converse, and there were associations of happiness, and of joy, and of friendship about the quiet vineyards and hills of Galilee. Remember that His joy was our joy, His sorrow our sorrow. Jesus Christ chose to be found at the marriage supper of Cana as well as at the grave of Lazarus. He did not seek to check mirth, to crush pleasure ; He came that we might have joy, and have it more abundantly. Pleasure for Himself or for others was not the pursuit of His life, but His life-work radiated goodness, from whence came enjoyment and satisfaction, exhilaration, happiness."
Rev. H. R. Haweis.

"It is easy in the world to live after the world's opinion; it is easy in solitude to live after our own; but the great man is he who in the midst of the crowd keeps with perfect sweetness the independence of solitude."

Ralph Waldo Emerson.

"Seldom comes the moment
In life, which is indeed sublime and weighty.
To make a great decision possible,
Oh! many things, all transient and all rapid,
Must meet at once: and, haply, they thus met
May, by that confluence, be enforced to pause
Time long enough for wisdom, though too short,
Far, far too short a time for doubt and scruple."

S. T. Coleridge.

"Our little lives are kept in equipoise
    By opposite attractions and desires;
The struggle of the instinct that enjoys,
    And the more noble instinct that aspires.

These perturbations, this perpetual jar
    Of earthly wants and aspirations high,
Come from the influence of an unseen star,
    An undiscovered planet in our sky.

And as the moon from some dark gate of cloud
    Throws o'er the sea a floating bridge of light,
'Across whose trembling planks our fancies crowd
    Into the realm of mystery and night,—

So from the world of spirits there descends
    A bridge of light, connecting it with this,
O'er whose unsteady floor, that sways and bends,
    Wander our thoughts above the dark abyss."

Henry W. Longfellow.

"The great unhappiness of men is, that they live abroad, they lose themselves in the accidents around, they are engrossed by outward events, by the changes of the natural or political world They do not explore the grander world within."

W. E. Channing, D.D.

"The great lesson to be learned in life is to make the right choice—to refuse the evil and to choose the good, to distinguish between them, and to prefer the one to the other."

Thomas Erskine.

"If you mean to act nobly, and seek to know the best things God has put within reach of men, you must learn to fix your mind on that end, and not on what will happen to you because of it. And remember, if you were to choose something lower, and make it the rule of your life to seek your own pleasure, and escape from what is disagreeable, calamity might come just the same ; and it would be calamity falling on a base mind, which is the one form of sorrow that has no balm in it, and that may well make a man say,—'It would have been better for me if I had never been born.'"

George Eliot.

"All life is full of opportunities of choice, and as we choose in them, and abide by our choice, such are we. It is by the often repeated choice in little things that our characters are fixed."

Bishop Wilberforce.

"The more inward the life the more potent it becomes."

"The present complexity of life and relation settles surely into a Simplicity in which only Self and God remain—Self alone with God! Hence, life in its full sense, ideal life, is simply a true adjustment and interplay between these two, self living unto and in God, and God returning upon self with joy,—a process more stable than the universe, and as enduring as God Himself."

Rev. John Pulsford.

"As our outward life widens, our inward one must deepen. That which is spreading itself broadly in the light must be ever more securely rooting itself in the darkness. Germination begins in darkness, but its first movement is towards the light. If light be attained, then growth is twofold—the hidden and the visible ; and because of the hidden, the visible will be stable and productive. If light be not attained, then all growth ceases. Live outwardly, or you cannot have health—live inwardly, or the outward life will be futile and worthless."

Rev. T. T. Lynch.

" Life is a series of surprises. We do not guess to-day the mood, the pleasure, the power of to-morrow, when we are building up our being. Of lower states,—of acts of routine and sense,—we can tell somewhat; but the masterpieces of God, the total growths and universal movements of the soul, He hideth; they are incalculable. I can know that truth is Divine and helpful; but how it shall help me I can have no guess, for *so to be* is the sole inlet of *so to know.* The new position of the advancing man has all the powers of the old, yet has them all new. It carries in its bosom all the energies of the past, yet is itself an exhalation of the morning."

Ralph Waldo Emerson.

" To live is to vary; in death only is sameness. Where the dew of the Lord is wanting, there surely will be uniformity—the uniformity of emptiness and barrenness, but where the dew falls, there will be variety—the blossoming of the lily, the root striking of the mountain forests, the dusky olive's branch, and Lebanon's smell."

Rev. S. A. Tipple.

" *Life* always appears to us beautiful and good. It is a very synonym for good, indeed. But wherever we see a whole there we see life; therefore if we saw the whole, we should see it to be life; *i.e.,* absolute beauty and good. Ugliness and evil are *not life;* types of sin, which is death. Ugly, evil, false, mean simply that we do not see the life; they are phenomena of which we are unable to see that they are vital parts of a living whole."

James Hinton.

" The living Life of God perpetually lightens;
And created life is nothing but a radiant shadow fleeing
From the unapproachèd lustres of that Unbeginning Being."

F. W. Faber, D.D.

" If I may but touch the hem of His garment—that is sufficient for the commencement of spiritual life. But they who do so will soon seek to converse with Him; they will look into His face: faith grows into fellowship; the joy of trust passes into the higher joy of oneness with Him in character and purpose."

Alexander Mackennal, B.A.

"This life is but the childhood in which we are to be trained up to the manhood of eternal life."

Thomas Arnold, D.D.

"O life! how like the common-breathèd air,
Which is thy outward instrument, thou liest
Ever about us, with sustaining force,
In the calm current of our usual days
Unfelt, unthought of; nay, how dense a crowd
Float on upborne by the prolific stream,
Even to the ridges of the eternal sea,
Spending profuse the passion of their mind
On every flower that gleams on either bank,
On every rock that bends its rugged brow,
Conscious of all things, only not of thee.

Yet some there are, who in their greenest youth,
At some rare hours, have known the dazzling light
Intolerable, that glares upon the soul,
In the mere sense of Being, and grown faint
With awe, and striven to press their folded hands
Upon their inner eyes, and bowed their heads,
As in the presence of a mighty Ghost,
Which they must feel, but cannot dare to see.
It is before me now, that fearful truth,
That single solitary truth, which hangs
In the dark heaven of our uncertainties,
Seen by no other light than its own fire,
Self-balanced, like the Arab Magian's tomb,
Between the inner and the outer World;—
How utterly the wretched shred of Time,
Which in our blindness we call Human Life,
Is lost with all its train of circumstance,
And appanage of after and before,
In this eternal present; that we are!
No when,—no where,—no how,—but that we are,—
And nought besides.

* * * * *

He was a bitter Mocker, that old Man
Who bade us 'know ourselves,' yet not unwise;
. For though the science of our life and being
Be unattained and unattainable
By these weak organs, though the athlete mind,
Hardened by practice of unpausing toil,
And fed to manhood with robustest meats,
Never can train its sinews strong enough
To raise itself from off the solid ground,
To which the mandate of creating Will
Has bound it; though we all must patient stand,
Like statues on appointed pedestals,
Yet we may choose (since choice is given) to shun
Servile contentment or ignoble fear,
In the expression of our attitude :
And with far-straining eyes, and hands upcast,
And feet half raised, declare our painful state,
Yearning for wings to reach the fields of Truth,
Mourning for wisdom, panting to be free."

Lord Houghton.

"Men nowhere, east or west, live yet a natural life, round which the vine clings, and which the elm willingly shadows. Man would desecrate it by his touch, and so the beauty of the world remains veiled to him. He needs not only to be spiritualized, but *naturalized*, on the soil of earth, who shall conceive what kind of roof the heavens might extend over him, what seasons minister to him, and what employments dignify his life! Only the convalescent raise the veil of nature. An immortality in his life would confer immortality on his abode. The winds should be his breath, the seasons his moods, and he should impart of his serenity to Nature herself."

H. D. Thoreau.

"There is a trial and probation throughout man's whole life— but the trial is subservient to the education; he is tried that he may be educated, he is not educated that he may be tried."

Thomas Erskine.

" By the sacrifice of life, voluntary or involuntary, and by that alone, can other and higher life exist."

Rev. F. W. Robertson.

" Life is, for the most part, a varied web. It is woven of glow and gloom, thunder purple and shining gold. Even in the midst of our darkest days deep joy rushed in ; even that which we now most sorrow for had in it, when we lived in it, inexplicable pleasure. Often, as we look back, that which was our happiness in hours gone by—so strangely mixed is life—is now our tragedy, and that which was our tragedy is now our blessedness. And on the whole the greater number of us have more joy than sorrow, though in the weight of sorrow we forget the multitude of joy. For sorrows keep together, while joys are dispersed through life, and in the centre of sorrow we cannot recall the joys that are scattered all over the circle of life."

Rev. Stopford A. Brooke.

" Accident does very little towards the production of any great result in life." *Samuel Smiles.*

" Let us consider now this life of the Vine,
　　Whereof we are partakers : we shall see
　　Its way is not of pleasure nor of ease.
　　It groweth not like the wild trailing weeds
　　Whither it willeth, flowering here and there :
　　Or lifting up proud blossoms to the sun,
　　Kissed by the butterflies, and glad of life,
　　And glorious in their beautiful array ;
　　Or running into lovely labyrinths
　　Of many forms and many fantasies,
　　Rejoicing in its own luxuriant life.

　　The flower of the Vine is but a little thing,
　　The least part of its life ;—you scarce could tell
　　It ever had a flower ; the fruit begins
　　Almost before the flower has had its day.
　　And as it grows, it is not free to heaven,
　　But tied to a stake ; and if its arms stretch out,

It is but cross-wise, also forced and bound,
And so it draws out of the hard hill-side,
Fixed in its own place, its own food of life ;
And quickens with it, breaking forth in bud,
Joyous and green, and exquisite of form,
Wreathed lightly into tendril, leaf, and bloom.
Yea, the grace of the green vine makes all the land
Lovely in spring-time ; and it still grows on
Faster, in lavishness of its own life ;
Till the fair shoots begin to wind and wave
In the blue air, and feel how sweet it is.
But so they leave it not ; the husbandman
Comes early, with the pruning-hooks and shears,
And strips it bare of all its innocent pride,
And wandering garlands, and cuts deep and sure,
Unsparing for its tenderness and joy.
And in its loss and pain it wasteth not :
But yields itself with unabated life,
More perfect under the despoiling hand.
The bleeding limbs are hardened into wood ;
The thinned-out bunches ripen into fruit
More full and precious to the purple prime.

And still, the more it grows, the straitlier bound
Are all its branches ; and as rounds the fruit,
And the heart's crimson comes to show in it,
And it advances to its hour,—its leaves
Begin to droop and wither in the sun ;
But still the life-blood flows, and does not fail,
All into fruitfulness, all into form.

Then comes the vintage, for the days are ripe.
And surely now in its perfected bloom,
It may rejoice a little in its crown,
Though it bend low beneath the weight of it,
Wrought out of the long striving of its heart.
But ah ! the hands are ready to tear down
The treasures of the grapes ; the feet are there

To tread them in the winepress, gathered in ;
Until the blood-red rivers of the wine
Run over, and the land is full of joy.
But the vine standeth stripped and desolate,
Having given all ; and now its own dark time
Is come, and no man payeth back to it
The comfort and the glory of its gift ;
But rather, now most merciless, all pain
And loss are piled together, as its days
Decline,. and the spring sap has ceased to flow,
Now is it cut back to the very stem ;
Despoiled, disfigured, left a leafless stock,
Alone through all the dark days that shall come.
And all the winter-time the wine gives joy
To those who else were dismal in the cold ;
But the vine standeth out amid the frost ;
And after all, hath only this grace left,
That it endures in long, lone stedfastness
The winter through :—and next year blooms again ;
Not bitter for the torment undergone,
Not barren for the fulness yielded up ;
As fair and fruitful towards the sacrifice,
As if no touch had ever come to it,
But the soft airs of heaven and dews of earth ;—
And so fulfils itself in love once more.

  *   *   *   *   *

Measure thy life by loss instead of gain ;
Not by the wine drunk, but the wine poured forth ;
For love's strength standeth in love's sacrifice ;
And whoso suffers most hath most to give."
         H. E. Hamilton King.

" The connections of human life stretch before us, and are
lost in the endless ages which are needed to accomplish God's
designs."   *W. E. Channing, D.D.*

" Many ministries are necessary for every single life."
         H. Allon, D.D.

"Life has its hum even in the dead hush of a midsummer noon. When the air seems so still that silence grows oppressive, lay your ear to the ground, and listen to the stir of the myriad insects that are keeping their summer festival. You will not marvel that simple hearts, in the good old times, believed that the grasses and the flower-cups were haunted, and that all the earth and air was thronged with troops of joyous invisible sprites, dancing in the sunbeams, swinging in the gossamer chains, hiding in the flower-bells, and making the summer air musical with the breath of their merriment and song. It needs a more trained and observant ear to catch the same undertone through the sighing winds and swirling leaves of autumn, but it is there; life has but drawn back to its source awhile, and there it is gathering up its forces, renewing its youth, and preparing for the outburst of the spring. It is the sense that there is no death in nature, that she but weaves the dress of Him who ever liveth, and has commission to weave on while He liveth, which robs the autumn and the deepening winter of all but a passing breath of sadness, and makes their twilight hour the season of our most peaceful and happy musings. We, too, if we have caught the Divine keynote, are content to rest with them when the main toil of our life-work is over; to rest and ripen, and lay up in the inner cells the sap which shall make the flowers of our eternal spring."   *Rev. J. Baldwin Brown.*

"There are moments when the liberty of the inner life, opposed to the trammels of the outer, becomes too oppressive; moments when we wish that our mental horizon were less extended, thought less free; when we long to put the discursive soul into a narrow path like a railway, and force it to run on in a straight line to some determined goal."

Anna Jameson.

"Gather up the fragments. In every human life there are sure to be some. Every one of us has a secret chamber somewhere, filled with inhabitants whom none but himself can see; it rests with himself alone whether they shall be decaying corpses or only beautiful ghosts."

Dinah M. Muloch.

" To embody is to define, to limit, to fix ; but the Ideas which are the life of man's soul are not thus comprehensible : they are so akin to the Divine as to be illimitable. What man has made, man can measure ; he can extract from it all its meaning, and that meaning is substantially ever the same. But that which is emphatically of GOD has many meanings, and in each there is more than man can ever discern or comprehend. Life in themselves, this is what man's works have not and GOD'S have. Light and shadow, perpetual motion and visible happiness, these only give endless significance to form ; and these are God's works alone." *Frederick Myers.*

" As in geometry so in life, distinct threads of influencing truth are often introduced abruptly, presently to be interwoven with one or with several of the many-threaded and related lines of truth." *Rev. T. T. Lynch.*

" There are numerous fragments of life which, so far as action or enjoyment is concerned, might be subtracted without injury. Yet these very seasons may afford peculiar advantages for the cultivation of patience, which is often more important than either action or enjoyment." *W. B. Clulow.*

" Life is a revelation." *Joseph Parker, D.D.*

" Our God in hours retired
   Can open in our heart
A fount of good desired,
   And such supplies impart,
That more it has, the more it gives,
And all our life upon it lives.

O sacred stream of love,
   Hast thou begun thy flow,
And from the hills above
   Reached now the lands below ?
Then blessed by thee, life's common field
Will corn, and fruit, and herbage yield."
                                       Rev. T. T. Lynch.

" The Life of the body may complete itself in the physical world ; that is its legitimate Environment.   The Life of the senses, high and low, may perfect itself in Nature.   Even the Life of thought may find a large complement in surrounding things. But the higher thought, and the conscience, and the religious Life, can only perfect themselves in God."

Professor Henry Drummond.

" The faith that life on earth is being shaped
    To glorious ends, that order, justice, love
    Mean man's completeness, mean effect as sure
    As roundness in the dewdrop—that great faith
    Is but the rushing and expanding stream
    Of thought, of feeling, fed by all the past.
    Our finest hope is finest memory,
    As they who love in age think youth is blest
    Because it has a life to fill with love.
    Full souls are double mirrors, making still
    An endless vista of fair things before
    Repeating things behind : so faith is strong
    Only when we are strong, shrinks when we shrink.
    It comes when music stirs us, and the chords
    Moving on some grand climax shake our souls
    With influx new that makes new energies.
    It comes in swellings of the heart and tears
    That rise at noble and at gentle deeds—
    At labours of the master-artist's hand
    Which, trembling, touches to a finer end,
    Trembling before an image seen within.
    It comes in moments of heroic love,
    Unjealous joy in joy not made for us—
    In conscious triumph of the good within
    Making us worship goodness that rebukes.
    Even our failures are a prophecy,
    Even our yearnings and our bitter tears
    After that fair and true we cannot grasp ;
    As patriots who seem to die in vain
    Make liberty more sacred by their pangs.

Presentiment of better things on earth
Sweeps in with every force that stirs our souls
To admiration, self-renouncing love,
Or thoughts, like light, that bind the world in one:
Sweeps like the sense of vastness, when at night
We hear the roll and dash of waves that break
Nearer and nearer with the rushing tide,
Which rises to the level of the cliff,
Because the wide Atlantic rolls behind
Throbbing respondent to the far-off orbs."

George Eliot.

" Worship expresses, though it may be feeble, the worshipper's supreme ideal of life." *Joseph Parker, D.D.*

" The life *unto* God flows out of the life *of* God in the soul."
H. R. Reynolds, D.D.

"Our first life is spontaneous and instinctive. Our second life is reflective. There is a moment when the life spontaneous passes into the life reflective. We live at first by instinct; then we look in—feel ourselves—ask what we are and whence we come, and whither we are bound. In an awful new world of mystery, and destinies, and duties, we feel God, and know that our true home is our Father's house which has many mansions."
Rev. F. W. Robertson.

" Life, as it has been, is a book always at hand, in which the tale of God's individual mercies to ourselves may plainly be read; and with this view it is good for us to look back upon it at our leisure in its great outlines, and to endeavour to regard it as a history belonging to some other person, which we are permitted to read."

"Every man's life, however outwardly uneventful, is full of importance the moment he looks back upon it, for it becomes to him a history, and he is able to see it in its true light, its relation to Eternity." *Elizabeth M. Sewell.*

" Life, for the most part, blooms only once, and, like the aloe, it blooms late." *F. W. Faber, D.D.*

> " We abide
> Not on this earth ; but for a little space
> We pass upon it : and while so we pass,
> God through the dark hath set the Light of Life,
> With witness for Himself, the Word of God,
> To be among us Man, with human heart,
> And human language, thus interpreting
> The One great Will incomprehensible,
> Only so far as we in human life
> Are able to receive it ; men, as men,
> Can reach no higher than the Son of God,
> The perfect Head and Pattern of mankind.
> The time is short, and this sufficeth us
> To live and die by ; and in Him again
> We see the same first starry attribute,
> ' Perfect through suffering,' our salvation's seal
> Set in the front of His Humanity.
> For God has other Words for other worlds,
> But for this world the Word of God is Christ.
> And when we come to die we shall not find
> The day has been too long for any of us
> To have fulfilled the perfect law of Christ.
> Who is there that can say, ' My part is done
>   In this ; now I am ready for a law
> More wide, more perfect for the rest of life ' ?
> Is any living that has not come short ?
> Has any died that was not short at last ?"

H. E. Hamilton King.

> " How many lives, made beautiful and sweet
>   By self-devotion and by self-restraint,
>   Whose pleasure is to run without complaint
>   On unknown errands of the Paraclete,
> Wanting the reverence of unshodden feet,
>   Fail of the nimbus which the artists paint
>   Around the shining forehead of the saint,
>   And are in their completeness incomplete ! "

Henry W. Longfellow.

" Degeneration compasses Degeneration. It is only a character which is itself developing that can aid the Evolution of the world, and so fulfil the end of life. For this high usury, each of our lives, however small may seem our capital, was given us by God. And it is just the men whose capital seems small who need to choose the best investments."

Professor Henry Drummond.

" The Life of man is made of many lives,
His heart and mind of many minds and hearts,
And he in inward growth most surely thrives
Who lets wise Nature order all the parts."

Lord Houghton.

" Life is seldom so varied or so adventurous as to enable a man to unfold all that is in him."

F. W. Faber, D.D.

" In dreams we see ourselves naked, and acting out our real characters, even more clearly than we see others awake. . . . , Our truest life is when we are in dreams awake."

H. D. Thoreau.

" The next life must be a state of retribution. Thither we carry nothing but ourselves, our naked selves. Our fortune we leave behind us ; our honours and rank return to such as gave ; even our reputation, the good or ill men thought we were, clings to us no more. We go thither without our staff or scrip ; nothing but the man we are. Yet that man is the result of all life's daily work : it is the one thing which we have brought to pass."

Rev. Theodore Parker.

" There is in life no blessing like affection :
It soothes, it hallows, elevates, subdues,
And bringeth down to earth its native heaven."

Letitia E. Landon.

" The bread of life is love ; the salt of life is work ; the sweetness of life poesy ; the water of life faith."

Anna Jameson.

" Life catches its ruddiest hue from the glow of the household fire. And just in the measure in which men and women, however isolated to the eye their lives may seem, learn the secret of fatherly, motherly, brotherly, or sisterly ministry to the men and women and little ones around them, does their life rise into nobleness and beauty, and become harmonic with the life of heaven."   *Rev. J. Baldwin Brown.*

> " Life . . . is energy of love,
> Divine or human, exercised in pain,
> In strife, and tribulation, and ordain'd,
> If so approved and sanctified, to pass,
> Through shades and silent rest, to endless joy."
>   *William Wordsworth.*

" There are many trials in life which do not seem to come from unwisdom or folly. They are silver arrows shot from the bow of God, and fixed inextricably in the quivering heart. They are to be borne. They were not meant, like snow on water, to melt as soon as they strike. But the moment an ill can be patiently borne, it is disarmed of its poison, though not of its pain."
>   *Henry Ward Beecher, D.D.*

> " When life from death's dark shade looks back,
> How different all the past appears
> To him who tries each well-known track
> Far through the dim and silent years !
> He sees it all ; the lesson taught
> In Sorrow's school by slow degrees,
> Now—with its last conviction brought
> Home to his heart—he clearly sees.
> The Love that led him by a way
> He knew not, sore against his will ;
> The Love that, changeless, day by day
> Watches and waits around him still ;
> The Love that crown'd his life with bliss,
> Making it all one happy dream ;
> The Love that woke him, lest he miss
> Through over-love the Love supreme ;

The Love that when it bid him part
  From all on earth he loved so well,
Folded him closer to the heart
  In which eternal mercies dwell,—
He sees it all, and is content ;
  The travail of his soul is o'er ;
The weary hours in anguish spent
  His joy remembereth no more.
Daily his cross had grown more light ;
  Now, from his shoulder it doth glide,
And rises to his dying sight
  The cross on which his Saviour died.
It was his death in life, to bow
  His broken heart submissive down :
It is his life in death, and now
  Points through the shadow to the Crown."

" Life below
Is but the school of life above."
Rev. J. S. B. Monsell, LL.D.

" Physical life is a growth ; so is intellectual, so is spiritual. But the condition of growth is use, exercise ; use what you have got, keep your mind open, do no violence to your reason, keep your heart pure, and you may safely lay aside fears about not having a right faith, or not believing enough. You will grow as infallibly as the corn grows in summer. Even here, your light will begin to shine before men ; you will begin to adorn Christ's doctrine in some things, and yonder, when the clouds roll away, you will see face to face ; and being changed from glory to glory, you shall then adorn the doctrine of God your Saviour in all things." *Rev. H. R. Haweis.*

" The life of man is a self-evolving circle, which, from a ring imperceptibly small, rushes on all sides outwards to new and larger circles, and that without end. The extent to which this generation of circles, wheel within wheel, will go, depends on the force or truth of the individual soul." *Ralph Waldo Emerson.*

"Every life has three aspects. All of us live, it may be said, three lives in one. *We live to one another.* A large part of every day is spent in the exercise of relations, in the discharge of offices, which have to do with others. These relations may be well or ill exercised. These offices may be well or ill discharged. But in some way or other they must of necessity be exercised and discharged by all of us. No man (in this sense) can live altogether to himself. He must affect others. He must, unless he would absolutely go out of the world, act upon and act towards other men. *We live to ourselves.* There is a secret life in each one of us, as well as an outward. Every man, well or ill, manages and directs himself. Every man holds the reins of his inner being, and for good, or else for evil, is (in the last resort) his own ruler, and his own counsellor, and his own physician. *We live to God.* Either negligently or else watchfully, either presumptuously or else reverently, either disobediently or else dutifully, each one of us must behave and deport himself somehow and in some manner toward the Most High God; towards Him in whom, whether he will or no, he lives, and moves, and has his being. To have nothing to do with God, is to have cast aside utterly the first law of our being, and in the highest possible degree to be blaspheming and defying Him daily. The creature must have a life towards the Creator; the only question is, What manner of life? A life of rebellion, or a life of love?" *Dean Vaughan, D.D.*

"Live daily, constantly, with a high purpose, putting forth moral energy in the minute conflicts of desire with the sense of right." *W. E. Channing, D.D.*

"If you are rooted in Christ, you are rooted in all the holy powers of God and of eternity." *Rev. John Pulsford.*

"Only by being filled with a higher Spirit than our own, which, having caused our spirits, is one with our spirits, and is in them the present life principle, are we or can we be safe from this eternal death of our being." *George Macdonald, LL.D.*

"Never does any part or province of life become independent of knowledge." *Rev. J. Llewelyn Davies.*

" Every human being is now forming, though unconsciously, a picture of his life, which he must hereafter present before God. If we would have ours such as we shall not shrink from then offering in Christ's name, we must work at it in the same child-like spirit, copying in every minute detail the picture of holiness which Jesus has set before us, until the finishing stroke shall be put to it in the moment of death, and our picture be confided to God's keeping, never to be seen by us again till, in the Day of Resurrection, we discover that we have, unknown to ourselves, and through God's grace, caught—though in an immeasurably faint degree—the form, and colour, and spirit of the Great Original." *Elizabeth M. Sewell.*

" How cruel life is to the wicked man ! Take him at his best estate,. reckon up the pains he takes, the efforts he makes, the activity he expends, how he is burnt up with the fever of insatiable desires, running a race after impossible ends, impoverishing heart and mind with excitements which are their own punishment ; what a tyranny the slow lapse of time is to him, what a bitter step-mother the world he has so adored ! The flood-tide of irritation and then the ebb of helpless languor, who would live a life of which those are the incessant alternations ? The wilful sinner is but a man who, in order to get rid of God, explores, to his own cost, every species of disappointment, and nowhere finds contentment or repose." *F. W. Faber, D.D.*

" The art of life is to know how to enjoy a little and to endure much." *W. Hazlitt.*

" Strange is the life of man, and fatal or fated are moments,
Whereupon turn, as on hinges, the gates of the wall adaman-
tine !" *Henry W. Longfellow.*

" Life is but thought.

*   *   *   *

Dewdrops are the gems of morning,
But the tears of mournful eve !
Where no hope is, life's a warning
That only serves to make us grieve."

S. T. Coleridge.

"Those to whom *life is a succession of particular businesses*, how-ever intelligent, energetic, and conscientious, must rank in the scale of human excellence below those to whom *life is rather the flow of one spirit.*   In the former there is always to be noticed a certain want of *porportion* in the parts and methods of their career.   It has not the unity of a pervading aim, the ground-colouring of a latent affection.   It is not the spontaneous expression of a given mind, but the activity provoked by a given lot ; so that its highest energy is that of adaptation rather than creation. . . . But a soul kindling with devout aspiration cannot mistake instrumental details for ultimate ends.   The act of the hour belongs to the business of the day ; the business of the day has its place in the scheme of years ; the scheme of years is but the element of an eternal work ; and all is the expression of a constant spirit, conversing with God in the present, and in quest of his higher mind in the future.   To such a one life is not a mere voyage by the log and line,—an experimental cruise over waters unexplored ; but a course computed by the everlasting stars over an ocean unvisited indeed, but not unknown ; with its relations to the heavens discerned, and sunny inlets and blessed islands ever in the thoughts.   The difference between a life pieced together from even the stoutest remnants, and a life woven, though with fragile woof and fading colours, from the continuous warp of a pure heart, is conspicuous especially in the *temper* with which the ills and wrongs of the human lot are borne."   '   *James Martineau, D.D.*

"The new life cannot be led except as new sensibilities to goodness are awakened.   Sufficient ability for living it is not acquired by our independent contemplation of the Holy Pattern."
                                        Rev. T. T. Lynch.

"It is the strange truth of life that unknowingly we are continually hovering close to our destiny.   We think again and again, in the street, at night before sleep attack us with her envious silence, that perhaps to-day we met, or perhaps to-morrow we shall meet, him or her who will upturn our life and make it new.   To come truly into contact with another human soul, whom you feel, it seems, that you have known before, and with whom friendship seems but a renewal of some forgotten life ; or to feel the revelation of a wholly new life to yours, so that you are renewed in absorbing that life,—there are few pleasures in life so profound as that, so eagerly desired, so rarely made the most of, so recklessly squandered when they come. It is God who sends them, but we often act as if it were the devil ; and that is a sore pity and a great wrong.

"Many a seed lies in the soil of a field unable to germinate. The rain falls on the land, the sun sends his heat into the ground, but all in vain. At last a new element is added to the soil ; the rain dissolves it around the seed, and now life awakens in its husk, it pushes up its trembling spear of green, the sunlight touches   and a new thing is born on earth."

Rev. Stopford A. Brooke.

'We, too, are deathless ; we,
  Eternal as the Earth,
We cannot cease to be
  While springtide comes or birth.
If our being cease to hold
  Reflected lights divine
On budding lives, they day by day do shine
  With unabated gold.
Though lost, it may be, to our mortal sight,
It cannot be that any perish quite—
Only the baser part forgets to be,
And if within the hidden Treasury
Of the great Ruler we awhile should rest,
Or issue with a higher stamp imprest,
With all our baser alloy purged and spent,
  Were we not thus content?
 *   *   *   *   *   *
The nobler portions of ourselves shall last
Till all the lower rounds of life be past,
  And we regenerate.
We, too, again shall rise
  The same, and not the same,
As daily rise upon the orient skies
  New dawns with wheels of flame.

12

So, if it worthy prove,
Our being, self-perfected, shall upward move
To higher essence, and still higher grown,
Not sweeping idle harps before a throne,
Nor spending praise where is no need of praise,
But through unnumbered lives and ages come,
Of pure laborious days,
To an eternal home,   .
Where spring is not, nor birth, nor any dawn,
But life's full noontide never is withdrawn."

Lewis Morris.

"Each advancing form of life, which God takes up, springs out of the failure of that which has preceded it."

Rev. Andrew Jukes.

"The ideal Christian life is a life in God—a life under the absolute control of the laws of an invisible, eternal, and Divine kingdom." *R. W. Dale, D.D.*

"It is *now*, in this earth life, we weave our heaven robes ; *now* we set the jewels in our heaven crown ; *now* we learn the heaven songs ; *now* we become fitted in choice, and love, and character for the realms of the holy. The whiteness of heaven is a further glory which comes upon the whitened earth-robes of an earnest Christian life." *Rev. R. Tuck.*

"Life, whether we build the pyramid of jasper or of common clay, however broad we make its base, mercifully narrows to the top ; and as on our upward path we successively leave behind us the beauty and joy of childhood, and the strength of manhood, and the few interests that survive, like pale flowers on the Alpine turf, to those days in which we shall say that we have no pleasure in them, as all things fall away from us, and leave us on our little narrow standing-place amid the cold, barren snows of old age, eternity is seen to be more and more beneath us as well as around us and above us ; the heavenly world becomes more and more part of our own home, and the transition in the end is easy and immediate.

" The life of faith exists behind the life of sense,—the life hid with Christ in God behind and beneath the life lived with men. Just as our world is even now among the stars, so is our life even now, in the spiritual and eternal world, covered and hid by the material frame and the circumstances of external life, as the flame of a lamp covers and conceals the changes of the elements on which it feeds and by which it lives."

Rev. Hugh Macmillan.

" The events of life sometimes startle us by an apparent eccentricity. Some line of thought or current of enterprise has been carrying us, and we feel that the path of the future is beginning to be plain. We shall go forward as we are ; the aim we have in view will be slowly accomplished, and every day will add something to its realization ; to-morrow will be as to-day, and the steady weeks will succeed one another with monotonous resemblance. Such are our thoughts ; but the thread which our imagination pictures as running on straight and firm in the future as in the past, is often broken with startling suddenness, and the whole of our life overspread with the hues of uncertainty. Such events are out of harmony with our plans—they cross our purposes or our expectations ; they are disturbing to our sense of repose ; they break up the petrifactions which the constant routine of life tends to form over the surface of the spirit. But there are other moods which succeed. There are times when our stirred and agitated minds are ready for any event. We have seen how life is constantly broken up, and its old combinations displaced, and new ones created. The wayward progress of Fortune has angered us, or terrified us, or depressed us ; we cease to be surprised at any of her whimsical deeds—she cannot astonish us with anything. There is a recklessness about us which obstinately refuses to be surprised ; there is an anger at everything in life, which is almost eager to anticipate every misfortune."

Bishop Boyd Carpenter.

" Life lies behind us as the quarry from whence we get tiles and cope-stones for the masonry of to-day."

Ralph Waldo Emerson.

"Our lives are not the accidental and purposeless fragments they often seem to us to be. God is so disposing them as that we may be sifted from all evil, converted to all goodness, His end for us being that we may become perfect and entire, lacking nothing."   *Samuel Cox, D.D.*

"Life is not mere continuance or development; it is not a harmony, but a struggle. It continues, it develops, it may reach a harmony, but these are not now its main aspects. It is this element of struggle that separates us from other creations. A tree grows, a brute develops what was lodged within it; but man chooses, and choice, by its nature, involves struggle. It is through choice and its conflicts that man makes his world, himself, and his destiny; for in the last analysis character is choice ultimated. The animals live on in their vast variety and generations without changing the surface of the earth, or varying the sequences wrought into their being; but man transforms the earth, and works out for himself diverse histories and destinies. One is perfectly co-ordinated to nature; the other is but partially so, and is man-like just in the degree in which he gets out of the formal categories of nature into the freedom of his own spiritual and eternal order; great just in the degree in which he rises above instincts, and gets to living out of moral choices."

Rev. Theodore T. Munger.

"I love a life whose plot is simple,
    And does not thicken with every pimple;
    A soul so sound no sickly conscience binds it,
    That makes the universe no worse than 't finds it.
    I love an earnest soul,
    Whose mighty joy and sorrow
    Are not drowned in a bowl,
    And brought to life to-morrow;
    That lives one tragedy,
    And not seventy;
    A conscience worth keeping,
    Laughing not weeping;
    A conscience wise and steady,
    And for ever ready;

Not changing with events,
Dealing in compliments;
A conscience exercised about
Large things, where one *may* doubt.
I love a soul not all of wood,
Predestinated to be good,
But true to the backbone
Unto itself alone,
And false to none;
Born to its own affairs,
Its own joys and own cares;
By whom the work which God begun
Is finished, and not undone;
Taken up where He left off,
Whether to worship or to scoff;
If not good, why then evil,
If not good god, good devil.
Goodness!—you hypocrite, come out of that,
Live your life, do your work, then take your hat,
I have no patience towards
Such conscientious cowards.
Give me simple labouring folk,
Who love their work,
Whose virtue is a song
To cheer God along."

H. D. Thoreau.

"To man, in the realization of his own personality, there is open the life that is infinite. . . . God suffers the limitations of the finite, that man may rise to the life that is infinite. God becomes subject to the conditions of time that man may enter into the life that is eternal."

Elisha Mulford, LL.D.

"There is no death! What seems so is transition.
This life of mortal breath
Is but a suburb of the life elysian,
Whose portal we call Death."

Henry W. Longfellow.

" The immortal life we hope for is not the mere continuance of our personal life in happiness ; it is its continuance in labour, in sacrifice, in love, and all these not for self, but for others. It is not isolation in comfort or in rest, apart from human interests ; it is a deeper and more passionate life in the whole of man, and in all its knowledge, art, and love. It is not a life in which self or self-objects can enter in, which the world can even touch ; it is a life which God will fill to its remotest vein with Himself, so that we shall become one burning flame of love—love which will make goodness certain, which, making us see into the heart of things, will make our knowledge of them clear, and our enjoyment of them even greater than our knowledge—love which will make our aspirations endless and our effort endless also. And this—which is God's activity of life in each of us—will be in all, for ever and ever, till, in that world to come, we shall know and rejoice to live in the knowledge that mankind will grow, labour, love, and enjoy, with a zest which ages will not lessen but increase."

Rev. Stopford A. Brooke.

" Ask yourselves whether *this* is not the true ideal of our life ?— That, while we are on earth, we should be as the reed shaken by and serving the wind, yielding to the Divine Spirit, following Him, and bearing witness to Him in all our changes ; loyal to Him, even though to be loyal we must often lash the earth, or be bruised against the tumultuous waters, or be torn on the hard, sharp rocks. Our language may be often nothing but a sigh over the mysteries of life, over the dark problems we cannot solve ; and, indeed, reeds that lie under the heavy and the weary weight of all this unintelligible world have but a hard time of it, and may well sigh, and even groan. But if we are faithful to the promptings of the Divine Spirit, if we yield to His constraints, we are gathering strength and sweetness of character ; we are attuning ourselves for His uses ; we are preparing ourselves for happier service. When Death cuts us down, *we* may become instruments more meet for the Spirit's hands, and pour forth clearer, richer strains. *Then* we shall beat our music out at last, and all the discords of earth and time will pass away from us for ever."

Samuel Cox, D.D.

" We must learn to reawaken and keep ourselves awake, not by
mechanical aids, but by an infinite expectation of the dawn, which
does not forsake us in our soundest sleep. I know of no more
encouraging fact than the unquestionable ability of man to elevate
his life by a conscious endeavour. It is something to be able to
paint a particular picture, or to carve a statue, and so to make a
few objects beautiful ; but it is far more glorious to carve and
paint the very atmosphere and medium through which we look,
which morally we can do. To affect the quality of the day, that
is the highest of arts. Every man is tasked to make his life, even
in its details, worthy of the contemplation of his most elevated
and critical hour."   *H. D. Thoreau.*

" Each hour has its lesson, and each life ;
And if we miss one life, we shall not find
Its lesson in another ; rather, go
So much the less complete for evermore,
Still missing something that we cannot name,
Still with our senses so far unattuned
To what the Present brings to harmonise
    With our soul's Past."
                          H. E. Hamilton King.

" This life, for the most part, is but a ripple that stirs the surface
of our being ; the depths of that being, like the depths of the sea,
are holden of a deep sleep."   *Ellice Hopkins.*

" The service of God must be co-extensive with our whole life,
and reach over our whole compass of duties, without a single
exception."   *Dean Goulburn.*

" A great deal of our heart-life is cryptogamous—mosses and
inconspicuous blooms hidden in the grass, thoughtlets, the *intents*
of the heart. We are hardly aware of this life ; but as God sees
in winter all the flowers which are yet sleeping beneath the soil,
so He sees all the hidden feelings of our hearts. He knows
every root, and what will spring from it, and comprehends its
intents, which are yet but germs, as well as its thoughts, which
have already blossomed."
                          Henry Ward Beecher, D.D.

" The nner life reveals itself, not in detail, but in its spirit."

Rev. Stopford A. Brooke.

" Life, in its very essence, is movement and transition. Not what we have, but what we gain or lose; not what we are, but what we are becoming; not where we stand, but whence we come and whither we go, constitute its real interest and worth; and the only value of that ease and virtual stagnation at which men delusively aim is to provoke their desires, and stir up the fermenting energies that contradict and exclude it."

James Martineau, D.D.

" The experience of life nearly always works towards the confirmation of faith. It is the total significance of life that it reveals God to man; and life only can do this ;—neither thought, nor demonstration, nor miracle, but life only, weaving its threads of daily toil, and trial, and joy into a pattern on which at last is inscribed the name God." *Rev. Theodore T. Munger.*

" There is a subtle law of assimilation whereby man, in his deepest life, receives an impress from the object on which his gaze is habitually fixed." *Canon Liddon.*

" Could we but turn upon ourselves the eyes
　　With which we look on others, life would pass
　　In one perpetual blush and smile.
　　The smile, how bitter!—for 'tis scorn's worst task
　　To scorn ourselves; and yet we could not choose
　　But mock our actions, all we say or do,
　　If we but saw them as we others see.
　　Life's best repose is blindness to itself."

Letitia E. Landon.

" Is not all our life—our lower life, at least—a miserable and fruitless attempt to reconcile the indulgence of our low desires for a summer holiday with the infinite and ever-increasing calls of conscience and law? Is not all our higher life a perpetual struggle to reach a horizon of duty, which is unbounded and ever-widening before us, as we fulfil its claims? "

Rev. F. W. Robertson.

' In this wild element of a Life man has to struggle onwards ; now fallen, deep-abased; and ever, with tears, repentance, with bleeding heart, he has to rise again, struggle again still onwards That his struggle *be* a faithful unconquerable one : that is the question of questions."   *Thomas Carlyle.*

" How near to good is what is *wild !* "

" Life consists with wildness.   The most alive is the wildest. Not yet subdued to man, its presence refreshes him.   One who pressed forward incessantly, and never rested from his labours, who grew fast and made infinite demands on life, would always find himself in a new country or wilderness, and surrounded by the raw material of life.   He would be climbing over the prostrate stems of primitive forest trees."   *H. D. Thoreau.*

" The value of life is measured by the richness and variety of its experiences.   Life ought to be worth double to your child what it has been worth to you.   Your life ought to be his vantage ground, from which, through the culture which God has strengthened you to give him, he may gather in the impressions of a far wider world."   *Rev. J. Baldwin Brown.*

" Out of the attempt to harmonize our actual life with our aspirations, our experience with our faith, we make poetry,—or, it may be, religion."   *Anna Jameson.*

> " One adequate support
> For the calamities of mortal life
> Exists—one only—an assured belief
> That the procession of our fate, howe'er
> Sad or disturb'd, is order'd by a Being
> Of infinite benevolence and power,
> Whose everlasting purposes embrace
> All accidents, converting them to good."
> *William Wordsworth.*

" The events of life are not appointed as testing us, whether we will choose God's will or our own, but real lessons to train us into making the right choice."   *Thomas Erskine.*

"To respect myself, to develop myself—this is my true duty in life."
Samuel Smiles.

"Your life is a school, exactly adapted to your lesson, and that to the best, last end of your existence."
H. Bushnell, D.D.

"The best test for Life is just *living.*"
Professor Henry Drummond.

"Life lives with youth, and its first rush is wonderful. Thoughts break out into leaf, feelings into blossom; a single day in that time of sun and rain may make the whole heart like a woodland; when the foliage of sweet thoughts first appears the grass is not seen for flowers. The first touch of love, the touch of a new aspiration, the winning of one new knowledge, may loosen the bonds of a thousand seeds of thought, and set them shooting upwards into growth and life. We are often born in a day; life then begins, and I hold it our duty in youth to put our whole force into living. But how? It is life, some say, to indulge our passions and desires to the full, and to send all the ardour of youth by the wild will to the service of the senses and the appetites. But is that really life, or death in the garb of life? It is said, with wisdom just and deep, that he that liveth in such pleasure is dead while he liveth. The germs of death are hidden in such life—the germ of weary exhaustion, the germ of consuming satiety; and where deathful things are hidden, there is no true life. Men call this a fast life. It is the fast life of a field flower in a hothouse, so driven beyond its due speed, overworked towards the production of the flower, that when it has finished flowering it is worthless, and will flower no more. And winter kills it; but its brothers of the field that have lived as swiftly only as Nature bade them, sleep unexhausted till the sunshine of the spring. The forced life is itself disease, and the lesson youth should learn from the life of the woods in spring is that in natural life only is to be found quick life. . . . Along with the leaves is born the cup of the flower, and with the flowers are involved the seeds. In all true life future life is hidden; provision is made for that production which is the first mark of life, for continuance of life and for its flower. Think of that truth as the spring moves your blood. Is there the element of continuance in anything you do? In your life are there seeds which, when decay comes, will insure a new outburst of life? Have you some certainty that you have life enough to flower? Is the true flower of a beautiful or useful life already formed in you? Are you showing forth already the beauty, and sweetness, and charm which tells that the flower is coming? If these things be so, then you are living the fullest and the quickest life, the life of which Spring is the image, of which God is the reality."

Rev. Stopford A. Brooke.

" There is a *releasing* power in life."

Joseph Parker, D.D.

"*Enough* is an ever-receding goal. These ideals and aspirations after something which the world cannot give, are to man, in the material body and the material world, what the organization of the sparrow is to the egg. They are voices implanted in man's nature prophesying another world, that shall be adequate to his largest desires. These stirrings of a higher life within us, these surgings of mighty impulses against the walls of clay, are the struggles of the unfledged bird for a new state of being. They are not, they cannot be, the mockings of some tormenting fiend; they are the powerful voices of an all-merciful, all-wise Father, who has provided a better world for us than this—voices of love, and hope, in which He calls us to believe in that world, and prepare for it."

Chauncey Giles.

" The discipline of our souls determines half the temptations of our life."

Henry Allon, D.D.

" Life is God's school, and they that will listen to the Master there will learn at God's speed."

George MacDonald, LL.D.

" There is no wind but soweth seeds
   Of a more true and open life,
Which burst, unlooked for, into high-souled deeds,
   With wayside beauty rife."

J. Russell Lowell.

" Every man has within him rudiments of Divine life as well as rudiments of diabolic life."

Rev. T. T. Lynch.

" The active life which has only the service of man for its end, and therefore gathers flowers, with Leah, for its own decoration, is indeed happy, but not perfectly so ; it has only the happiness of the dream, belonging essentially to the dream of human life and passing away with it. But the active life which labours for the more and more discovery of God's work, is perfectly happy, and is the life of the terrestrial paradise, being a true foretaste of heaven, and beginning in earth, as heaven's vestibule. So also the contemplative life, which is concerned with human feeling, and thought, and beauty—the life which is in earthly poetry and imagery of noble earthly emotion—is happy, but it is the happiness of the dream ; the contemplative life which has God's person and love in Christ for its object, has the happiness of eternity."

John Ruskin.

" We are always *doing*—too much so for finest being; are always *striving*—too much so for highest attaining. There is no life, indeed, no healthy and wholesome soul life, without the bustle and swelter of action ; and many a man is acquiring and growing more divinely in his daily buying, and selling, and manifold mundane anxieties and labours, than others in their cloistered stillness and seclusion, and amid the quiet of meditative days. But are we not, as a rule, too unbrokenly busy, for ever eagerly hearing something, reading something, pursuing something, inquiring into something ; rarely resting from the strain of desire and enterprise, to bathe in the waters of leisurely thought, rarely pausing to breathe and inspire at large, rarely allowing ourselves the mental hush and silence, in which the finest sounds may be heard, and that which is hidden be able to come forth and show itself; as when the noisy merry-makers or travellers have passed, and all is profoundly still again, the hidden life of the forest steals out, and many a beautiful timid creature, whose adjacency had not been suspected, glides into the open from behind the trees."

Rev. S. A. Tipple.

" Our life is twofold : sleep has its own world,
A boundary between the things misnamed
Death and existence : Sleep hath its own world,
And a wide realm of wild reality,
And dreams in their development have breath,
And tears, and tortures, and the touch of joy ;
They leave a weight upon our waking thoughts,
They take a weight from off our waking toils,
They do divide our being ; they become
A portion of ourselves as of our time,
And look like heralds of eternity ;
They pass like spirits of the past,—they speak
Like sibyls of the future ; they have power—
The tyranny of pleasure and of pain ;
They make us what we were not—what they will,
And shake us with the vision that's gone by,
The dread of vanish'd shadows.   Are they so ?
Is not the past all shadow ?   What are they ?
Creations of the mind ?—The mind can make
Substance, and people planets of its own
With beings brighter than have been, and give
A breath to forms which can outlive all flesh.

*　　*　　*　　*　　*　　*

　　　　　For in itself a thought,
A slumbering thought, is capable of years,
And curdles a long life into one hour."

Lord Byron.

" Life is but the long phantasm of the sleep-walker ; replete
with the consciousness of nimble thoughts, and vivid passions,
and precarious glories, and strenuous deeds,—a perfect conflict of
awful forces to him that is within it ; but to the eye of waking
truth outside, still and passive as the sculptured slumber of a
marble image ; a casket of mimic battles and ideal woes."

James Martineau, D.D.

" Faith's moonbeams softly glisten
Upon the breast of life's most troubled sea."

F. W. Faber, D.D.

" There are episodes in most men's lives in which their highest qualities can only cast a deterring shadow over the objects that fill their inward vision. . . . Only those who know the supremacy of the intellectual life—the life which has seed of ennobling thought and purpose within it—can understand the grief of one who falls from that serene activity into the absorbing, soul-wasting struggle with worldly annoyances."

" Life never seems so clear and easy as when the heart is beating faster at the sight of some generous self-risking deed. We feel no doubt then what is the highest prize the soul can win ; we almost believe in our own power to attain it."

George Eliot.

" There exist moments in the life of man
When he is nearer the great Soul of the world
Than is man's custom, and possesses freely
The power of questioning his destiny."

S. T. Coleridge.

" Never is our true life greater, never is it more consciously precious to us, than when we hold to it, and pursue its highest aims, amid the wintry gloom of some present disappointment, and with the withered leaves of present failure rustling on our path."

Alexander Raleigh, D.D.

" It is far easier to scatter blessings than to stoop to the low, and to live with them as a friend. The Son of God walking amidst the band of His disciples as an equal, sitting at their table, inviting to it the publican, and conversing with all He met on the highway and in the palace with like sympathy and interest, displays to my mind a charity stronger than when He employed His power to raise the dead. In every act and relation of common life, we see that His very life and spirit was benignity."

W. E. Channing, D.D.

" For ah ! life's stream is bitter,
When too greedily we drink."

Robert Buchanan.

" The thought of God will be as a true talisman of strength ; it will give simplicity and directness to our life. Over the intervening crowd of daily difficulties will rise clear and high before us the mountain of God's presence, drawing to itself our advancing steps." *Bishop Wilberforce.*

" Life is a festival to the wise."
Ralph Waldo Emerson.

"Whatever has the deepest place in our life has also the chief dominion over us, and whatever has the chief dominion over us is our Lord. Memory, conviction, sentimentality, conscience, habit, etc., etc., may *call* Jesus 'Lord and Master,' while a very different Lord inspires and rules our life. Let us not deceive ourselves. What we are when we are most free, that we really are." *Rev. John Pulsford.*

" There is one solitude common to all—one solitude which God alone invades. There is a world which the vulture's eye hath not seen, nor foot of man hath trod. It is the world in a man's own heart. It belongs often to the present. There he is ever solitary. No ear hears the songs sung in its woods ; no eye sees the tears which water its fields ; none the battles which make its plains terrible ; none the graveyards there, where are broken vows, abandoned plans, worn-out hopes, joys blind and deaf, faiths betrayed or gone astray, lost, lost love ; silent spaces where only one mourner ever comes. Stillness as of death dwells in this world, yet work as of infinite life is wrought therein. A hundred thoughts and emotions meet and interchange in the present, and we only hear the conclusion of all this toil in our companion's heart in a single sentence, or see it in a single act. It belongs often to the past. In that rushing swiftness of thought which suggests our immortality, we resume within a few minutes the memories of years gone by, embody all their sadness in a sigh, conclude all their experience into a thought ; and no one sees aught of this labour but a new touch of expression in the face which alters it for a moment and flits away. It belongs often to the future. Far into the coming time, years and years away, we wander, slaves of the imagination, building our air-wrought castles, picturing what we shall be when we walk by alien streams, and have lost the love and interests of the present; dreaming of fame, or love, or death, or of life brought at last out of shadow into quick reality. And of all this wild world of activity created in an hour there is no trace that man can see but an eye dimmed for an instant or a smile which hides itself. And more, within that lonely world there are long histories in which the soul exhausts itself and finds no end, trials which keep life for ever on the strain, this way and that dividing the swift mind, till the battle rages round the thing as raged of old the fight around the body of Patroclus, from morn till even, and is taken up again next day, and the day after, and for year after year, incessant as the waves, and as changeful in its force. And not the nearest and the dearest to our life knows that beneath the quiet commonplace is hidden a tragedy, a comedy, or a romance. Only now and then, in some moment of imperious passion, or in some crisis in which life concentrates, some touch, some trace of it, rushes to the lips in dim, confused expression. Sometimes it is not these things which have no connection with our outward life, but a life opposed to it which we lead in the solitary soul. There are currents in the ocean, deep below, which stream the contrary way to those that flow above; and no one guesses their existence, save when the sounding line visiting the deeps is borne away, and comes to the surface tangled; save when some plant or shell that cannot live in the warm surface waters trending northwards, comes up and tells that below a tide is streaming southwards from the pole. Many lives are such, and they are lonely and stern enough God knows. The artist-nature is caught in business; the soldier-heart has to mount the pulpit, not the breach; the woman made for one life has slid into its opposite; the sceptical nature has to fight for faith in a life which demands faith; the believing nature is thrown into a world of doubt. Above, to men's eyes, their lives trend all one way; far, far below, and only known when one casts the plummet deep, or a strange thought appears on the surface, the whole true current of the life sets steadily and always the other way. Yet there, and there only, in that silent sphere is the true enthusiasm, joy, and sorrow; there only is life known and felt. And yet, because to disclose it, or to let it rise to the surface, would tangle life inextricably, would overthrow and slay the necessary duties—or because it is too sacred, from long hiding and long worship, to expose to the coarse wonder of the world, it is never known. These die, and make no sign. No one has known them but God alone. This is something of the solitude of the inner life, and no one can say that it is an evil solitude, unless one should dwell in it always to the loss of duty, and then it is solitude no longer; or unless its thoughts and emotions be evil in themselves."

Rev. Stopford A. Brooke.

"It is the life within which truly corresponds to the life to come; so he that dwells most in himself, dwells most in hell or in heaven. In the outward world there is an inward soul. We may commune with peace and goodness as we gaze on sky and meadows; and there is that within God's work which brings sympathy for what is within man's heart. So that when we sit upon a ledge of rock, and enjoy a hush filled only with murmuring sounds, and look upon the bloom of the world,—so wide, so bountiful,—there rises a longing for heaven; for we are indeed now tasting heaven. We have gone within our heart, and have gone, as it were, within the veil of visible things. The life beyond all we see is the life within all we see. And the life most within ourselves is the life, then, that must needs look farthest, and sustain itself most by expectations."

Rev. T. T. Lynch.

"Life it not a little cup dipped from the stream of time. It is itself a *stream;* and though at its birth it may dance and send forth cheerful murmurs as it does not afterwards, still it is intended to flow, as it advances, through more beautiful regions, and to adorn its shores with richer verdure and more abundant harvests."

W. E. Channing, D.D.

"The voyage of human life under any other Head than Christ, and under any other wind than the wind of His Spirit, is sorrowful beyond all expression."

Rev. John Pulsford.

"If we live truly, we shall see truly. It is as easy for the strong man to be strong, as it is for the weak to be weak. When we have new perception, we shall gladly disburden the memory of its hoarded treasures as old rubbish. When a man lives with God, his voice shall be as sweet as the murmur of the brook and the rustle of the corn."

Ralph Waldo Emerson.

"The material, operating upon our senses, is always asserting its existence; and if our inner life is not equally vigorous, we shall be moved, urged, what is called actuated, from without, whereas all our activity ought to be from within."

George MacDonald, LL.D.

"But often, in the world's most crowded streets,
    But often, in the din of strife,
    There rises an unspeakable desire
    After the knowledge of our buried life :
    A thirst to spend our fire and restless force
    In tracking out our true, original course ;
    A longing to inquire
    Into the mystery of this heart which beats
    So wild, so deep in us—to know
    Whence our thoughts come and where they go.
    And many a man in his own breast then delves,
    But deep enough, alas ! none ever mines.
    And we have been on many thousand lines,
    And we have shown, on each, spirit and power ;
    But hardly have we, for one little hour,
    Been on our own line, have we been ourselves—
    Hardly had skill to utter one of all
    The nameless feelings that course through our breast,
    But they course on for ever unexpress'd.
    And long we try in vain to speak and act
    Our hidden self, and what we say and do
    Is eloquent, is well—but 'tis not true !
    And then we will no more be rack'd
    With inward striving, and demand

Of all the thousand nothings of the hour
Their stupefying power;
Ah yes, and they benumb us at our call!
Yet still, from time to time, vague and forlorn,
From the soul's subterranean depth upborne
As from an infinitely distant land,
Come airs, and floating echoes, and convey
A melancholy into all our day.

Only—but this is rare—
When a belovèd hand is laid in ours,
When, jaded with the rush and glare
Of the interminable hours,
Our eyes can in another's eyes read clear,
When our world-deafen'd ear
Is by the tones of a loved voice caress'd—
A bolt is shot back somewhere in our breast,
And a lost pulse of feeling stirs again.
The eye sinks inward, and the heart lies plain,
And what we mean, we say, and what we would, we know.
A man becomes aware of his life's flow,
And hears its winding murmur, and he sees
The meadows where it glides, the sun, the breeze.

And there arrives a lull in the hot race
Wherein he doth for ever chase
That flying and elusive shadow, rest.
An air of coolness plays upon his face,
And an unwonted calm pervades his breast.
And then he thinks he knows
The hills where his life rose,
And the sea where it goes."

Robert Buchanan.

"The only life which is not worth living is not of God's giving, but of our own creation—the life of no duty, no love, no trust; which is indeed separated by an immeasurable interval from its opposite, and amounts to a spiritual suicide of our humanity."

James Martineau, D.D.

" *Christ is the inward rectification of the life of man*, the pure strong germ of the new heart within the big, rough old one. When the busy energies of the world are ordered 'according to the love of God in Christ Jesus,' nothing will pass away but that it may exist in a nobler form; nothing will be excluded by the laws of *spirit* that appertains to the nature of man. Though all that appertains to the nature of man did not *outwardly* appear in the life of Christ, the life of Christ, as He was and is, will *inwardly* appear in all departments of this nature. *God in Christ, is Christ in the world; and Christ in the world, is the world in God.*" *Rev. T. T. Lynch.*

" Man cannot well face life without some shield between. He may fight ever so bravely, but the spears of life will be too many and too sharp for him. And no shield will thoroughly defend him but God. The lowest, by its very condition, demands the highest; the weakest calls out for the strongest,—none but the strongest can succour the weakest; the saddest can be comforted only by the most blessed; the finite can get deliverance from its binding and torturing condition only in the eternal one. When Hamlet caught sight of life, and saw what he had got to do and bear, he said, 'I'll go pray.' You have but to name God before sorrow, and it changes colour; name Him before burdens, and they grow less; name Him before the vanity of life, and it disappears. The whole sphere and scene of life is changed, lifted into a realm of power, and wisdom, and gladness. With the incoming of God there is a sense of reversal, everything that is sad, and poor, and dark, and wrong is turned about, and gathers meaning and purpose. A prophetic sense enters into us, and these wandering, disorderly, fragmentary features and experiences of life are built up into a city that hath foundations in which we repose by faith." *Rev. Theodore T. Munger.*

"So materialistic is the course of common life, that we *ask daily* new Messiahs from literature and art, to turn us from the Pharisaic observance of law to the baptism of spirit. But stars arise upon our murky sky, and the flute *soupire* from the quarter where we least expect it." *Margaret Fuller Ossoli.*

"The consciousness of deadness is itself a sign of life—
equivocal, unworthy, unsatisfactory, but still there is life."

W. Morley Punshon, D.D.

"Noble thought produces
Noble ends and uses,
Noble hopes are part of Hope wherever she may be ;
Noble thought enhances
Life and all its chances,
And noble self is noble song,—all this I learn from thee !
And I learn, moreover,
'Mid the city's strife, too,
That such faint song as sweetens Death can sweeten the
Singer's life, too ! "   *Robert Buchanan.*

"Not in a close and bounded atmosphere
Does life put forth its noblest and its best ;
'Tis from the mountain's top that we look forth,
And see how small the world is at our feet
There the free winds sweep with unfettered wing ;
There the sun rises first, and flings the last,
The purple glories of the summer eve ;
There does the eagle build his mighty nest ;
And there the snow stains not its purity.
When we descend, the vapour gathers round,
And the path narrows ; small and worthless things
Obstruct our way ; and in ourselves we feel
The strong compulsion of their influence."

Letitia E. Landon.

" However mean your life is, meet it and live it ; do not shun
it, and call it hard names. It is not so bad as you are. It looks
poorest when you are richest. The fault-finder will find faults
even in Paradise. Love your life, poor as it is. You may
perhaps have some pleasant, thrilling, glorious hours, even in
a poor-house. The setting sun is reflected from the windows of
the alms-house as brightly as from the rich man's abode ; the
snow melts before its door as early in the spring."

H. D. Thoreau.

" The purest joys of a man's life are strangely independent of his surroundings. What he *has* in the way of pleasures and possessions is literally nothing in the account ; what he *is*, and what he has in the inward treasure-house, is all in all."

Rev. J. Baldwin Brown.

" Love is ever busy with his shuttle,
Is ever weaving into life's dull warp
Bright, gorgeous flowers and scenes Arcadian ;
Hanging our gloomy prison-house about
With tapestries, that make its walls dilate
In never-ending vistas of delight."

Henry W. Longfellow.

" How much nobler the inspirations of all true life than its realizations ! How we picture the holiness, and love, and service of our discipleship—what we are to be, what we are to do. We do not realize the serpent that finds its way into every Eden, the failure that mars every purpose, the element of disenchantment and disappointment that corrects every illusion. The chief pathos of later life is the mournful contrast between the promise and the performance—'I am not better than my fathers were.' Still the idealism has its great uses ; it is not delusion that discredits it, so much as shortcoming. What would life be without it ? Perhaps it could not be as we imagine it ; but it may be better for our imaginings."

Henry Allon, D.D.

" As you penetrate the labyrinth of life in pursuit of Christian duty, you will often be surprised and charmed by meeting your Master Himself amid its windings and turnings, and receive His soul-inspiring smile."

Elizabeth Prentiss.

" We cannot tell of what elements our life is made up. It is no one shower of rain that makes the summer green. We are gathering from every point all day long ; we are daily at school, and every providence that passes before us leaves some impress on our life."

Joseph Parker, D.D.

" Death itself is only one among many beginnings ; walking in newness of life."

Elizabeth Charles.

" There are myriads of illusions which, colouring the scenes of life as they arise, pass away as shadows, and are forgotten, but which have a function and a significance somewhat as the leaves of a tree, that after flourishing for a while in the summer sun, at length fall off and perish, yet leave behind some addition to that solid structure which expands itself in the trunk and branches. Viewed as a system of transient but inevitable mental changes, the later outgrowing or obliterating the earlier, the whole of our present existence is but a species of prolonged illusion, or rather a succession of illusions; not to be interpreted apart from those ulterior aims comprehended in our destiny, whose consummation is no more to be estimated by its introductory stages, than the grandest choral strain by its elemental notes on the gamut. Yet if mankind could always know to what extent their hopes are visionary, or how impressions now familiar are to vanish before others that will steal on them as insensibly as the light of morning, existence would almost arrive at a stand, a great portion of its happiness be lost, and duty itself often remain undischarged."

W. B. Clulow.

" There are moments in the life of every contemplative being when the healing power of Nature is felt—even as Wordsworth describes it—felt in the blood, in every pulse along the veins. In such moments converse, sympathy, the faces, the presence of the dearest, come so near to us, they make us shrink ; books, pictures, music, anything, any object which has passed through the medium of mind, and has been in a manner humanised, is felt as an intrusive reflection of the busy, weary, thought-worn self within us. Only Nature, speaking through no interpreter, gently steals us out of our humanity, giving us a foretaste of that more diffused, disembodied life which may hereafter be ours. Beautiful and genial, and not wholly untrue, were the old superstitions which placed a haunting divinity in every grove, and heard a living voice responsive in every murmuring stream."

Anna Jameson.

" How much more the happiness and usefulness of life depend on a right balance of mind than on remarkable gifts ! "

W. E. Channing, D.D.

" Our lives here are mostly in the power
    Of other lives, and each of us is bound
    To be his brother's keeper."
                              H. E. Hamilton King.

" Our life is an act of dying ; and we die just as fast as we
live."   *Rev. William Mountford.*

" Happy is he who lives to understand
    Not human nature only, but explores
    All natures, to the end that he may find
    The law that governs each ;· and where begins
    The union, the partition where that makes
    Kind and degree among all visible beings ;
    The constitutions, powers, and faculties,
    Which they inherit,—cannot step beyond,—
    And cannot fall beneath ; that do assign
    To every class its station and its office,
    Through all the mighty commonwealth of things,
    Up from the creeping plant to sovereign man.
    Such converse, if directed by a meek,
    Sincere, and humble spirit, teaches love ;
    For knowledge is delight ; and such delight
    Breeds love ; yet, suited as it rather is
    To thought and to the climbing intellect,
    It teaches less to love, than to adore ;
    If that be not indeed the highest love ! "
                              William Wordsworth.

" Nothing admits culture, but that which has a principle of
life capable of being expanded."
                              W. E. Channing, D.D.

" The interest of man in men, and of God in all men, shown
by deeds of love, and the irresistible power of a holy life, that
. . . is the heart and marrow of Christianity, as it is sketched
lightly but firmly by the Master's own hand in the Sermon on
the Mount ; and that was, and ever must be, the only life, and
heat, and radiance which the Christian Church ever had or ever
can have."   *Rev. H. R. Haweis.*

" The life of the Spirit is the eternal life of man. It is not
spatial nor temporal ; it is not bounded by these coasts of time
it is here and now, but it is not at this place to be described by
the location of the place, and it is not at this time to be measured
by the termination of this time. It is not in the past, and it is not
to be foisted away into the future ; *he that believeth hath eternal life.*
There is in man the suspect that in the transient course of things
there is yet an intimation of that which is not transient. The
grass that fades has yet in the folded and falling leaves of its
flower that perishes the intimation of a beauty that does not fade.
The treasures that are frayed by the moth and worn by the rust
are not as those in which love, and faith, and hope abide. There
is a will that in its purpose does not yield to mortal wrong.
There is a joy that is not of emulation. There is a freedom that
is other than the mere struggle for existence in physical relations,
and is not determined in its source or end by these finite conditions. This is the life of the Spirit. It is born of God ; it is of
the uncreated Spirit ; it is begotten, not made ; it proceeds from
the Father and the Son ; it is in *the fellowship of the Holy Ghost.*"

Elisha Mulford.

" We become conscious of Life in the degree that our minds,
though at work, are in repose ;—not unemployed, but at ease
and peaceful. Work and repose are not antagonistic ; they are
each other's complement. The grandest workings of nature are
precisely those which present to us, along with movement, the
sublimest pictures of tranquillity, as the roll of the sea, the
circling of the constellations round the pole. Great workers, or
those who most largely realize life, are always at rest. They
accomplish so much because they have learned the secret of
tranquillity. Free from those contentions of spirit which most
men allow to distract them from the true ends and prerogatives
of life, the tranquil find the time and the opportunity which the
mass of mankind so loudly complain that they have *not.* Like
the calm flowing river, they reflect every tree and cloud, while
the brawling and troubled stream shows not a single picture. It
is the tranquil who truly ' inherit the earth.' "

Leo H. Grindon.

" Is it nothing that we can withdraw from the beaten roadside of this outer life, and enter a world, which always tranquillizes us and fills us with wonder and worship ?   To this higher world we are indebted for the lasting sublimity and freshness of human life."   *Rev. John Pulsford.*

" We are to make mercy the trust of our life, because we are learning to make justice the rule of our life."

Rev. T. T. Lynch.

" We keep but what we give,
And only daily dying may we live."

Lewis Morris.

"What if we live many and various lives, each providing us its peculiar opportunities of acquiring some new good, and casting away the slough of some old evil ; so that the course of our existence should include a series of lessons, and the world be indeed a stage on which every man fills many parts?   If the doctrine of transmigration has never been taught in this form, such is perhaps the idea embodied in the $\mu\hat{\nu}\theta\mathrm{os}$."

Archdeacon Julius C. Hare.

" Using the sensuous life aright, is taking the crystal from the quarry, and converting it into a magnifying lens."

Leo H. Grindon.

" The summer life of the soul.   It abides in the light of God's countenance ; it glows beneath His blessing ; the sound of living waters is among its woods, the colours and life of God's character are in its flowers ; the freshness of immortal being falls on it like dew ; deep sunlight from God's love streams into its glades, songs of joy are often heard therein ; in the air it breathes is the Peace that passeth all understanding."

" Few sights are fairer than that seen autumn after autumn round many an English homestead, when, as evening falls, the wains stand laden among the golden stubble, and the gleaners are scattered over the misty field ; when men and women cluster round the gathered sheaves, and rejoice in the lovingkindness

of the earth ; where, in the dewy air, the shouts of happy people
ring, and over all the broad moon shines down to bless with its
yellow light the same old recurring scene it has looked on and
loved for so many thousand years.   It is the picture of a fruitful
human life when its autumntide has come ; and blessed are they
of whom men can feel the same as when they share in a harvest-
home, of whom they can say, ' He has reached his autumn, we
reap his golden produce, and we thank him in our hearts ' ;
and in whose own spirit glimmers fair the moonlight of peace
in the evening of life, the peace that is born of work completed,
the humble, happy knowledge that can say, ' Men will feed on
my thoughts, my work shall nourish them, and God, in whose
strength I have lived, will garner all for me.'   There is no
blessedness in life to be compared with' that ; it is the true,
unselfish joy of harvest."

"Look beneath the surface of the earth, under the shroud of
snow.   What do you see ?   In every root the force of life
upstoring, round every seed the close embrace of the earth
inducing that slow movement that will enable it to bring forth
life out of its death—from the snow-water as it filters down
taking up new elements from the earth in its passage, the powers
brought to the seed that send its green lance above the ground
in spring to meet the light and win the flower of light.   Beneath
the winding-sheet is, not death, but life in preparation—hidden,
but in slow activity.   The forces are being laid up which will be
the green leaves of a thousand woods, the roses and lilies of a
thousand gardens, the fountain rush of spring.   That is what
winter tells the man who knows.   It is the story it tells also to
the Christian, who has found and known the Fatherhood of God.
He comes to the wintry time of age.   Decay deals hardly with
him.   The senses fail, the brain refuses work ; he knows that
death cannot be far away.   But he has an inward life that refuses
death.   It takes to itself, during this dark time, all things that
are faithful, loving, clear, and pure.   The winter of age has
frozen his outward activity.   But in the patient waiting and
repose of a faithful age the spiritual forces which will make the
form, and colour, and power, and work of his coming life are

gathering together into a store that waits but the touch of death to break into immortal enegry.   He will sleep beneath the snow, but it will be to awaken."   *Rev. Stopford A. Brooke.*

" The small events of life, taken singly, may seem exceedingly unimportant, like snow that falls silently, flake by flake; yet, accumulated, these snowflakes form the avalanche."

Samuel Smiles.

" We write our lives, indeed,
But in a cipher none can read,
Except the author.   He may pore
The life-accumulating lore
For evermore,
And find the records strange and true
Bring wisdom old and new.
But though he break the soul,
No power has he to give the key,
No license to reveal.
We wait the all-declaring day,
When love shall know as it is known.
Till then, the secrets of our lives are
ours and God's alone."

Frances Ridley Havergal.

"The worth of life lies in a man's own hands."

Dinah M. Muloch.

" Life, that is, action, is alone the human condition into which the light of the Living can penetrate; life alone can assimilate life, can change food into growth."

George MacDonald, LL.D.

" The true problem of the spiritual life may be said to be, do the opposite of neglect.   Whatever this is, do it, and you shall escape.   It will just mean that you are so to cultivate the soul that all its powers will open out to God, and in beholding God be drawn away from sin."

Professor Henry Drummond.

" Human life, as a great whole, is very wonderful to look at in its vastness and complexity ; we may contemplate it from the outside, as a spectacle, as a growth, as a machine, in which individuals are swallowed up in countless numbers, in which even the greatest men count but for little, and are not long missed. But it is, besides, a scene of innumerable separate responsibilities, each of them as real, as grave, as stringent, as if there were no others.   The spectator of it suddenly finds that what he watches and judges has recoiled on himself; that he himself is called on to give an account, that he himself is on his trial, that he himself is the object of judgment.   The mightiest is not excused; the most obscure cannot escape.   In the midst of the world's changes, the world's debate, each has his separate life to live."

Dean Church.

" To the receptive soul the river of life pauseth not, nor is diminished." *George Eliot.*

" We are born to crave ; we live by longing ; our life is tested, and proved, and prolonged, by the activity of our desires."

H. R. Reynolds, D.D.

" Within the graven lintels of the gate
That here divides our vision and our fate,
The dreams we walk in and the truths of sleep,
All sense and spirit have life inseparate.

There what one thinks is his to grasp and keep ;
There are no dreams, but very joys to reap,
No foiled desires that die before delight,
No fears to see across our joys and weep."

Algernon C. Swinburne.

" Man's spiritual life consists in the number and fulness of his correspondences with God."

Professor Henry Drummond.

" Prayer is the bringing of one's heart into the sunshine, of that, like a plant, its inward life may thrive for an outward development." *Rev. T. T. Lynch.*

" We need pray for no higher heaven than the pure senses can furnish, a *purely* sensuous life. Our present senses are but the rudiments of what they are destined to become. We are, comparatively, deaf, and dumb, and blind, and without smell, or taste, or feeling. Every generation makes the discovery, that its divine vigour has been dissipated, and each sense and faculty misapplied and debauched. The ears were made, not for such trivial uses as men are wont to suppose, but to hear celestial sounds. The eyes were not made for such grovelling uses as they are now put to and worn out by, but to behold beauty now invisible. May we not *see* God? Are we to be put off and amused in this life, as it were with a mere allegory? Is not Nature, rightly read, that of which she is commonly taken to be the symbol merely? When the common man looks into the sky, which he has not so much profaned, he thinks it less gross than the earth, and with reverence speaks of ' the Heavens,' but the seer will in the same sense speak of 'the Earths,' and his Father who is in them. Did not He that made that which is *within* make that which is *without* also ? "
H. D. Thoreau.

" If God be consciously in your life, there is nothing He does not make divine."
Rev. Stopford A. Brooke.

"Everything depends upon the level of your life. It is possible to live so high up in intellectual and spiritual companionship as to receive, with grateful ease and friendly recognition, appearances and communications, which at one time would have afflicted us with the surprise of a miracle. We must ourselves be miracles ; then every opening of Providence, how bright soever or startling, will be accepted as one of the assured blessings of daily life."
Joseph Parker, D.D.

" To succeed in life, . . . must be to acquire that inwrought likeness with God which constitutes the creature's capacity to receive and enjoy the Divine favour."
Rev. John Pulsford.

" Life is too precious to spend in a treadmill."
Elizabeth Prentiss.

"It is he whose life has the most frequent Easters, who is always getting up to new affection, and a loftier standard, and a purer tone, and a clearer atmosphere,—who has the best justification for his hope, that in that great day when Jesus shall come he shall take his part in the heavenly celebration, and mingle his love and joys with 'the whole family' of the saints, in those blessed meetings of the resurrection morning."

Dean Vaughan.

"In duty, and in duty only, does the individual begin to come into real contact with life; therein only can he see what life is, and grow fit for it."

George MacDonald, LL.D.

"We may prove what we like or what we can about the documents of which the Bible is composed, but the life-receipts are hung up out of the reach of criticism; and these are the soul's true Jacob's ladder; by these we climb up to God; once uttered they are uttered for all time, and they are true, experimentally true, for all time; the promise is to you and to your children, the banquet is spread, 'And the Spirit and the Bride say, Come.'"

Rev. H. R. Haweis.

"The world is full of crystals. Swift, or slow, .
　Or dark, or bright their varying formation;
　From pure calm heights of fair untrodden snow,
　To fire-wrought depths of earliest creation.
　And life is full of crystals, forming still
　In myriad-shaped results from good and seeming ill.

　Yes! forming everywhere; in busiest street,
　In noisiest throng. Oh, how it would astound us,
　The strange soul-chemistry of some we meet
　In slight and passing talk! For all around us,
　Deep, inner silence broods o'er gems to be."

Frances Ridley Havergal.

"Our lives are never fairly poised or truly rich, unless there is something outside our own orbit which we can love and enjoy without coveting to possess. What would the earth be without the sunbeams?"

Edward Garrett.

"Energy enables a man to force his way through irksome drudgery and dry details, and carries him onward and upward in every station in life. It accomplishes more than genius, with not one-half the disappointment and peril. It is not eminent talent that is required to ensure success in any pursuit, so much as purpose,—not merely the power to achieve, but the will to labour energetically and perseveringly. Hence energy of will may be defined to be the very central power of character in a man—in a word, it is the Man himself. It gives impulse to his every action, and soul to every effort. True hope is based on it,—and it is hope that gives the real perfume to life. There is a fine heraldic motto on a broken helmet in Battle Abbey, 'L'espoir est ma force,' which might be the motto of every man's life. 'Woe unto him that is faint-hearted,' says the son of Sirach. There is, indeed, no blessing equal to the possession of a stout heart. Even if a man fail in his efforts, it will be a satisfaction to him to enjoy the consciousness of having done his best. In humble life nothing can be more cheering and beautiful than to see a man combating suffering by patience, triumphing in his integrity, and who, when his feet are bleeding and his limbs failing him, still walks upon his courage."

Samuel Smiles.

"There is a Gethsemane in every noble life."

Joseph Parker, D.D.

"Sometimes our path in life seems like a lane full of windings, where the steep banks shut out the light and air, and all we can do is to trudge steadily on through the thick mire. But if we look high up in front of us we shall see, as Israel saw, the faint blue hills of the Land of Promise rising up against the sky. The path will come out at length in full view of the Celestial City; and at last we shall be at home."

Bishop Thorold.

'Life is variety of power; it is full and rich where there are many and diverse abilities, poor and mean where there are few."

J. F. Stevenson, LL.B., D.D.

"The only true way to live in this world, constituted just as we are, is to make all our employments subserve the one great end and aim of existence—namely, to glorify God and to enjoy Him for ever. But in order to do this we must be wise task-masters, and not require of ourselves what we cannot possibly perform. Recreation we must have. Otherwise, the strings of our soul, wound up to an unnatural tension, will break."

Elizabeth Prentiss.

"That which in lifeless things ennobles them by seeming to indicate life, ennobles higher creatures by indicating the exaltation of their earthly vitality into a Divine vitality; and raising the life of sense into the life of faith,—faith, whether we receive it in the sense of adherence to resolution, obedience to law, regard-fulness of promise, in which from all time it has been the test as the shield of the true being and life of man, or in the still higher sense of trustfulness in the presence, kindness, and word of God; in which form it has been exhibited under the Christian dispensation. For whether in one or other form, whether the faithfulness of men whose path is chosen and portion fixed, in the following and receiving of that path and portion, as in the Thermopylæ camp; or the happier faithfulness of children in the good giving of their Father, and of subjects in the conduct of their King, as in the 'Stand still, and see the salvation of God,' of the Red Sea shore, there is rest and peacefulness, the 'standing still' in both, the quietness of action determined, of spirit un-alarmed, of expectation unimpatient: beautiful, even when based only, as of old, on the self-command and self-possession, the persistent dignity or the uncalculating love of the creature, but more beautiful yet when the rest is one of humility instead of pride, and the trust no more in the resolution we have taken, but in the hand we hold."

John Ruskin.

"No life, however long, will suffice to take us into the deepest depths of the Gospels; but it is not a slight thing to be always going deeper, or even to be only learning more and more how astonishingly deep they are."

F. W. Faber, D.D.

14

"When the regularities of habit and the perseverance of will become simply automatic, they lose their claim to moral admiration : however they may pace with heavier grist the mill of wealth, they have ever less to offer at the shrine of worship : the windows are darkened through which gleams of Divine and solemn light once entered and enriched the soul : the voice loses its mellow tones, and is no longer flexible enough to sing a song of hope to the heavy hearts of sorrowing men. No withered unconcern, no dead exactitude, is fitted for a life like ours,—a life full of free elements, related not merely to the punctualities of material nature, but to the heaving passions of living men ;—a life strewed with various sorrows and full of struggling nobleness, where no open ear is ever far from the curse, the sigh, the prayer :—a life of outward heats and inward thirst, that no sleeping mill-pond can keep clear and fresh, but only the running waters of the pure soul descending from the upland wilds."

James Martineau, D.D.

"Thought is for ever enlarging its horizon. Were man destined to live only in this world, his desires and powers would have been fitted wholly for this world, and his capacities would have been limited to the means of present enjoyment. But his faculties are now continually overleaping the bounds of earth ; he delights in discoveries which have no relation to his existence on this planet ; he calls to his aid the arts, not merely to render life comfortable, but to assist him in the most remote researches ; invents instruments which extend his sight beyond these visible heavens, and reveal hidden stars and systems ; and presses on and on to fathom the profoundest secrets of the universe. The human mind has an intense delight in what is vast and unexplored. Does such a mind carry with it no proof that it is destined to wider spheres of experience than earth affords,—that it is designed to improve for ever in the knowledge of God's wonderful works ? "

W. E. Channing, D.D.

"Life is the true reality in death, the immortal germ that survives all its ravages, and perpetuates itself indefinitely in new forms."

Rev. Hugh Macmillan.

" Life may be lyric or epic, as well as a poem or a romance."
Ralph Waldo Emerson.

" Life has no higher end than to come into a conscious love
of God."   *Rev. Theodore T. Munger.*

> " We know not what we shall be, but are sure
> The spark once kindled by the eternal breath,
> Goes not out quite, but somewhere doth endure
> In that strange life we blindly christen death."
>   *Lewis Morris.*

" We are the children of God, the heirs of immortality, but a
little lower than the angels, crowned with glory and honour.
This is the only thought that can give true ' grandeur to the
beatings of the heart ' ; this is the only thought which, however
mean and narrow be the stage whereon our life is played, can yet
make the drama of stately and most regal argument.   Oh, if we
could but grasp the thought, we should live lives nobler and more
beautiful ; we should breathe a purer, a sweeter, and a calmer
air ; time would present to us a richer aspect, and its daily voices
echo in our ears with a sweeter melody ; for then, from the cradle
to the grave, the dark waters of life would be illuminated, and its
dense clouds would be pierced through and through with the
splendour of heaven—with the unchangeable sunlight of that
eternal life which is hid with Christ in God ! "
                                      Archdeacon F. W. Farrar.

> " Life's smallest miseries are, perhaps, its worst :
> Great sufferings have great strength : there is a pride
> In the bold energy that braves the worst,
> And bears, proud in the bearing ; but the heart
> Consumes with those small sorrows, and small shames,
> Which crave, yet cannot ask for sympathy."
>   *Letitia E. Landon.*

" When the strain of life is great it is not the counterfeit of
the heavenly life man wants, however clearly executed, but its
grand reality."   *Sarah Doudney.*

" The whole of this life is one grand march toward life indeed and life in earnest."

Henry Ward Beecher, D.D.

"Most of us are far less happy than we might be, if we had learned the Divine art of wringing the last drop of good out of everything. After our rude attempts at smelting there is a great deal of valuable metal left in the dross, which a wiser system would extract. One wonders when one gets a glimpse of how much of the raw material of happiness goes to waste in the manufacture in all our lives. There is so little to spare, and yet so much is flung away."

Alexander Maclaren, D.D.

" So near along life's stream are the fountains of innocence and youth making fertile its sandy margin; and the voyageur will do well to replenish his vessels often at these uncontaminated sources. Some youthful spring, perchance, still empties with tinkling music into the oldest river, even when it is falling into the sea, and we imagine that its music is distinguished by the river gods from the general lapse of the stream, and falls sweeter on their ears in proportion as it is nearer to the ocean. As the evaporations of the river feed thus these unsuspected springs which filter through its banks, so, perchance, our aspirations fall back again in springs on the margin of life's stream to refresh and purify it. The yellow and tepid river may float his scow, and cheer his eye with its reflections and its ripples, but the boatman quenches his thirst at this small rill alone. It is this purer and cooler element that chiefly sustains his life."

H. D. Thoreau.

" It is in life—in the wear and tear of life—that those graces must be wrought and fashioned which perfect the soul, immortal, over death."   *Dean Stanley, D.D.*

" We live by admiration, hope, and love ;
    And, even as these are well and wisely fix'd,
    In dignity of being we ascend."

William Wordsworth.

" The home-life is the sphere of the most intense of human experiences. It is life in the keenest tension and to the loftiest strain."
                                Rev. J. Baldwin Brown.

" The true philosophy of life consists in great thoughts being habitually connected with little things ; how the discipline of life consists principally of small matters ; how these may exercise the divinest principles, call forth the deepest sympathy, and nourish and perfect the highest excellence ; how we are to be interested in each other with respect to the ordinary events of life, as well as with respect to what is to be evolved in a higher world ; how the little accidents and duties of time are the proper preparation for the revelations of eternity ; how, in short, the true spiritual greatness of man in this life is not to be looked for in his doing great things, but in his doing small things after a great and serious manner."
                                Rev. Thomas Binney.

" Christianity is help from without, that enters to commune with and assist what is most inwardly within ; it is the action of life on life, the holy life on the sinning one ; it wakens the slumbering, frees the enslaved, who, shaking off slumber, are yet at first amazed and dreamy, and, losing chains, do not at once lose stiffness and the pain of limbs."
                                Rev. T. T. Lynch.

" A complete human life must have in it not only submission but resistance ; the fighting against evil and in defence of good ; the struggle with Divine help to overcome evil with good ; and finally the determination not to sit down tamely to misery, but to strive after happiness—lawful happiness, both for ourselves and others. In short, not only passively to accept joy or grief, but to take means to secure the one and escape the other : to ' work out our own salvation,' for each day, as we are told to do it for an eternity. Though with the same Divine limitation —humbling to all pride, and yet encouraging to ceaseless effort— ' for it is God that worketh in us, both to will and to do, of His good pleasure.' "
                                Dinah M. Muloch.

" All our earthly life is but a *beginning.* Nothing is finished on earth ; the world is full of unfinished undertakings. We begin sentences that we hope to conclude in heaven. We are always stammering through alphabets, and lisping the first syllables of a never-ending song." *H. R. Reynolds, D.D.*

" Let me move slowly through the street,
    Filled with an ever-shifting train,
Amid the sound of steps that beat
    The murmuring walks like autumn rain.

* * * * *

Each, where his tasks or pleasures call,
    They pass, and heed each other not.
There is who heeds, who holds them all,
    In His large love and boundless thought.

These struggling tides of life that seem
    In wayward, aimless course to tend,
Are eddies of the mighty stream
    That rolls to its appointed end."

W. C. Bryant.

" No distinct boundary can be discerned to limit our personal life on the inward side ; and however deeply we may reflect on that constancy in variation which makes our identity, we are always dimly aware of a lower depth, which, while it is continuous with our consciousness, is utterly beyond sounding or measurement. Thus we get an idea—vague, it may be, but unspeakably impressive and real to those who feel the ultimate oneness of all existence—of a measureless ocean of living energy, which rolls its tide, as it were, into the little creek that is bounded by our senses, there to take the form of finite personal life. This flowing tide ripples on the shore of the objective world, and toys with pebbles, and drinks the scent of flowers ; but, behind, is the broadening flood which widens out beyond vision or sounding-line into the inconceivable grandeur of God."

J. Allanson Picton.

" No man ever lived whose acts were not smaller than himself."
Rev. F. W. Robertson.

" Death ever fronts the wise ;
Not fearfully, but with clear promises
Of larger life, on whose broad vans upborne,
Their outlook widens, and they see beyond
The horizon of the Present and the Past,
Even to the very source and end of things."

J. Russell Lowell.

" It is a wonderful life, this of ours,—
Every child at its birth is an Elnathan, a gift of God."

William Mountford, M.A.

"The brook represents to us our present life—limited, and yet restless ; narrow, yet with capabilities of opening into what is very great.   And the sea represents what that greatness is—the endless power, and strength, and life of that to which our souls may come if we will be faithful."

Archbishop Benson.

" What the skin is to the human body, holding all the parts of the inner machinery compactly to their work ; what the simple constitution is to a highly-elaborated state, enveloping all its functions with a few great first principles which none of those functions must violate or transcend,—such to the manifold actions of a man is some great simple conception of what life is and what it means surrounding all details, giving them unity, simplicity, effectiveness."

Rev. Phillips Brooks.

" There are two lives to each of us, gliding on at the same time, scarcely connected with each other ;—the life of our actions, the life of our minds ; the external and the inward history ; the movements of the frame, the deep and ever-restless workings of the heart.   They who have loved know that there is a diary of the affections, which we might keep for years without having occasion even to touch upon the exterior surface of life, our busy occupations—the mechanical progress of our existence ; yet by the last are we judged, the first is never known.   History reveals men's deeds, men's outward characters, but *not themselves*.   There is a secret self that hath its own life 'rounded by a dream' unpenetrated, unguessed."

Bulwer Lytton.

"Our life, like the fancies of our sleep, is blended of the inter-mingling realities of the unseen and the seen. All of us live two lives in one : the outward, temporal, accidental life of routine and circumstance; and that inward, invisible life, which is unlimited by time or space, which can either soar into the heaven of heavens, gaze undazzled upon the very throne of God, and move untrembling, the Arm that moves the world; or which, sinking downwards into the very deepest and deadliest abysses, can dwell familiarly in the evil darkness, with all monstrous and prodigious things. And this inner and outer life are often wholly disparate ; in some men they brighten and fade into alternate prominence and oblivion; in some the outer life is all, the inner nothing ; in some the inner is the awful reality, the outer but a passing and inconsiderable dream. And again, the relations between these two lives often wholly differ. In some the outer life is false—a mere hypocrisy : a whitened sepulchre covering the deep uncleanness ; a fair face hiding the inward leprosy ; the network of sunbeams over a treacherous and turbid sea. In some this outer life is not false but inadequate ; it fails somehow to express and reflect the inward goodness ; it creates an unjust prejudice like the rough robe that conceals a king, or the stained fringe of the shallow waves that are so poor an outcome of the mighty sea. And there are some again—oh, happy they !—whose two lives, the outer and the inner, are mutually expressive, exquisitely har-monious. Sings our great poet :—

> ' How sour sweet music is
> When time is broke, and no proportion kept ;
> So is it with the music of men's lives ! ' "
>
> *Archdeacon F. W. Farrar.*

" 'Seek ye first the kingdom of God.' There should be some-thing strong, steady, settled as the under-current of life. There are plenty of little eddies, plenty of little gusts of wind coming and breathing fitfully upon the surface of the waters, which may be extremely healthy and delightful, but down below should be calm depths—something deep and permanent must strike the keynote of your life—a moral something."

Rev. H. R. Haweis.

" Nothing worth calling good can, or ever will be, started full grown. The essential of any good is life, and the very body of created life, and essential to it, being its self-operant, is growth. The larger start you make, the less room you leave for life to extend itself. You fill with the dead matter of your construction the places where assimilation ought to have its perfect work, building by a life-process, self-extending, and subserving the whole. Small beginnings with slow growings have time to root themselves thoroughly.

God's beginnings are imperceptible, whether in the region of soul or of matter."

George MacDonald, LL.D.

" Our life is turn'd
Out of her course, wherever man is made
An offering or a sacrifice, a tool
Or implement, a passive thing employ'd
As a brute mean, without acknowledgment
Of common right or interest in the end ;
Used or abused, as selfishness may prompt,
Say, what can follow for a rational soul
Perverted thus, but weakness in all good,
And strength in evil?   Hence an after-call
For chastisement, and custody, and bonds,
And ofttimes death, avenger of the past,
And the soul guardian in whose hands we dare
Intrust the future.   Not for these sad issues
Was man created; but t' obey the law
Of life, and hope, and action.   And 'tis known,
That when we stand upon our native soil,
Unelbow'd by such objects as oppress
Our active powers, those powers themselves become
Strong to subvert our noxious qualities :
They sweep away infection from the heart,
And by the substitution of delight,
Suppress all evil; whence the being moves
In beauty through the world."

William Wordsworth.

"To take up our life as it is, and do the best we can to make it great and good—our best to make it fit to give back one day to the God who gave it—that is—to *live*."

Mrs. Leith Adams.

"So little turns
The stream of our lives from the right;
So like is the flame that burns
To the hearth that gives warmth and light;
So fine the impassable fence,
Set for ever 'twixt right and wrong,
Between white lives of innocence
And dark lives too dreadful for song."

Lewis Morris.

"All knowledge which alters our lives penetrates us more when it comes in the early morning: the day that has to be travelled with something new and perhaps for ever sad in its light, is an image of the life that spreads beyond."

George Eliot.

"Our every day's life reveals the accumulated effects of a past lifetime; each day's life adds to that effect, whatever it may be, and prepares the way for the character of every to-morrow."

H. R. Reynolds, D.D.

"God has as many plans for men as He has men; and, therefore, He never requires them to measure their life exactly by any other life."   *H. Bushnell, D.D.*

"How little we know the moments which decide the destinies of life. We live on as usual. The day is a common day, the hour a common hour. We never thought twice about the change of intention, which by one of the accidents (accidents!) of life determined for good or for evil, for happiness or misery, the colour of our remaining years. The stroke of the pen was done in a moment which led unconsciously to our ruin; the word was uttered quite heedlessly, on which turned for ever the decision of our weal or woe."   *Archdeacon F. W. Farrar.*

" So slender is
The boundary that divideth life's two paths."

S. T. Coleridge.

" Life only avails, not having lived."

Ralph Waldo Emerson.

" If a man has not the whole of himself with himself, he ought
to inquire into it ; for it is hard to be a man and not to have the
enjoyment of a man. There is always a peculiar charm about
the man who lives wholly and heartily while he lives. The man
himself has the first enjoyment of this charm. Heaven and earth
make one in a man's life, when he has the consent of his whole
nature for what he is, and for what he does."

Rev. John Pulsford.

" It has been well believed through many ages that the beginning of compunction is the beginning of a new life; that the mind
which sees itself blameless may be called dead in trespasses—in
trespasses on the love of others, in trespasses on their weakness,
in trespasses on all those great claims which are the image of our
own need." *George Eliot.*

" In every new relation of life into which we come, we find out
finer shades, higher colours, nicer distinctions, and wider circuits
of justice." *Henry Ward Beecher, D.D.*

" For strong souls
Live like fire-hearted suns to spend their strength
In farthest striving action ; breathe more free
In mighty anguish than in trivial ease."

George Eliot.

" A merely ascetic life is an unsympathetic one ; and a life
without sympathy is a life without God."

Rev. T. T. Lynch.

" We live in a system of approximations. Every end is prospective of some other end, which is also temporary ; a round
and final success nowhere. We are encamped in nature, not
domesticated." *Ralph Waldo Emerson.*

"The greatness that inspires also weakens : the perfection that stimulates our finer qualities presses heavily on our weaker ones. We hold our lives under this two-fold condition of perfect require-ment and human weakness, and the result is an experience sharing in the qualities of each. But it is better that there should be fluctuation under high requirement than uniformity under low requirement. For the kingdom of Heaven aims only at the best; it does not concern itself with what is inferior; it is gauged throughout upon the scale of the perfect and the infinite."

Rev. Theodore T. Munger.

"Once the void of life revealed,
It must deepen on for ever,
Unless God fill up the heart
With Himself for once and ever."

Lord Houghton.

"Who can look upon the marvellous effects of spring-time, as the generations of the sun by the earth, and not rather as witnesses of the coming forth of a universal energy from Heaven—namely, from the Spirit and power of God in Heaven? by which He brings forth, in temporal nature, the best and loveliest representation possible of that higher world of life and beauty. If the subject-matter were of a more heavenly sort, the manifestation would be more heavenly. But crude as the earthly material is, see the hedges and woods, bud and leaf,—see the fruit trees blossom, hear the song-birds giving utterance to their new life and delight, let the genial spirit of the atmosphere embrace and inspire you, and say, whether Heaven is not in the effort to bring itself forth in a physical form? 'Canst thou restrain the sweet influences of Pleiades?' Is there not present throughout all elements, all fields, and woods, a loving and love-generating sea of life? Is it not as though all the virtues of Heaven said, 'Come, let us embody ourselves in the earth : let us rejoice together before the eyes of the children of men, that they also may rejoice with us'?"

Rev. John Pulsford.

"The aids to nobler life are all within."

Matthew Arnold.

" Wherever there is life it must go on and on, growing from one stage to another; not resting at any one point of attainment, but advancing until it has covered every branch and twig with fruit."

Rev. Hugh Macmillan.

" Life has its pauses. There come times when we are forced away from the treadmill of our daily occupation, and set free from the necessity of fixing our attention upon external objects, or the care of others. We are left to ourselves ; we have only to consult ourselves about the disposal of the day. We can rise when we please, go where we please, see whom we please ; we can be idle, and none will chide us ; we can be industrious, though then perhaps some gentle voice will bid us lay aside our work, and take the rest which our leisure time affords.

The mind gains freedom and strength at such seasons ; new topics are considered, and old ones come before us in new lights ; the atmosphere which surrounds the thoughts is no longer laden with conventionalisms ; best of all, care no longer frets us, and our minds grow calm from clearer notions."

Bishop Boyd Carpenter.

" We are not the birds and butterflies, but the labourers of the earthly vineyard. To discover one's right work and do it, must be the grand secret of life." *Dinah M. Muloch.*

" God is the hidden spring, the open river, and the ocean fulness of universal life and being."

William Pulsford, D.D.

" Such is, more or less, our life-trial—to cultivate trust in God, and other good things, without allowing them to run into evil— without suffering them to ferment toward corruption ; to carry our graces safely through and above all the weakness, and folly, and disorder in us, that lies around them, and tends to mix with and mar them ; to learn to be pure and self-denying, high-principled and devout, with *no less* of humanity, or natural fluency and sweetness ; to come out purged and sanctified at last, with no incidentally contracted *twist* or *narrowness.*"

Rev. S. A. Tipple.

"To go to Christ and get the perfect idea of life, and of every action of life, and then to go forth, and by His strength fulfil it,—that is the New Testament conception of a strong, successful life.

"We are like a Moses, who, at any moment, whenever the building of the tabernacle flagged and hesitated, was able to turn and go up into the mountain and look once more the pattern in the face, and come down strong, ambitious for the best, and full of hope. So any moment we may turn from the poor reality to the great ideal of our own lives, which is in Christ, with one earnest question, 'Lord, what wouldst Thou have me to be?' We may pierce through the clouds and reach the summit, and there, seeing His vision of our possibilities, be freed at once from our brethren's tyranny, and from our own content and sluggishness, and set to work with all our might to fulfil God's image of our lives, to be all that He has shown us that it is possible for us to be, to make all things in these valley lives of ours after the pattern showed to us in the mount."

Rev. Phillips Brooks.

"A life regardful of duty is crowned with an object, directed by a purpose, inspired by an enthusiasm, till the very humblest routine, carried out conscientiously for the sake of God, is elevated into moral grandeur ; and the very obscurest office, filled conscientiously at the bidding of God, becomes an imperial stage on which all the virtues play."

Archdeacon F. W. Farrar.

"Life, the patient and universal teacher, has its various zones of experience, and in each of them we are at school with our Father. Sometimes we feel to be dwelling in a sluggish lagoon oozing through sunny flats of marsh and osier beds. Then the scene changes, and it is an Alpine valley, where jagged peaks lose themselves in frozen vapour, and gloomy ravines, never rosy with the dawn, depress us with their indescribable solitude. Let us be sure that our heavenly Father speaks to us all in turn, as and when we need Him."

Bishop Thorold.

. . . " Study to make prevail
One colour in thy life, the hue of truth."

Matthew Arnold.

"Thou hadst no youth, great God!
An Unbeginning End Thou art;
 Thy glory in itself abode,
And still abides in its own tranquil heart:
No age can heap its outward years on Thee:
Dear God! Thou art Thyself Thine own eternity!

 Without an end or bound
Thy life lies all outspread in light;
 Our lives feel Thy life all around,
Making our weakness strong, our darkness bright;
Yet is it neither wilderness nor sea,
But the calm gladness of a full eternity."

F. W. Faber, D.D.

"Life is the one universal soul, which, by virtue of the
enlivening BREATH, and the informing Word, all organized bodies
have in common, each *after its kind.* This, therefore, all animals
possess, and man as an animal. But, in addition to this, God
transfused into man a higher gift, and specially inbreathed :—
even a living (that is, self-subsisting) soul, a soul having its life
in itself. 'And man became a living soul.' He did not merely
possess it, he *became* it. It was his proper *being*, his truest *self*,
the man is *in* the man. None then, not one of human kind, so
poor and destitute, but there is provided for him, even in his
present state, a *house not built with hands."*

S. T. Coleridge.

"A moral life, easily and habitually, though not at the cost
of any great suffering, *kind*, is a lovable one; but, like much
that is ornamental and attractive, it beareth not the root, but the
root it. Much may be done to the tree by training, much to the
man by teaching, but you cannot *learn* to do what you have not
the heart to do. You cannot learn to manage, on any stream, a
vessel that draws more water than the depth of the stream
supplies."

Rev. T. T. Lynch.

"A man's life may be *influenced*, but it is not *determined*, by his circumstances. No aid, save that which comes from above to every man, can help him to climb the mountain path of life, or enter the wicket-gate of righteousness; nor can any will or power except his own retard his ascent or forbid his ingress."

Archdeacon F. W. Farrar.

"If there is any failure in the force of our religious life now, it is not a new ideal that we want, but only an expansion of Christ's Spirit. Why should you be alarmed at the responsibility of living in the spirit instead of on the letter? God is with you, God is in you; and because He is with you He asks, 'Why even of yourselves judge ye not that which is right?' He will not condemn you for any intellectual mistake, but only for the disloyalty of soul, which will not follow the guidance of His Spirit towards a higher tone of life and a larger-hearted faith."

J. Allanson Picton.

"Waste is the rule of life : the gay flowers spring,
The fat fruits drop, upon the untrodden plain ;
Sea-sands at ebb are silvered o'er with pain ;
The fierce rain beats and mars the feeble wing ;
Fair forms grow fairer still for deep disease ;
Hearts made to bless are spent apart, alone."

Lewis Morris.

"Life is comic or pitiful as soon as the high ends of being fade out of sight, and man becomes near-sighted, and can only attend to what addresses the senses."

Ralph Waldo Emerson.

"We live together years and years,
And live unsounded still
Each other's springs of hopes and fears,
Each other's depths of will :
We live together day by day,
And some chance look or tone
Lights up, with instantaneous ray,
An inner world unknown."

Lord Houghton.

"The free-will, the reason, and the power of self-command, struggle perpetually with an array of chance incidents, of mechanical forces, of material causes, beyond foresight or control, but not beyond skilful management. This gives a delicate zest and point to life, which it would surely want if we had the power to frame it as we would. We did not make the world, and are not responsible for its state, but we can make life a fine art, and, taking things as we find them, like wise men, mould them as may best serve our own ends."

John Inglesant.

"As the broad ocean endlessly upheaveth,
With the majestic beating of his heart,
The mighty tides, whereof its rightful part
Each sea-wide bay and little weed receiveth,—
So, through his soul who earnestly believeth,
Life from the universal Heart doth flow,
Whereby some conquest of the eternal Woe,
By instinct of God's nature, he achieveth."

J. Russell Lowell.

"The indication of a capacity for a higher life is ever a dissatisfaction with the present."

James Hinton.

"It is through loss that all gain in this world is made. The winter leaves must fall that the summer leaves may grow. But in heaven a different law of development will prevail. In the trees of warm climates the buds have no winter leaves or protective scales, being simply formed of the ordinary leaves rolled up ; consequently they expand in growth without losing anything. And so it will be in the eternal summer above. There will be a constant unfolding of the fulness of immortal life from glory to glory ; but there will be no loss of the processes and experiences through which the unfolding will take place. The means and the end will be one and the same. There will be a constant reaching forth unto those things which are before, but there will be no forgetting the things that are behind."

Rev. Hugh Macmillan.

15

" A life of prayer is a life whose litanies are ever fresh acts of self-devoting love."   *Rev. F. W. Robertson.*

" The tenses of Christian life are not mere narrative tenses. They are perfect and present. 'Thou *hast redeemed* us to God by Thy blood, and hast made us kings and priests.'"

Elizabeth Charles.

"We school our manners, act our parts—
But He, who sees us through and through,
Knows that the bent of both our hearts
Was to be gentle, tranquil, true.

And though we wear out life, alas !
Distracted as a homeless wind,
In beating where we must not pass,
In seeking what we shall not find ;

Yet we shall one day gain, life past,
Clear prospect o'er our being's whole ;
Shall see ourselves, and learn at last
Our true affinities of soul.

We shall not then deny a course
To every thought the mass ignore ;
We shall not then call hardness force,
Nor lightness wisdom any more.

Then, in the eternal Father's smile,
Our soothed, encouraged souls will dare
To seem as free from pride and guile,
As good, as generous, as they are."

Matthew Arnold.

" *God's fatherliness.* This is the one unfailing key to all the problems of life—its denials and its bountifulness, its sunshine and its storm, its voices and its silence."

Bishop Thorold.

" Without thought, we live a parasitic life, and, having no root in ourselves, are strangers to the world's great wonder to God."

W. Pulsford, D.D.

"Love excites the profoundest life of man ; and each lower degree of love prepares the way for one which is higher. The love of God is the end of all, and I suppose that all must drop off, leaf by leaf, till that fruit is matured. The *withering*, no doubt, is often exquisitely painful ; still we find that the heart cannot grow here of itself, and that it retains to the last its strong necessity of loving. In the ordinary appointment this goes on gradually through the successive stages of filial tenderness, fraternal affection, intense love, wedded purity and confidence, friendship, patriotism. In other cases it is done by wrenches, as there are some flowers that blossom with a loud crack, when the old covering, once green and tender, falls off; and the great thing, then, seems to be to go on to the next stage humbly, if one has been missed, instead of sinking to the same level again."

Rev. F. W. Robertson.

"The circumstances of our lives are not unmeaning, but infinitely otherwise ; but this we very often do not see for want of vision. High as heaven and wide as the earth is the atmosphere of holy opportunity, in which our souls have their being." *William Mountford.*

"Live in the calm clear light,
The sunlight of God's loving fatherhood.
Small things are only great to little men,
And an unruffled mind is no mean wealth.
It is the tallest tree i' th' wood enjoys
Most of the sunshine. To the soul erect,
And living far above the dust of things,
Joy shall be strength, to do and to endure ;
For 'tis the heavenliest spirit has most strength,
As the top leaf falls last."

S. W. Partridge.

"In many of our neighbours' lives there is much not only of error and lapse, but of a certain exquisite goodness which can never be written or even spoken—only divined by each of us, according to the inward instruction of our own privacy."

George Eliot.

"Animal and vegetable life both form round a nucleus, or centre, which is at first a mere point or speck undiscernible except by the microscope, but which contains in it the germ of the animal or plant which is to be formed by expansion from it. And in some eminent servants of God the spiritual life has all formed itself from this one centre, developed itself from this one nucleus,—the realization of the Presence of God."

Dean Goulburn.

"And if I list to sing of sad things oft,
It is that sad things in this life of breath
Are deepest and divinest.   Tears bring forth
The richness of our natures, as the rain
Sweetens the smelling brier."

Robert Buchanan.

"The orbs of heaven introduce curves and turning-points into the path of life, which relieve its monotony, and impart interest and variety to it.   Life is not a continuous drudgery, a going on wearily in a perpetual straight line; but a constant ending and beginning.   We do not see all the road of life before us ; the bends of its days, and months, and years hide the future from our view, and allure us on with new hopes and fresh expectations, until at last we come without fatigue to the end of the journey.   The lights which God hath set in the firmament divide our life into separate and manageable portions.   Just as the horizon takes out of the great globe a landscape which does not bewilder us with its vastness, but spreads around our home and sphere of labour a sufficient variety of scenery and objects to draw out and exercise our faculties of mind and body ; so the horizon of each day, or week, or month, or year takes out of our whole existence a part, which enables us most efficiently to transact on its stage the business, and carry on the relations of life.   We have to deal, not with the whole of life, but with small portions of it, as they are measured out to us one by one."   *Rev. Hugh Macmillan.*

"All our life must be a selection."

Thomas Arnold, D.D.

"There are many mornings in our lives, many moments which are as fountains, from which the rest of our life continues to flow." *Elizabeth Charles.*

"What is our life but an endless flight of winged facts or events? In splendid variety these changes come, all putting questions to the human spirit. Those men who cannot answer by a superior wisdom these facts or questions of time, serve them. Facts encumber them, tyrannize over them, and make the men of routine the men of *sense*, in whom a literal obedience to facts has extinguished every spark of that light by which man is truly man. But if the man is true to his better instincts or sentiments, and refuses the dominion of facts, as one that comes of a higher race, remains fast by the soul, and sees the principle, then the facts fall aptly and supple into their places; they know their master, and the meanest of them glorifies him." *Ralph Waldo Emerson.*

"The intelligence of Nature's life is intelligence within her own sphere; but it pierceth not Nature's veil, and knows nothing of absolute truth." *Rev. John Pulsford.*

"The seed must rot ere life come out of it. What is carnal in us must be mortified ere some fresh burst of life manifest it." *Thomas Guthrie, D.D.*

"There is no infinite in Nature. All
　　Is finite, set within a self-made bound.
　　Thought builds round space itself a brazen wall,
　　And hates the barren cycle's endless round.
　　Life grown too perfect is not life at all;
　　Some hidden discords sweeten every strain;
　　No virtue is, where is no power to fall,
　　Nor true delight without a touch of pain." *Lewis Morris.*

"In some regions of infinity, and from among its splendours, this earth will be looked back on like a lowly home, and this life of ours be remembered like a short apprenticeship to duty." *William Mountford.*

"Who could recite all the marvels of water, which now hardens to a stone, and now softens to a feather; which you may find distributed into innumerable portions, every one of which has form, and every one of which reflects loveliness, in the morning dew; which comes upon us from the fulness of the cloud with power that overpowers not, disparting itself into innumerable tiniest drops, distilling gently on us, so that neither we nor our husbandries may be borne away by its strength, the blessing which God thus accommodates to our wants and weakness? Truly, water is itself an emblem of life—life for ever moving, life for ever bounteous, life capable of assuming conditions full of awe and of dread, and other conditions of tranquillity, and abounding ease, and power; life that enables us to perform all the various offices by which we secure and advance our own vitality; life which is simple and yet manifold, inexhaustible, and yet now appearing in constancy, as a river that ever runs, and now awhile inconstant to us, as a brook which the summer beams dry up, but which the winter rains bring back."

Rev. T. T. Lynch.

"The life in time is a life of defect, of passion, of getting, from the pressure and torment of our want. The life of heaven, the life eternal, is the life of being, of action, of giving from the riches of our having." *James Hinton.*

"Opportunities for doing *greatly* seldom occur—life is made up of infinitesimals." *Rev. F. W. Robertson.*

"It is the way with half the truth amidst which we live, that it only haunts us, and makes dull pulsations that are never born into sound." *George Eliot.*

"The healing of Christianity can only come into a human life as Christianity itself comes. We must take the whole cure, or we shall not feel it perfectly in any of its parts."

Alexander Raleigh, D.D.

"How often has the Spirit chosen the time, when no ray came from without, to descend upon the orphan life!"

Margaret Fuller Ossoli.

"As soon as the soul quits its own life, the life of God enters in, and possesses that soul. Strictly speaking, the life of man is the Divine life in him. Hence the repeated teaching of our Lord: That, whoever keepeth his fallen life, shall never regain his original life." *Rev. John Pulsford.*

"Left to ourselves to peer about from the dull prison of our grosser mind,—unaided by the mighty spirits of our race, who emancipate us by their greatness and snatch us by their genius into the free light,—how little should we see of the sanctity and glory of this world! What a dim and subterranean life we should live! Yet the instant we are taken aloft we find that the darkness was the dream, and the splendour is come true!" *James Martineau, D.D.*

"Life has dark secrets; and the hearts are few
That treasure not some sorrow from the world—
A sorrow silent, gloomy, and unknown,
Yet colouring the future from the past.
We see the eye subdued, the practised smile,
The word well weighed before it pass the lip,
And know not of the misery within." *Letitia E. Landon.*

"The idea of Christ in the holy mind becomes gradually blended with all the actions of its daily life; thought goes out to Him as by a Divine instinct; an ever-acting attraction draws the heart upwards to its great and first object, and life becomes an unconscious yet continuous prayer. The transition from motive to act, from holy intention and design to holy doing, becomes less and less marked, until at last the will acquires an almost mechanical certainty, an almost unconscious smoothness and rapidity of action. And so, with the unfettered ease of one 'who playeth well upon an instrument,' from the many-stringed harp of life the soul renders up to God the sweet melody of holy deeds." *John Caird, D.D.*

"He who leaves a holy life behind him, to bless and guide his fellows, bequeaths to the world a richer legacy than any book." *W. E. Channing, D.D.*

" Why, who would live if unto mortal eye
    The things lay glaring, which within our hearts
    We treasure up for God's ? "
                                    Felicia Hemans.

" Our life is a vapour that appeareth for a little, and then
vanisheth away ; but this brief vapour life of ours is laden with
eternity, and is a fact so real and grand as to strike the imagination
with amazement.   We can make it very beautiful or very gloomy.
Let it not be to any of us the mere thick mist that broods over
the ceaseless machinery of toil and care, or the foul exhalation
that rises from the muddy pools of the world's pleasures ; but let
it be what God intended it to be, a cloud in the height of heaven,
in the world, but not of it ; brightened by the sun of righteousness,
and assuming fairer and more heavenly hues as it nears the gates
of the west ! "   *Rev. Hugh Macmillan.*

" The tree of life
    Must strike its roots in secret in the earth ;
    The well-spring gush from hidden depths."
                                    Bishop Bickersteth.

" All life is a history of the power of involuntary, unconscious
influences. . . . Our conscious influence is the result of intention,
and on the whole does little ; but our unconscious influence is
the aggregate result of our whole character, manifesting itself
in words, looks, acts, that are not meant to effect anything, but
which inevitably mould others.   Our conscious and intentional
influence may fail or may be false, but our involuntary is inevitable, and every moment operative, and must be true."
                                    Rev. F. W. Robertson.

" We may study the laws of matter at and for our convenience,
but a successful life knows no law.   It is an unfortunate discovery
certainly, that of a law which binds us where we did not know
before that we were bound.   Live free, child of the mist,—and
with respect to knowledge we are all children of the mist.   The
man who takes the liberty to live is superior to all the laws, by
virtue of his relation to the law-maker."
                                    H. D. Thoreau.

"Whatever a man lives for is his faith."

Joseph Parker, D.D.

" Every life is a pilgrimage, seeking its goal in some Canaan of rest." *Henry Allon, D.D.*

" If death is only the completion of the first little round in life —the first short flight; if it marks the end only of man's seed-time ; if his budding hopes, his lofty aspirations, and dawning consciousness of desires which no earthly good can fill, are but the swelling germs of faculties that are to blossom and bear immortal fruit ; if he leaves in the grave only the swaddling clothes of his spiritual infancy, and rises, as from a sleep, in perfect human form, with all his memory, his consciousness of individual being, to enter upon an endless career, in which hope is changed into fruition, and aspiration into attainment; then death is the grand step in life. It solves all its enigmas ; it is the fulfilment, of which this life is but the prophecy ; and to the wise and pure it opens the shining portals of an endless day."

Chauncey Giles.

" Life carries with it its own signet." *John Ker, D.D.*

"Under every guilty secret there is hidden a brood of guilty wishes, whose unwholesome, infecting life is cherished by the darkness. The contaminating effect of deeds often lies less in the commission than in the consequent adjustment of our desires —the enlistment of our self-interest on the side of falsity ; as, on the other hand, the purifying influence of public confession springs from the fact, that by it the hope in lies is for ever swept away, and the soul recovers the noble attitude of simplicity."

George Eliot.

" A word may be recalled, a life can never be."

S. T. Coleridge.

" The soul's life is written in itself. Nothing is lost, nothing omitted. Whatsoever is hiddenly done in the closet of the soul, shall come into manifestation in eternity; and the raiment without shall express all 'the beauty of holiness,' which has been acquired within." *Rev. John Pulsford.*

" Praise God, creature of earth, for the mercies linked with secrecy,
   That spices of uncertainty enrich thy cup of life.
   Praise God, His hosts on high, for the mysteries that make all
      joy ;
   What were intelligence, with nothing more to learn, or heaven,
      in eternity of sameness ? "

Martin F. Tupper, D.C.L.

"At first our everlasting life will be like a summer's day, so calm, and beautiful, and long. But it will prove a day that will last on, and on, and on. And when no night comes, and we do not get weary, and all things keep on brightening about us, as the eyes of our understandings open, then, little by little, we shall begin, in awe and wonder, to feel what it is to be immortal."

William Mountford.

" All experience is a correction of life's delusions—a modification, a reversal of the judgment of the senses; and all life is a lesson on the falsehood of appearances."

Rev. F. W. Robertson.

" What is time past but to-day,
      Mirror'd in still pools peacefully ;
   The future but the same to-day,
      Reflected in a heaving sea ?
   Only the present hour has life,
   The home of work, the field of strife.
   Choose not thy bride among the dead,
      But press the present to thy breast ;
   In her, thy soul shall find its bread,
      Thy mind its sphere, thy heart its rest.
   Till God shall speak another ' Let there be,'
   And time, like darkness before light, shall flee
   Before the *Now* of His eternity."

Elizabeth Charles.

" The course of God for man is always from lower things to higher, from an inferior to a nobler life. The course of nature is birth and death, but the Divine order for human life is birth, and birth, and birth."

Rev. John Pulsford.

" Life here, it is spring's fickle time,
        Alternate blight and balm ;
But Heaven will be our summer's prime,
        One bright unending calm."
                                    Rev. T. T. Lynch.

" It is very mistaken to think that the *great* occasions of life
only demand religious feeling and principle ; it is in the every-day
petty annoyances, the constant call upon our charity, forbearance,
and meekness, that we feel the constant want of some stronger
and more powerful stimulant than the feeling of the moment,
to smooth down the rubs of life, and make our existence one of
peace and happiness."   *Maria Hare.*

" With the sinking of high human trust, the dignity of life
sinks too ; we cease to believe in our own better self, since that
also is part of the common nature which is degraded in our
thought ; and all the finer impulses of the soul are dulled."
                                              George Eliot.

" Living by faith, we wait for the new heavens and new earth
wherein dwelleth righteousness ; for the beautiful glory of the
last, the happy day ; for Christ coming to be admired by those
who love Him ; for the Paradise of God, with its trees, and bloom,
and fruit ; for the city of God, with its order, wealth, and
grandeur ; for the satisfaction of our souls when we wake up
in the likeness of the Son of man, and see Him as He is.   Then
may we say, ' As it was in the beginning so it never more shall
be.   Sorrow and doubt are gone.'"
                                    Rev. T. T. Lynch.

" As the law of our life is, ' first, that which is natural ; and,
afterwards, that which is spiritual,' we should expect the certitude
of our hearts, in relation to spiritual things, to fluctuate with our
own state.   There will be times of spiritual apathy, when we
shall be glad to fall back upon the letter of the Word, saying,
' Thus it is written, and therefore *must* be ' ; and there will be
other times of spiritual fervour, when, with ' the eyes of the heart,'
we enjoy open vision, and in light see light."
                                    William Pulsford, D.D.

" Man receives life only in that plane of his nature which he exercises."
Chauncey Giles.

" The law of Christ is a law of service: to the man who is penetrated with the Spirit of Christ, the humblest place is the highest place if it is the place in which he can do most for God and for man, and the obscurest duties are the most honourable, if, by discharging them, he can contribute most effectively to the triumph of the Divine love over the miseries and sins of mankind. To serve men for Christ's sake, in Christ's name, as His representative, though the service wins no praise, though it is met with coldness, ingratitude, calumny, by those to whom it is rendered—this is the true Christian life."
R. W. Dale, D.D.

" There is no form of spiritual life which in its progress towards the perfect man must not be tried to the uttermost. The form of the trial varies with the growing form of the elect life, for that which tries us at first is not the trial of the riper and more advanced spirit; but a cross and trial there must be at every stage, to purify the elect from the hereditary evil which still so perseveringly cleaves to him. Many, therefore, are the inward groans and deaths, which must be passed through in the journey towards perfection. For as the vine draws its sap from the impure earth, and so yields a fluid fruit, first sour, then sweet, which, being crushed in the wine-press, is then turned into wine by fermentation, and thus by successive changes spiritualized and advanced unto a more powerful and enduring form of being, so in the great change of man's renewal unto God, the new life, growing out of, and in part, and for a season sustained by the defiled and earthly nature, is dissolved and purified by successive changes and ferments, till it is transformed and rectified into that which is immortal."
Rev. Andrew Jukes.

" That deep awful rest which is the most endearing of all the attributes of the life that shall be—the rest which is order instead of disorder, harmony instead of chaotic passions in jar and discord, and duty instead of the conflict of self-will with His loving will."
Rev. F. W. Robertson.

" True love
Takes joy as solace, not as aim,
And looks beyond, and looks above ;
And sometimes through the bitterest strife
First learns to live her highest life."
Adelaide A. Procter.

" About the river of human life there is a wintry wind, though a heavenly sunshine ; the iris colours its agitation, the frost fixes upon its repose. Let us beware that our rest become not the rest of stones, which so long as they are torrent-tossed and thunder-stricken maintain their majesty, but when the stream is silent, and the storm passed, suffer the grass to cover them and the lichen to feed on them, and are ploughed down into dust."
John Ruskin.

" To live through but one perfect hour of life,
With hope enlarging all the space beyond,
Is better than a lifetime, and more long,
Looking back on it."
H. E. Hamilton King.

" Wherever healing power is, there is life. And so any great process of redemption is bright with the tokens of a living God."
J. Allanson Picton.

" ' It is a fearful thing to fall into the hands of the living God.' The 'hands of the living God' are what we call the 'laws' of Nature. When God is spoken of as the 'living,' it is ever with special reference to Nature. It is Nature, the Creation, that is the *life* of God. It is thus in respect to ourselves ; our life is that which we produce by our self-sacrifice ; we are living in respect to that which we have so created by self-control. Thus the passage means what we daily see. It *is* a fearful thing for a man living in this universe to be wicked. Nature infallibly and fearfully avenges every wrong." *James Hinton.*

" Life is no series of chances with a few providences sprinkled between to keep up a justly failing belief, but one providence of God." *George MacDonold, LL.D.*

" The growing good of the world is partly dependent on unhistoric acts; and that things are not so ill with you or me as they might have been, is half owing to the number who lived faithfully a hidden life, and rest in unvisited tombs."

George Eliot.

" Our most solemn moments are never as we picture them. God's angels are generally entertained unawares; when we most look for the gleam of their white wings at some mysterious turn of our life's path, we come instead on some common linen whitening on the hedge, some utterly trivial occurrence of daily life, wholly impervious to the sublime and to high-wrought sentiment."

Ellice Hopkins.

" Our life, as a whole, embraces our past, which is absolutely unchangeable, and our future, which is not yet within our reach; we are conscious of no present power over either. Our separate acts are perceptibly subject to our own control; nay, it is by the use of our free-will in our separate acts that we are able to change the character of our life or to preserve it from change; and with this corresponds our responsibility."   *Bishop Temple.*

" We get accustomed to mental as well as bodily pain, without, for all that, losing our sensibility to it; it becomes a habit of our lives; and we cease to imagine a condition of perfect ease as possible for us. Desire is chastened into submission; and we are contented with our day when we have been able to bear our grief in silence, and act as if we were not suffering. For it is at such periods that the sense of our lives, having visible and invisible relations beyond any of which either our present or prospective self is the centre, grows like a muscle that we are obliged to lean on and exert."   *George Eliot.*

" Say thou not sadly, ' never,' and ' no more,'
    But from thy lips banish those falsest words;
 While life remains, that which was thine before
 Again may be thine, in Time's storehouse lie
        Days, hours, and moments, that have unknown hoards
            Of joy, as well as sorrow."

Frances A. Kemble.

"Unbroken stands the scheme before us. Life infinite and boundless, throbbing in our veins with a tiny thrill of the vast pulse that courses through the infinitude of space, the joy and sorrow in our hearts calling us to an universal sympathy, guaranteeing to us a sympathy that is universal in return."

James Hinton.

"When we have panted past life's middle space,
    And stand and breathe a moment from the race,
        These graver thoughts the heaving breast annoy :
    Of all our fields how very few are green !
        And ah ! what brakes, moors, quagmires, lie between
    Tired age and childhood ramping wild with joy."

W. S. Landon.

"It is the hardness of life which gives us power. Patience, courage, generosity, can never be learned, or practised, unless there be trial, danger, temptation. Life is an education ; we may make it help us to grow nobler, and more fair to God."

Bishop W. Boyd Carpenter.

"Life has its perspective for us ; bright forms and slanting gleams and shadows in the past ; a haze not without its glory in the future ; both, looked at with a sigh from thorny ways and wasting heats in the present. In relation to lower existence, our human consciousness of time is a prerogative ; in comparison with God's life, it is an infirmity, or at least a limitation. And, according as we use or abuse it, we may verge towards either extreme, sinking ourselves into nature or merging into God. Do we use change, or does change use us ? Do we drift into the currents of necessity, or keep the open sea, where, with the good winds of heaven, a course may yet be steered ? Do we surrender the eternal in us to the temporal, and yield the soul to the seasonal pressures of life ? Then do we go over to the side of mere nature, and claim our slave-lineage with pride. Or do we convert the temporal in us into the eternal, and appropriate all change and loss to feed imperishable love and glorify divinest truth ? Then do we draw nearer unto God, and humbly own our heavenly filiation." *James Martineau, D.D.*

"A life of constant action and unwearied exertion excludes universal knowledge."   *W. E. Channing, D.D.*

"Life is a unity, not a group of results ; a power, not a mere effect."   *James Hinton.*

"The golden moments in the stream of life rush past us, and we see nothing but sand ; the angels come to visit us, and we only know them when they are gone.

"It is a sad weakness in us, after all, that the thought of a man's death hallows him anew to us ; as if life were not sacred too—as if it were comparatively a light thing to fail in love and reverence to the brother who has to climb the whole toilsome steep with us, and all our tears and tenderness were due to the one who is spared that hard journey.

"There are moments when by some strange impulse we contradict our past selves—fatal moments, when a fit of passion, like a lava stream, lays low the work of half our lives."

George Eliot.

"When we look towards winter from the last borders of autumn, it seems as if we could not encounter it, and as if it never would go over. So does threatened trouble of any kind seem to us as we look forward upon its miry ways from the last borders of the pleasant greensward on which we have hitherto been walking. But not only do both run their course, but each has its own alleviations, its own pleasures ; and very marvellously does the healthy mind fit itself to the new circumstances ; while to those who will bravely take up their burden and bear it, asking no more questions than just, 'Is this my burden?' a thousand ministrations of nature and life will come with gentle comfortings. Across a dark, verdureless field will blow a wind through the heart of the winter which will wake in the patient mind not a memory merely, but a prophecy of the spring, with a glimmer of crocus, or snowdrop, or primrose ; and across the waste of tired endeavour will a gentle hope, coming he knows not whence, breathe spring-like upon the heart of the man around whom life looks desolate and dreary."

George MacDonald, LL.D.

" Life hath its high and its ignoble tasks,
Fitted to every nature.   Will the free
And royal eagle stoop to learn the arts
By which the serpent wins the spell-bound prey ? "
Felicia Hemans.

" Man is judged by man ; nothing else were fit.   The deflections from perfect humanity cannot be measured by the standard of perfect humanity.   Hence it is the Son of man, the humanity of God, who judges.   When man meets Him, all is plain.   His perfection is the test ; He furnishes the contrast that repels, or the likeness that draws.   This, then, is judgment : man revealed by the unveiling of his life, and tested by the Son of man."
Rev. Theodore T. Munger.

" Egypt is a good school for God's Son, while He is a junior, but Egypt cannot complete His education.   Israel must go forth out of Egypt, yet not empty, as though Egypt contained nothing worth preserving, but full rather.   Egypt ruins the Egyptians, because it is their all, but it serves Israel as a stepping-stone to a higher life."
Rev. John Pulsford.

" Let thyself die—
And dying, rise again to fuller life.
To be a whole is to be small and weak—
To be a part is to be great and mighty
In the one Spirit of the mighty whole—
The spirit of the martyrs and the saints."
Canon Kingsley.

" What is the end and essence of life ?   It is to expand all our faculties and affections.   It is to grow ; to gain, by exercise, new energy, new intellect, new love.   It is to hope, to strive, to bring out what is within us, to press towards what is above us.   In other words, it is to be Free."
W. E. Channing, D.D.

" Practical life does all for a purpose ; yet it is precisely in a reasonable ultimate purpose that it is most likely to be wanting."
John Sterling.

" What any life, however humble, can do, is a secret with God ;
it may widen its influence through ages, or it may leave a trace
seen only to Him." *F. Cunningham Geikie, D.D.*

" To hope and wait for the highest and best we can conceive,
this expands life, this stretches out its short span. This affords
a field for the solution of its mysteries, for the cure of its ills,
for regaining what is lost, for recomposing the 'sweet societies'
of earth, for that realized oneness with God which is the unceasing
cry of the God-created spirit."

Rev. Theodore T. Munger.

" Carry religious principle into common life, and common life
will lose its transitoriness.

" Live for Christ in the world, and you carry out with you
into eternity all the results of the world's business that are worth
the keeping. The river of life sweeps on, but the gold grains
it held in solution are left behind, deposited in the holy heart."

John Caird, D.D.

" A manly life is the best gift you can leave mankind ; that can
be copied for ever." *Rev. Theodore Parker.*

" Life is a chase,
And Man the hunter, always following on,
With hounds of rushing thought or fiery sense,
Some hidden truth or beauty, fleeting still
For ever through the thick-leaved coverts deep
And wind-worn wolds of time.   And if he turn
A moment from the hot pursuit to seize
Some chance-brought sweetness, other than the search
To which his soul is set,—some dalliance,
Some outward shape of Art, some lower love,
Some charm of wealth and sleek content and home,—
Then, if he check an instant, the swift chase
Of fierce untempered energies which pursue,
With jaws unsated and a thirst for act,
Bears down on him with clanging shock, and whelms
His prize and him in ruin."

Lewis Morris.

" An ignoble life genders ignoble thoughts. A spiritual life
will give rise to spiritual thoughts."

Rev. John Pulsford.

"The tackings of the vessel are not its destination ; the
wanderings of life are not its end."

Rev. George Dawson.

" The religious life is one of sacred obligation and self-revision."

Rev. T. T. Lynch.

> " All your lives on high
> Are written fair, but mortal history
> Is traced upon the sand that may not keep
> The dint of wave, so quick the dash and leap
> That follows on—a picture on the wall—
> A name upon the stone—a leaf whose green
> Less quickly fades, because it once hath been
> Within the dove's soft beak, and this is all."

Dora Greenwell.

" Out of God's boundless Bosom, the fount of life, we came.
Through selfish, stormy youth, and contrite tears—just not too
late ; through manhood not altogether useless ; through slow and
chill old age, we return from Whence we came, to the Bosom of
God once more. Go forth again, it may be, with fresh knowledge,
and fresh powers, to nobler work. Amen."

Canon Kingsley.

> " Lo ! out of beauty cast away
> Another beauty grows :
> What Death reaps in the fields of life
> In fairer fields he sows.
>
> And through a thousand gates of gloom,
> With tracts of life between,
> The creatures that the Father made
> Creep on, now hid, now seen ;
>
> And duly out of every doom
> A sweeter issue flows."

Robert Buchanan.

"In a life in which all duties meet, there is a harmony which is favourable to all. One spirit circulates through all. They grow like the limbs of a well-proportioned body."

W. E. Channing, D.D.

"Life consists, not in equilibrium, but in the passage towards equilibrium. In man it is the leap from the potential, through the actual, to repose. The passage often involves a fight. Every natural growth is more or less of a struggle with other growths, in which, in the long run, the fittest survives."

Professor Tyndall.

"The prospect of eternal life must be inconceivably more dear to a benevolent heart than to any other being, because this heart is fixed on an object so glorious and extensive, that it wants an eternity to enjoy and pursue it."

W. E. Channing, D.D.

"How many things make one feel as if one's whole life was only a confused dream! Wouldn't it be odd to wake at the end, and find one had not lived at all? Many perhaps will wake at the end, and find it so indeed in one sense."

Frances A. Kemble.

"Till life is coming back, our death we do not feel,
Light must be entering in, our darkness to reveal."

Archbishop Trench.

"A lonely childhood and youth may make a great man, a good man, but it rarely makes a happy man. Better all the tussles and troubles of family life, where the angles of character are rubbed off, and its inclinations to morbidness, sensitiveness, and egotism knocked down." *Dinah M. Muloch.*

"The life of *faith* means the life which comes nearest to Christ's in never forgetting the unseen Father in the activities of the present." *Dean Church.*

"God has made us so that there is no *certainty*, however dreadful, to which the life-forces do not in time adjust themselves." *Harriet B. Stowe.*

"The real beauty of life is in health of mind, strength of will, vigour of purpose. The real poetry of life is in the noble effort which does not rest till it has accomplished its end; in the undying pursuit of that which we know to be best; in the battle for right, in the resolution and the power to live above the standard of the world; in the ravishment which is born of seeming truth, love, justice, purity, as they are seen of God, not as they are seen by men, and in unresting, yet unhasting endeavour to become at one with them.

"It is faithful; and what beauty is like the beauty of faithfulness, what poetry is so glorious as that which is heard in the Doric music of a life, marching with unshaken will to the Highest, and suffering all things, rather than give way?"

Rev. Stopford A. Brooke.

"The Christian life is often like a mountain rill, all excitement, and bubble, and foam at first; but which, when it gets to level ground, becomes slower, and sometimes looks as if it were almost stagnant. At other times it is like the rising sun, which, before it appears above the horizon, sends forth some rays of light to commence the advent of another morning, and then shines brighter and brighter until the perfect day."

Hubert Bower.

"This life, which seems so fair,
Is like a bubble blown up in the air,
By sporting children's breath,
Who chase it everywhere,
And strive who can most motion it bequeath."

William Drummond.

"The life of every individual may be compared to a river: rising in obscurity, increasing by the accession of tributary streams, and, after flowing through a longer or shorter distance, losing itself in some common receptacle. The lives of individuals also, like the course of rivers, may be more or less extensive, but will all vanish and disappear in the gulf of eternity." *Rev. Robert Hall.*

"A man lives by believing something; not by debating and arguing about many things." *Thomas Carlyle.*

" In every earnest life, there are weary flats to tread, with the heavens out of sight,—no sun, no moon,—and not a tint of light upon the path below; when the only guidance is the faith of brighter hours, and the secret Hand we are too numb and dark to feel. But to the meek and faithful it is not always so. Now and then, something touches the dull dream of sense and custom, and the desolation vanishes away: the spirit leaves its witness with us; the divine realities come up from the past and straightway enter the present; the ear into which we poured our prayer is not deaf; the infinite eye to which we turned is not blind, but looks in with answering mercy on us. The mystery of life and the grievousness of death are gone; we know now the little from the great, the transient from the eternal; we can possess our souls in patience; and neither the waving palms and scattered flowers of triumph can elate us, nor the weight of any cross appear too hard to bear." *James Martineau, D.D.*

" Beside a well-reap'd field at eventide,
 One laid him down to rest who'd wandered far,
 And fought and wounded been in Life's great war.
 ' These have done well their work,' he said, and sigh'd,
 ' But on mine armour blots of earth remain ;
 Nor blood, nor tears of mine, have wash'd that stain.'
 Then came a voice from heaven's blue depths profound,
 Beyond the shining of the evening star,
 And breathless awe thrill'd through him at the sound :
 ' I will make clean thine armour once again.'
 Then down that weary soul devoutly kneel'd,
 And lifted from the dust glad tearful eyes.
 Sweet sleep fell on him from the solemn skies,
 And perfect peace upon the well-reap'd field."
 Frances A. Kemble.

INDEX OF AUTHORS.

INDEX OF SUBJECTS.

Life.

Faculties.

Mental Desires.

Emotions.

RELIGIOUS.—

GENERAL.—

Death.

Printed by Hazell, Watson, & Viney, Ld., London and Aylesbury